When the Butterflies Came

ALSO BY KIMBERLEY GRIFFITHS LITTLE

The Healing Spell
Circle of Secrets

When the Butterflies Came

KIMBERLEY GRIFFITHS LITTLE

SCHOLASTIC PRESS/NEW YORK

All rights reserved. Published by Scholastic Press, an imprint of Scholastic Inc., *Publishers since 1920*. SCHOLASTIC, SCHOLASTIC PRESS, and associated logos are trademarks and/or registered trademarks of Scholastic Inc.

Library of Congress Cataloging-in-Publication Data

Little, Kimberley Griffiths.
When the butterflies came / by Kimberley Griffiths Little. — 1st ed.
p. cm.
Summary: Tara Doucet is grieving for her grandmother, and her family is falling apart around her, but it seems like her grandmother has preplanned an elaborate itinerary for her to follow which will lead her and her sister Riley from Louisiana to a South Pacific island and into danger — and everywhere she turns butterflies follow.
ISBN 978-0-545-42513-1 (jacketed hardcover) 1. Butterflies — Juvenile fiction.
2. Grandmothers — Juvenile fiction. 3. Sisters — Juvenile fiction. 4. Bereavement — Juvenile fiction. 5. Louisiana — Juvenile fiction. 6. Chuuk (Micronesia) — Juvenile fiction. [1. Butterflies — Fiction. 2. Grandmothers — Fiction. 3. Sisters — Fiction.
4. Grief — Fiction. 5. Louisiana — Fiction. 6. Chuuk (Micronesia) — Fiction.
7. Mystery and detective stories.] I. Title.
PZ7.L72256Whe 2013
813.6 — dc23
2012014722

10 9 8 7 6 5 4 3 2 1   13 14 15 16 17

Printed in the U.S.A.   23
Reinforced Binding for Library Use
First edition, April 2013

FOR MY MILLY,
A SPECIAL DAUGHTER WHO KNOWS THE POWER OF
CHARMS AND BUTTERFLIES AND MAGIC!

Chapter One

You can chase a butterfly all over the field and never catch it.
But if you sit quietly in the grass it will come
and sit on your shoulder.

~ANONYMOUS~

The first butterfly comes the day after the funeral.

I'm lying on the floor with my fingers in my ears — and I'm a girl who never sticks her fingers in her ears — when a pair of purple wings flutters across my bedroom window.

Jerking upright, I pull out my fingers to stare at the empty window glass. The butterfly, if there was one, isn't there any longer. I must be seeing things.

Disappointment settles in my chest as my sister's favorite

band, Kittie, keeps on shrieking through the walls. I swear the screaming — I mean singing — is gonna blister the faded wallpaper right off its glue.

"I'll hack Riley's speakers into a million pieces," I mutter, yanking the new dress I'd bought for the funeral down over my knees. It's yellow, because that's Grammy Claire's favorite color. Lying on the floor while wearing a dress is another one of those things I never do — unless I'm straightening rug fringe in the downstairs foyer.

But I can't hardly care about Riley or rug fringe. Not after staring at the closed lid of Grammy Claire's coffin for two hours. I can still smell the scent of mortuary formaldehyde inside my nose.

The sun shifts through the window, jabbing me right in the eyeball. The world ought to be dark and sinister and cranky. The sky should be gushing tears, drowning the streets, uprooting trees, and spitting at anybody who dares to be happy.

Grammy Claire is dead. The person I love more than anyone else in the whole world.

Fighting the burning in my eyes, I start counting dust particles as they float through the air like angel glitter. When I reach Dust Particle Number Forty-Three, all of a sudden the earth stops.

The dust floaties freeze.

Riley's insane rock music halts and the whole world goes silent. And very, very still. Even my stomach stops growling, although I can't remember the last time I ate. Maybe the funeral potatoes, clumped and cold.

Because, suddenly, through the open window, the butterfly returns. Deep purple wings swish the air, outlined in lemon yellow, reminding me of Grammy Claire's melt-in-your-mouth pound cake. The butterfly dips and swirls, and my eyes go crazy trying to follow its path.

First, it inspects my dresser and the spines of the books in my bookcase. Then it flies up to dance around the four posters of my bed and the drapes that hang in perfect folds along the floor. I'd fixed them myself just that morning.

Finally, the butterfly hovers right over my face, staring straight into my swollen, itchy eyes. The wings fold up tight, and then open again — so slow, it's like watching hundred-year-old molasses ooze out of a bottle. Never seen a butterfly move so deliberate, like it's thinking about its actions instead of trying to escape back out the window. Like that butterfly *knows* I'm watching it. The wings look soft as velvet and I want to touch it so bad, but I'm afraid of scaring it off.

The butterfly floats across my nose, moving its wings like the bayou on a sluggish, blistering hot day. Shades of purple and yellow, deep and brilliant and *dazzling*.

I lift my hand and stick out my finger. Three heartbeats later, the butterfly alights, its spindly feet touching the tip of my finger like an invisible breath of air.

I swear its wings *are* velvet. Softer than anything I've ever felt before. Softer than silk or marshmallows or bubble gum when it's brand-new.

The butterfly's tiny black eyes fix on mine. We stare at each other, and it's almost as if that butterfly is looking at me and knows who I am. Like it's got a *brain* and is *thinking*.

That's when I hear music again. Not Riley's rock music rattling my brain, making me want to crunch my teeth. This is angel music, delicate, unearthly, filling me up until my heart feels like it's gonna burst.

This butterfly ain't no regular butterfly.

"Are you magic?" I say real quiet, because I don't want it to fly away and disappear. "I wish Mamma could see this." Problem is, I don't even know where Mamma is because she actually *did* run off and disappear after the funeral was over.

A hole is shredding up my heart, and I can't believe I'm never gonna see my Grammy Claire again. I'd been counting down the days until she arrived. Now I wish she'd never gotten on that airplane. But for just a few minutes, the hurt in my heart begins to vanish.

All because a butterfly flew in the window and perched on my finger.

We're like a statue, me and that purple butterfly. If we were suddenly transported to a museum filled with halls of sculptures, we'd be called *Girl with a Butterfly*.

I glance at my dresser where the beveled glass figurine Grammy Claire gave me for my last birthday sits. It arrived wrapped up in tape and newspaper and postmarked from Guam. The crystal piece has a delicate butterfly inside sitting on a patch of flowers — and a girl stands next to it wearing butterfly wings, like she's a fairy.

Trying not to jiggle the butterfly tickling my finger, I fumble for the crystal with my other hand, but two seconds later, Riley starts hollering like the world is coming to an end. 'Course, with Grammy Claire gone, the world *has* come to an end.

And that's when the purple butterfly gently kisses the embroidery on my sundress, like it's kissing my heart, and flutters out the window.

Chapter Two

Butterflies are always following me, everywhere I go.
~MARIAH CAREY~

R iley's shrieking startles me so bad the glass butterfly tumbles off the dresser and lands on my big toe, smashing the glittery nail polish stars Mamma painted a week ago. *Ouch!*

Hopping on one foot, I race to the window. My heart lurches. There's no sign of the purple butterfly! Over there! Is that a bit of purple floating along the ribbon of green lawn?

I lean out farther and the purple disappears in a gust of invisible wind. My feet come off the floor and the edge of the windowsill digs into my stomach. The shingles of the first-story roof loom dangerously close. I flip back in and land on my backside. More pain shoots down my legs.

Walking on the opposite side of my injured big toe, I march to the door and throw it open.

Riley throws her bedroom door open, too, and we stand face-to-face, nose to nose.

My sister's blue hair sticks straight up, brittle and spiky with too much hair glue. She's wearing the same pair of ripped jeans she's had on for the last three days. I wonder how often she does her laundry. I have to wash my sheets every day. And iron them.

"*What* are you screaming about?" I screech at her.

"As if you care what I'm screaming about," Riley says in her lazy voice.

"What did I ever do to you?" My voice cracks.

"What did you ever do to me?" Riley repeats. "Try — *everything*!"

I hold myself still, like I do at school when someone's in my space or has messed with my desk. "So you're screaming just because . . . of nothing?"

Riley rolls her eyes. "I always have a reason. A moth tried to attack me."

"A moth tried to attack you?"

Riley throws her arm out dramatically. "It's over there."

My stomach quivers. Two minutes ago I had a butterfly sitting on my finger and now there's an attack moth in Riley's room.

"Do I have permission to enter Your Highness's abode?"

Riley can't bring herself to actually say yes. Finally, "I suppose" oozes out of her mouth. Crossing the threshold is always a huge deal. "Go ahead," she snaps.

I take three small steps and glance around. Her room is a wreck. Clothes are all over the place. A half-filled suitcase sits on the floor. Assorted mountains of makeup and hair junk are scattered across the bedspread. Heavy metal shatters the air. "Could you turn it down?" I yell.

"What?" she says, although it looks like she just mouths the word since I can't actually hear her.

"The music!"

She rolls her eyes and pushes the volume button on the remote control. The sudden silence makes my ears ring.

"Hey, what're you doing with a suitcase?"

"There!" Riley spits out, pointing to her dresser and ignoring my question. There's so much clutter, jewelry, papers, notes, photos, pencils, and school paraphernalia I can't tell what she's referring to.

"What?"

"*The moth!* What do you think I'm talking about?"

"I don't see any moth."

"You are so blind, Tara." She pushes me forward.

On the edge of the dresser lies a pair of soft wings, a black body, and spindly legs. I almost choke. "You smashed it! You *killed* it."

My legs feel wobbly as I stare at the broken pieces of what used to be a living creature.

"It's a *moth*. An ugly *insect*. They try to make you go crazy by flapping their wings in your eyes or trying to nest in your hair."

I want to strangle my stupid, self-centered sister. "It's not a *moth*. It's a *butterfly*! Can't you see the colors?" My eyes zero in on the deep blue smeared across the polished oak. There are faint tinges of a bright orange hue, too. "They're like — like — flying flowers or something. Would you crush a *flower*, a perfect *rose*? Or stuff Mamma's spring tulips in the garbage can?"

"Don't get so dramatic." Riley riffles through the closet, pulling clothes off hangers. "Butterflies have a short life span, don't they? Like a single day or something? And there's millions of them. One dead butterfly won't make a bit of difference in the ecosystem."

One dead.

The words sound so ominous. Like a bad omen. Boding evil.

I reach out and touch one of the broken wings, so small, so perfect, it feels like touching a breath of air. "But *this* butterfly was different. What did it do to you? Where did it come from?"

"Came flapping through my window, then tried to attack me."

"Butterflies don't attack! What did it actually *do*?"

"I was just sitting on my bed —"

Surreptitiously, I glance over and see paper, a letter, scrawled with male handwriting. You can always tell when it's a boy's handwriting. It's messier, jagged, and sloppy.

"— when that moth — butterfly — insect thing — tried to land on my eyelashes."

"You mean your head?"

"No, it came straight at my eyes! Like it was attacking me!"

"You never thought it might be a friendly butterfly? A butterfly trying to figure out who you were? To make sure it had the right address or the right person?"

Riley stares at me. "I think Grammy Claire's death has made you go crazy, little sister. Butterflies are bugs. They cannot read street addresses."

"Maybe it was trying to give you a message. An important message."

"Maybe I need to call Mrs. Begnaud to come stay with you."

"I'm not sick!" I stop, feeling dizzy, like I've been turned inside out.

"Maybe you're sick in the head. Ever think about that? Maybe you need someone to examine your crazy mind." She slams the closet door and walks to the window, staring into the hot, steamy afternoon. The fan overhead turns lazily, stirring the air. "Some days I think my whole family needs a psychiatrist."

"Are you planning on leaving?" My stomach starts to hurt again.

"Did the suitcase give it away?" Riley is pure sarcasm, but her voice softens just a little bit.

"You were going to leave me here all by myself?" I choke back a sob, holding it inside my chest, which *really* hurts. Me, Tara Doucet, Pantene Princess, crying? I never cry. Not in public. Not if I can help it. Mamma taught me to act cool and calm no matter what happens.

I whisper the words I've heard my mamma say a thousand times ever since my daddy left when I was six. Mamma didn't want nobody in Bayou Bridge talking behind her back. Reciting your pedigreed genealogy helps a girl not to lose her temper. "I'm Tara Doucet, daughter of one of the oldest families in New Iberia Parish, descendant of the original Paris Doucet family."

"What are you doing?" Riley lifts her eyebrows so high they disappear into her blue bangs. My sister was eleven when Daddy left, and it occurs to me that she's been angry ever since.

"You don't care about me or our family reputation or anybody but yourself."

"Just now you were talking to yourself."

"No, I wasn't."

"Yes, you were. Did Mamma tell you all that stuff?"

"I don't want to talk about it." I scramble to my feet, keeping my long hair in front of my face because I don't want to look at her. Picking up the pieces of broken butterfly, I hold them gently in my palms. Over my shoulder, I hiss at my sister, "Murderer!" and run back to my own room.

"Oh, please! Tara, come back here! I gotta talk to you!"

"No!" I scream, placing the torn pieces of blue-and-orange butterfly on my bureau. "I'm sorry," I whisper to it, and my heart turns over painfully.

Sweeping my eyes around the bedroom, a wiggly shiver runs up my spine. At exactly the same moment the purple butterfly came, this blue-and-orange one had flown into Riley's bedroom. I just *knew* that butterfly wasn't a normal butterfly!

"Grammy Claire," I whisper, breathing on the dead butterfly as if I could put its wings and body back together and wake it up again. "Grammy Claire, I *need* you. You were supposed to live until you were a hundred years old. You always said so!"

I begin counting dust motes again so I won't start crying. Riley's music cranks up, and a second later something slams against the wall. Probably the stiletto heels she wore for Prom three weeks ago.

Then I realize it's my bedroom door banging against the wall.

"Tara," Riley says behind me. When I whirl around, she holds out a piece of paper. "I came to show you this. A note I found."

"From Mamma?" We'd gotten home from Alucet Mortuary yesterday and disappeared into our own rooms, and I hadn't seen her since.

"Read it."

I don't want to, but finally I pluck the pink notepaper from Riley's fingers.

Tara, I'm not dead like Grammy Claire. I'm perfectly, miserably fine. But don't come looking, Riley. Don't worry; it's always darkest before the dawn. At least I keep telling myself that … but don't listen to me, girls. You'll know what to do.
With love from your mamma,
Becca Doucet

At first I can't believe the note is really from her, but Mamma always signs her full name. A funny little quirk she has. Plus I recognize her handwriting.

"What's she talking about, dark before the dawn? It's a blistering ninety degrees and the middle of the day." I love that word, *blistering*. Describes so many things. Weather. Moods. Or Riley most of the time.

"It's just an expression," Riley says, sounding weary. "Means when things look really horrible and sucky, just wait because eventually it'll get better. Like nightmares when they disappear with the alarm clock and five minutes later you forget why you were ever scared."

Mamma just . . . disappeared. With only a cryptic note left behind. She has a habit of disappearing once in a while, but she always comes back. At least eventually. I always worry that *this* is the time she'll leave forever and I'll never see her again. But to disappear on the day after Grammy Claire's funeral . . . I know she's been crying buckets. But what about *me*?

Mamma should be here. Daddy should live *here*, not in stupid California, and he should take me to dinner. Alyson should call me. Closing my eyes, I wish really hard that Alyson's mamma will show up with her gumbo and hug me real tight. Because something really strange is going on.

First, Grammy Claire dies coming home from the airport in New Orleans — after her fifth year living on that island. She was gonna take me and Riley and Mamma back to the South Pacific for the rest of the summer. She said there was something important she needed to show us. Or tell us. We were finally going to go snorkeling, and swim with sea turtles, and I'd planned on spotting a mermaid from my own private beach.

The funeral was closed casket. I didn't even get to see her one last time. The undertaker man said, "The accident, ah, left things, ah, less than, ah, pleasant," when I asked him why.

Mamma pinched my arm. She hissed at me that seeing a dead body was something properly bred ladies don't think about, let alone ask about.

I stare at the window, wishing the butterfly would come

back. What if a cat claws it out of the air? Or it gets smooshed by a car or drowned in the bayou? The thought makes me sick and I can feel myself shaking.

Then I realize that someone is pounding on the front door.

"Turn off your music!" I yell to Riley, taking the stairs two at a time.

The music lowers exactly one notch. Downstairs is silent as a tomb. Empty as a cavern. Friendless as enemy territory. The wallpaper is dingy and fading, the parquet flooring old as the hills. The shine Miz Landry put on it for Grammy Claire's visit is long gone, too.

I hear the buzz of a lawn mower through the open windows, and secretly hate how our old plantation house looks. Mamma always makes sure the lawns and gardens are pristine. Decorated in sparkly white lights for the December holidays. But the citizens of Bayou Bridge are not allowed to know that the interior of the main house is crumbling into shambles.

Mamma never lets anybody inside anymore. Teas and book clubs and garden parties are a thing of the past.

The doorbell rings again, twice real fast.

"Okay, okay," I mutter. When I jerk the door open, there's a short, skinny man with a cap on his head, ears sticking out, and wearing a starched uniform.

"Special delivery, miss," he says, touching the brim of his hat and thrusting a brown envelope at me.

I blink. "Who's it for?"

Without glancing at the address, he says, "Miss Tara Doucet. You're her, right?"

"You mean Becca Doucet?"

"Nope."

"Riley Doucet?"

He shakes his head.

I look at him sideways. "Grammy — I mean — Grammy Claire — well, guess her last name isn't really Doucet . . ."

"If you're Tara Doucet, then this letter is definitely for you." He smiles, and I can't help smiling back. First time I've smiled in days. The skin around my mouth feels weird and tight. "Sign right here, miss," he adds, handing over a clipboard.

I take the attached pen, and write *Tara Doucet* on the line marked with an X.

He tips his ball cap again. "Have a nice day."

I watch him jog down the brick walkway and jump into his truck. Just a regular old post-office truck.

I shut the door, staring hard at the envelope, my ears buzzing, like crazy.

Then I rip it open.

Chapter Three

Nerves and butterflies are a physical sign that you're mentally ready and eager. You have to get the butterflies to fly in formation, that's the trick.

~STEVE BULL~

Dearest Tara,

If you're reading this, that means I'm gone.

Oh, phooey! I hate even writing this, let alone thinking about it. What does gone mean, after all? Am I six feet under? Floating in the air or dancing on a cloud? Maybe I'm having tea with God and making Him answer the long list of questions I've been hungering after for decades.

I suppose I could be wandering Timbuktu with amnesia, but I made arrangements for that long ago — with Reginald Godwin, my butler, who doesn't leave my side for a moment. Even sleeps outside my bedroom door so there's no trouble with theft or ransacking.

Whatever the reason we can't be together and I'm writing this contingency letter, always know in the deepest regions of your soul that your Grammy loves you from the depths of her own crazy, old heart.

I miss you dreadfully already,
Grammy Claire

P.S. Now. On to business. Whatever happens, go with the flow. I'm watching out for you. Believe that completely. And I have a plan. Don't I always?

Your first job is to start packing, my girlie, because in just a few hours Reginald Godwin will be there to move you and Riley to my old house. Don't despair, even though the house is a bit untidy after a year of lying empty (I know that will drive you especially mad, Tara darling), Madame Erial See is a dam good cook. You're gonna eat good.

And then I have a few other tasks for you . . .
so keep your thinking cap on and your wits
about you.

Final Advice: Don't trust anybody who tells you
to do the opposite of my instructions.

Remember what Deborah Chaskin said:

"Just like the butterfly, I too will awaken in my
own time."

Even if that means I'll wake up in heaven next
time I see you. You can bet I'll be the first one in
line to hug you and smother you with kisses.

All my love forever,

G.C.

A letter from my Grammy Claire!

A letter from the dead — *beyond the grave*! Shivers race up my arms and legs like spiders are crawling along my skin.

How strange that it arrived the day after her funeral. Almost like Grammy Claire planned it. Well, I guess she did plan it. She'd written me this letter before she died so I would have something to comfort me when she actually did die. It's spooky and wonderful all at the same time.

The sound of her voice comes through the words on the

thick, creamy stationery so strong, so *real*, tears prick my eye-lids like sharp needles.

"You weren't supposed to die!" I whisper fiercely to the empty foyer. Polished parquet and meticulously straight rug fringes aren't particularly comforting at the moment. Holding the letter to my chest, I want to breathe in her words and the smell of the paper that she touched with her own hands.

My grandmother had always been a planner. The kind of person with a list of fascinating things to do every day, who didn't let nobody stop her from doing them. A grandmother who would think about me *before* she died so that *after* she actually did die, things would be okay. Just like folks write a will to make sure nobody fights over their stuff.

I read through the letter again, feeling a flush of warmth in my chest, as I think about her sitting down at her desk to write to me so that I wouldn't be so sad that awful day in the future after her funeral.

I read the letter again in the hall, lifting my right foot to rub my toes against the side of my left leg. Standing on one leg like a stork. It's something I do when I am thinking or puzzling something out. Definitely a trait with the girls in my family. We all do it: Mamma, Riley, me, *and* Grammy Claire. Guess we originally picked up the habit from her.

The doorbell rings a second time, but I keep staring at my letter, annoyed at the interruption. My eyes flip through the P.S. that's filled with all sorts of mysterious hidden messages.

The doorbell rings *again*, and now the person on the other side of the door holds it for several seconds so it rings and rings like a siren.

Hurriedly, I fold up Grammy Claire's letter, stick it in the envelope — then cram it down the front of my dress like I'm a spy.

When I open the front door, a tall, manicured, tanned man stands there. He's wearing a strange sort of suit. Not a tuxedo. Not a suit businessmen wear to their high-rise offices on television. It's tailored all wrong, Mamma would say. And I'm pretty sure he's blistering hot because a trickle of sweat drips down his nose and plops on the front step as he performs a deep bow.

He lifts his head, mops his brow, and says in a cultured voice with a trace of a British accent, "At your service, Miss Tara Doucet."

Grammy Claire's letter crackles inside my dress. I wonder if I should slam the door shut. He knows my name, but I don't know him from nobody! Where is Mamma when I need her?

The man takes out his handkerchief again and erases the sheen of sweat once more. "It's warmer here than I expected," he tells me.

That's when I realize he's wearing a butler kind of suit. With black tails and a pair of white gloves tucked in his pocket. He produces a letter from the inner coat pocket and hands it to me. "Reginald Godwin at your service."

I start to close the door, wondering if Riley will be able to hear me yelling over that dumb Kittie band — wondering if I *need* to start yelling.

"Go ahead," Reginald Godwin adds pleasantly. "Read the letter."

The note is short and to the point and my heart begins to pound.

Tara, the man standing before you is Reginald Godwin, my butler (chauffeur, handyman, and all-around employee). He will accompany you and Riley to my house. I've known him for decades and he's as trustworthy as anybody you'll ever meet. The question is: Have you packed yet? If not, then go. Go! There is no time to waste!

All my love forever,

G. C.

Grammy Claire's handwriting on *this* note matches the handwriting on the *previous* note. Handwriting I've seen all my life. And the man calling himself Reginald Godwin is in possession of it.

He stands perfectly upright on my porch. Behind him, the red and yellow roses of our garden waver in the heat. Hot, sticky July wafts into the air-conditioned house.

"Okaaay," I start to say, not sure what I'm supposed to do. Grammy Claire says I can trust him. He's actually fairly handsome for an old guy. Smudges of gray paint his temples, but other than the lines around his eyes, I can't tell how old he is.

When he gives me an assuring smile, I see a hint of a dimple. And he's got very, very blue eyes. As if his eyes absorbed the ocean's deep blue color.

This is the man who slept outside Grammy Claire's bedroom all these years to make sure she was safe from poisonous snakes and woman-eating tigers on that island in the middle of the South Pacific Ocean. So I know I'm going to like him.

Butler Reginald stifles a yawn behind the handkerchief he keeps taking in and out of his pocket. When I stare at him, he says, "Jet-lagged, I'm afraid. And I was raised in northern England. Not used to this southern humidity."

"Didn't you spend the last few years on a tropical island?"

"Most assuredly, but your grandmother and I, we usually wore shorts and shirts for our work there. When she sent me back to the States I assumed, wrongly, that I should wear more formal attire suitable to my position of employment."

"Oh. Well, I guess you can come in, then," I drawl real slow, thinking about how Mamma is gonna kill me for letting a stranger into her shabby, threadbare house.

"May I meet your mother and sister, Riley?" he asks with perfect politeness.

"Mamma's upstairs sleeping right now," I lie, cursing her again for disappearing.

Overhead, Riley's music makes a thrashing noise like someone is dying. Which, for the first time in my life, I'm actually happy about. At least Butler Reginald knows I'm not home alone. Not that I think he's dangerous. I'm just having a hard time taking everything in. Even an infuriating big sister is better than being home alone.

Butler Reginald seems to notice my hesitation. "Thank you, Miss Tara, but I can always wait outside for the —"

Just then a big yellow truck pulls in front of the house, its brakes screeching. The truck parks at the edge of the lawn where the oak tree branches lay like gnarled arms across the grass.

"Ah, it's here. Right on time. Are you ready?"

"Ready for what?"

"The adventure of a lifetime."

I squint at him, flipping my silky hair over my shoulder. "Did you know that you sound like a game-show host on television?"

He gives me another smile, and I think about how rude I must sound for a seventh-generation female of the Doucet family. "Before I forget, please take this and keep it safe."

A padded manila envelope comes out of his pocket, and when he hands it to me I feel something hard with an unusual shape sliding around inside. It's not a very big envelope, though. Just a few inches around.

He waves to the driver of the truck. "This is the correct address, my good man!"

We look at each other and I press the new note and the envelope with its odd contents to my thigh.

"Well," I say. "I guess I'd better start packing."

"Perfect," Butler Reginald replies. "I have a small list of items your grandmother would like us to take along. May I?"

"Um, sure. Come on in. I'll go get Riley."

As I walk back up the ragged carpeted stairs, my head is buzzing, my heart is thumping, and my hands are sweaty. Pulling the first letter from the top of my dress, I grip both of Grammy Claire's notes when I step into my bedroom — just as the second butterfly arrives.

Chapter Four

Someday, I will be a beautiful butterfly, and then everything will be better.

~A BUG'S LIFE (MOVIE)~

I stand still, hardly breathing.

This second butterfly isn't as shy as the first. It circles the room, its wings fluttering furiously as it begins to circle *me*. My eyeballs strain to see where it's going next — because *this* butterfly is practically invisible!

A set of gorgeous, nearly translucent, dainty wings beat at the air. The only reason I can see where it's going is because the wings are outlined in magenta red with a splash of white like the wisp of a feather.

The butterfly creates a magical breeze against my face, and I can see my alarm clock sitting on the night table right through it! Like the wings are pieces of shimmery cut glass.

"Can I hold you?" I say in my softest voice. It circles again, inspecting me, studying me. "I'll protect you," I whisper, holding out my hands. The transparent butterfly floats downward, and then actually sits inside my palms. I think we just had a conversation! "What are you?" I ask. "*Who* are you?"

Stupid questions. Of course it's a butterfly, but it's not like any butterfly I've seen flitting around our azalea bushes. But *why* did I ask *who* it was — crazy — and yet it's wonderful to think about. I feel myself relax as I hold the beautiful creature in my hands. My thoughts seem to change, too, and I don't feel so sad anymore.

"How can I help you?" My skin prickles as I realize that I'm talking to an insect! Every kid at school would laugh if they saw me. I know the boys would try to catch it and pin its wings to a board. My best friend, Alyson, would probably swat it away if the butterfly tried to touch her. She hates bugs and smashes cockroaches whenever she has a chance.

But a transparent butterfly isn't any old ugly cockroach. Not by a long shot.

I don't move a muscle as the butterfly's wings slowly open and close. Almost like the butterfly is absorbing my warmth, or my soul.

Do butterflies actually fly, or do they move on the wind, floating from flower to flower? I blink my eyes, wondering if I'm dreaming. "Do you know where you are?" I can't help asking. "Do you know who I am?" Peculiar tingles run down my neck. "I've never had a butterfly come flying into my room before. And today I've had two. Two in an hour. What does it mean? Where did you come from?"

The butterfly moves its head, looking up at me, as though it wants to answer my questions. The idea makes my heart pound so hard I'm afraid it's going to leap out of my chest.

Out in the hallway, Riley tosses a suitcase onto the landing with a wallop that makes the walls shake. The butterfly cocks its head like it can hear my sister, then lifts off, hovering above my fingers. The creature is so delicate, so exquisite, tears sting my eyes.

"Yeah, my sister sometimes scares me, too," I murmur. "Oh!" I cry as the butterfly quickly circles and floats out the window. "Don't go!" It turns once, closes its wings just like a wink, and disappears into the sunshine.

I race to the window again, but there's no sign of it, like it vanished into thin air. Well, I guess it *is* a transparent butterfly, after all. Much harder to see once it takes flight. Two butterflies in an hour. What is going on? I fall onto my bed, rumpling the sheets — and I'm a girl that never lies on my bed in the middle of the day. Wrinkles and lumps in the bedspread make me cringe.

I want to call Alyson, but I know deep in my heart she won't understand what just happened. Her daddy — the town sheriff — would call a doctor to come examine my head. Her mamma would bring me sweet tea and pat my hand and tell me I'm only imagining things because I'm grieving.

And they'd give me secret looks of pity because Mamma's gone missing again.

I wish I could show those butterflies to Grammy Claire. She wouldn't laugh at a conversation with a butterfly. Pulling out the letters, I read them one more time, memorizing the words, relishing the way she loved me. I've bawled my eyes out for days, and yet when they fill up with tears all over again, it actually *hurts* as though my heart is cracking into little pieces.

The next moment, I jump up from my bed and stand at the open door. I can't hear anything from downstairs, but soft rustling noises are coming from the other wing of the house. The wing beyond the staircase, just opposite Riley's and my rooms. The sneaky, furtive sounds send a chill right up my neck. Before I can investigate, Riley storms into my room without knocking.

"There's some kind of butler dude downstairs with a British accent examining the ratty Doucet antiques. And a noisy truck out front."

"I know."

My sister takes a step backward, surprised at my answer. She points to the letters I'm still clutching. "What do you have there?"

"Um, these are — they're from Grammy Claire."

"No, they're not. She's dead."

"Do you gotta *say* it like that?"

Her eyes are sorta cold, sorta vacant, sorta crazed. "It's just the truth."

Rage swells up inside my throat. "I think I hate you."

She shrugs, unapologetic. "I hate playing word games. I hate —" She stops, then gives my bed frame a good kick.

"Go ahead and say it. You hate me, too." But even as I give her permission to despise me, I regret saying I hate her and hope she wasn't going to tell me the same thing in return.

"Actually, I wasn't gonna say that at all. I hate Grammy Claire dying. We didn't even get to see her. I also hate funerals. And funeral potatoes. And Daddy not even coming out here because of his stupid new wife. And —" She breaks off and if she's fighting tears, that would be a first for my combat-boot-wearing sister.

"What?" I prod, wanting her to go on. Desperate for her to go on.

"— I hate that Mamma takes off and leaves us alone every time there's a crisis. She and Grammy Claire are *so* different it's like they don't even share the same gene pool."

"We have something in common, then." Riley gives me a half smile and my heart suddenly warms to her, even as fear takes over. "Are you leaving me, too? Are you running away with what's-his-name?"

30

She lets out a noisy sigh. "Brad. His name is Brad. And — no. I was going to, but I won't."

"Because you don't want to leave me alone?" My heart jumps with hope that my sister doesn't find me completely annoying.

"Get real. Guess I just decided to obey Grammy Claire's dying wishes."

"I knew you loved me!" I throw my arms around her neck and get stabbed in the ear by a wad of brittle hair glued together with super-duper-holding goop.

"Brad has to work a construction job with his uncle the next few weeks in Shreveport. He'll get overtime. Maybe when he comes back he and I'll run away together."

I blink at her. "For real?"

She rolls her eyes. "You're so gullible. But, yeah, maybe we will. You gonna make something out of it?"

I shrug my shoulders and flip my hair. "You gonna get married? Do you actually love him?" I wonder what it's like to kiss a guy with an earring in his tongue.

"I don't want to talk about it."

"Fine."

"Fine."

We stand there staring at each other.

The clock ticks.

Riley finally says, "You ready?"

My heart gives a jump. "For what?"

"Well, I declare, Tara Scarlett Doucet!" she says in an obnoxious Southern accent. "I coulda sworn you graduated sixth grade last month! What do you *think* I'm referring to? Are you packed for Grammy Claire's house? Unless I'm going alone and you're staying here by yourself."

"Don't you dare leave me behind, Riley Samantha Doucet! I'm going and you can't stop me!"

Her lips curve into a small smile. "Good, because that butler dude says we're leaving ASAP."

"I didn't think you'd met him yet."

"I know what's going on in this house more than you think, Tara. Believe me."

"Shh!" I suddenly hiss. "I hear funny noises." There's definitely the sweep of a door closing softly and the muffled sound of running water. "Is that the dishwasher?"

Riley's eyes flick away down the hall. "Nope."

"I think it's coming from the South Wing."

"You're so brilliant I can hardly contain myself."

I ignore her sarcasm. "Is someone breaking into our house?"

"Guess again."

That's when I *know*, and the knowledge makes my heart skip a whole beat. "It's Mamma, isn't it?"

"Give the girl the grand prize!"

"I thought she went away to some resort hotel so she could watch television twenty-four seven and order room service."

Mamma's note didn't actually *say* that, but I was sort of hoping that's all she was doing.

Riley gives me a look like I'm the dumbest person in the whole world. "We don't have any money for a resort hotel and room service."

"That's better than some mental hospital, ain't it?"

"You don't pay attention to anybody else in the world but yourself, Tara. Have you ever heard of the Doucet Family Trust Fund?"

She says it in capital letters like it's more important than the governor. I shrug, pretending I know all about it when I really don't.

"Read that note again. Mamma doesn't ever say what she's doing. She likes to be all vague and cryptic."

I don't like hearing her talk negatively about Mamma even though Mamma makes me angry, too. I'd spent the whole previous night wishing Mamma would come into my room and stroke my hair and tell me it was going to be okay without Grammy Claire.

I guess Mamma can't lie — because nothing will ever be the same again without Grammy Claire. Not for me, not for Riley, and not for Mamma neither. Grammy Claire rescued us all the time. She was our Superwoman Grammy. The person who made you smile and know that everything was gonna be fine. Nope, better than fine — you knew things were gonna be *good*.

Then I spy the corner of the small padded envelope sticking out from under my pillow where I'd hidden it — the one I haven't opened yet. The one with something inside.

"Pack," Riley tells me. "And fast. None of your silly dawdling and trying on clothes."

"Okay, okay," I say, pushing her out the door.

I'm packing but don't have a clue where we're really going or what I'm going to do once I get there. A strange butler is in my house. Mamma's gone off the deep end. Riley's being sort of nice. Best of all, I have two letters from Grammy Claire.

Running across my room, I reach under the pillow and bring out the soft, squishy envelope, ripping open the seal. I shake out the contents and a single brass key falls into my lap.

A white tag is stuck through the little hole of the key and on the tag is written the words *Number One*. Are my eyes playing tricks? I know exactly what door this key will open. And all of a sudden I feel a whole lot better.

Sticking the key into the pocket of my sundress, I start throwing underwear and socks and shorts and shirts into piles on my bed. Soon as I'm packed, I sneak down the hall of the South Wing, listening to the echoes of Riley's suitcases bumping down the stairs. One, two, three . . . for a girl who only wears ripped jeans and T-shirts accessorized with an occasional baggy sweatshirt, she sure has a lot of luggage. Must be a whole case just for her hair goop and neon hair dye.

The front door slams and the whole house lets out its breath. Silence invades the very air I'm breathing.

My heart starts to yammer inside my chest when I reach the splintered mahogany door to the guest suite. Rubbing my sweaty hands against my dress, I get up the nerve to knock. I'm trying to remember the last time I saw Mamma. Ever since the police arrived at our doorstep with news of the car accident, the days are a blur.

I make three taps with my fist — but there's no answer. 'Course, she's not gonna answer. She ran away from us, from the world, from her life, to the other side of this big ole house.

Wrapping my fingers around the fake crystal doorknob, I jiggle it back and forth. It's not locked so I push the old door open, slowly, slowly, and let myself inside.

Chapter Five

"Just living is not enough," said the butterfly.
"One must have sunshine, freedom, and a little flower."
~HANS CHRISTIAN ANDERSEN~

The master suite guest room is rarely used. We don't hardly have guests anymore. Grammy Claire used these rooms when she came to visit, but it's been a year. Yet I can still smell the faint scent of her perfume lingering, against a backdrop of lemon furniture oil.

I spot a dried-out bouquet of roses on one of the bureaus. Dusty petals lay scattered on top of the wood.

The room has a four-poster tester bed with damask drapes that reek of the decade Before the War. I remember Grammy

Claire telling me that a long time ago every plantation mistress wanted one of those expensive beds. I guess my great-great-great-grandfather did pretty good at sugar cane if he could purchase such a bed.

The rugs under my feet are worn and thin, the flowers fading inside the pattern. Ancient tables and bureaus and coat racks and gilt mirrors are stacked and shoved everywhere. I let out my breath and pivot on my toes, right smack in the middle of all those dusty, musty antiques.

So where is she? Thought for sure I'd see her bawling her eyes out on the pillows, but there's no one on the bed. The sheets and duvet are rumpled. The pillowcase looks sort of gray. Maybe all those scratchy noises I heard earlier weren't Mamma at all. Maybe it was just the automatic sprinkler system coming on. Creaks and groans from an old house with arthritis and a bad case of plumbing.

My bare feet don't make any noise as I cross the room, jumping softly from one rug to the next.

And then I see her.

The French doors are open, and my mamma is sitting on the upstairs porch that wraps around the back of the house.

"Mamma?" I call out real soft.

She doesn't move.

I walk closer and see her small figure wrapped in a blue sheet, knees tucked under her chin, eyes behind dark glasses, pale skin, and no makeup. She's staring at the fountain in the center of the lawn, which makes small gurgling noises. Masses of flowers spread out in five directions in the shape of a star from the fountain's shushing pool of blue. At least the perennials come back every year, or we probably wouldn't have any flowers at all anymore.

At the bottom of the lawn, the Bayou Teche runs sluggish and brown. A nutria paddles right down the middle, carrying a branch in his mouth. The rickety slave shacks from Before the War have gloomy black sockets for windows, giving me a shiver.

My mamma used to be president of the Garden Club, but nobody in Bayou Bridge knows she suffers from melancholy, especially since Daddy left us for the glamour of Hollywood and some woman named Crystal. Yeah, like the chandelier. But I realize that Grammy Claire dying hurts worse than my daddy leaving.

"Mamma, you okay?"

She's so silent my heart grips the inside of my chest like it's got sharp claws.

I kneel on the planks of the porch to get right in her face, but her eyes are closed behind the sunglasses, mouth turned down like she's in agony.

"Mamma, it's Tara."

There's a scary moment of silence while I wonder if she forgot how to talk, then she draws out a sigh and nods.

"How you doin'?" Feels like I'm five years old again, scared and small, even though I'm starting middle school at the end of summer. I want to ask a thousand questions, but I don't think she's going to give me any answers.

She shakes her head, tight and nervous.

"You been up here since the funeral?"

"Yeah," she whispers, her voice scratchy like she hasn't talked in days.

"You got something to eat?"

She shrugs and her thin fingers clutch the chair arms like she's afraid that lawn chair is going to launch her right over the balcony.

"Bet you haven't eaten at all," I accuse her. "Want me to bring you some lemonade? Or tea? Or cookies?"

"Miz Landry's comin' later."

Miz Landry is our once-a-week housekeeper, although she usually shows up more often than that. I guess Mamma might get hungry, but she won't starve.

I think about Riley making that crack about the Doucet Family Trust Fund.

"Mamma, how can we afford to pay Miz Landry still? I know we're keeping up appearances on the outside, but what happens if you gotta go to a hospital? How we gonna pay?"

My mamma's eyes are two dark holes behind those sunglasses, just like the slave shack windows. "A proper-bred lady doesn't worry about finances, Miss Tara."

"Well, you know you're gonna make yourself sick, Mamma."

"Riley says that, too. Thank goodness you girls are under your daddy's medical insurance."

"Riley's been here?" The words burst out of my mouth. Riley knew Mamma was here all along and never told me? That just irks me so bad I want to hit something.

"Gave her that note so you girls won't worry."

I rise to my feet, spittin' mad. "Riley is a stinking liar! She said you'd gone and disappeared to a hotel and left that note on your bureau! Some days I just hate her to pieces. Some days, I want to run away, too."

Mamma makes a noise in her throat, and for the first time since I came out here, she turns her head toward me. "Riley's just — Riley," she says in a strangled voice. She sounds sick. Tired. Worn-out. I don't even know what to call it.

I pace up and down the porch, then bang my forehead against one of the peeling white-painted pillars. The sprinklers come on, shooting sprays of water over the grass. I wish I was a little kid again running through the sprinklers while Daddy takes home movies of me in my Barbie swimsuit.

Finally, I go back over and lay my head in Mamma's lap. I try to see past the dark glasses, staring at her colorless lips and small, pointed chin. "Mamma," I bawl, clutching at the sheet. "I want Grammy Claire. She shouldn't have died. It just isn't fair!"

Mamma doesn't answer. There's a wall of silence like I never said anything.

Something catches the corner of my eye and I glance up, my hair sticking to my face in the heat. A butterfly dances along the tops of the elephant ears on the banks of the bayou. It's small and blue, so delicate and tiny, if I blinked I might miss it. The blue butterfly crosses the lawns and darts around the chugging sprinklers.

"Look, Mamma," I breathe out. "It's so darling. So pretty."

I've got her attention. She lifts her chin and looks out. I can see her eyes watching the butterfly behind the sunglasses.

The blue butterfly comes closer, looping over the railing of the porch and then spinning around our heads. It circles Mamma's chair, and she lets out a tiny gasp. Her lips begin to tremble into a smile.

Time seems to stand still and then the butterfly pauses, as if listening to something in the breeze. Zooming back over the porch, it skims across the grass and disappears down the bayou again.

The spell is broken. Mamma shifts in her seat, pushes my hands off her lap, then stumbles back into the dark room. Throwing herself on the bed, she jerks at the draperies to close herself in like a cocoon.

"Mamma! Don't! What're you doing?" I run over and grab her arm to stop her from shutting me out.

She rips off her sunglasses and takes my hand in her cold fingers. Her eyes are bloodshot and puffy and wrinkled. Like she's been crying nonstop for days.

"Well, haven't I been crying for days, too?" I cry out. "But *I* don't hide away and shut out the world." Anger builds inside my chest, like I got a ticking bomb inside me. I want to scream and scream, but she looks so frail, and so pathetic, I can't do nothing.

I pick up one of the empty vases stacked on a table and turn toward the wall, ready to smash it into smithereens just to get her attention. To snap her out of the hateful melancholy.

Mamma gives up on the curtains and falls back onto the bed. "Go on now, Tara. Do what Grammy Claire tells you to do."

I glare at her. "You know about that butler guy downstairs?"

She nods with her eyes closed. "Riley told me."

I make a face.

"I can't help you right now, just go — go!"

She rolls over onto her side. The mound of pillows smells unclean, as if Mamma hasn't showered in three days neither.

Words shoot out of my mouth like sharp, pointed needles. "Everybody always tells me to go! Go, go, go! You and Riley are the bosses of everything and keep all these secrets, but you don't care at all about how I feel! Maybe I will go! And maybe I'll never come back! How'd you like that?"

I pause to catch my breath and realize that the only thing I'm shouting at are the heavy burgundy drapes surrounding the bed. Nothing but a bunch of velvet folds Mamma's hiding behind. Shouting at my mamma who's sick, but won't go to a doctor. Mamma who says she cares, but is so broken she don't know up from down.

And I'm a girl who never shouts at her mamma. Last time it happened I was four years old and got a mouth full of Ivory soap. I'm so mad I want to spit, too, and I've never been tempted to spit in all my life. I don't know whether to drag her out of bed or slam the door until the walls fall down around our heads.

I decide to storm out.

Don't even say good-bye.

Except a few last hateful words come flying off my tongue: "Only Grammy Claire cared, and now she's gone, and I wish you'd died instead of her!"

Silence rings, hovering in the air, buzzing at the molding, curling up the carpet. I'm horrified, and let out a ragged gasp. But I don't take it back. I can't. Not yet.

Instead I grab at the knob with both fists, whip the bedroom door open, and crash right into Miz Landry coming in. I'm moving so fast, we smack heads and I see stars and diamonds and little black flecks. Tears spring to my eyes, but I'm so upset at my mamma that I hold in all the dumb tears. I let out a hiccup and start coughing. "I'm so sorry, Miz Landry!"

43

"Ah, honey, just an accident, darlin'," she says in her soft, mothery voice. "You hurt, baby?" She holds me, stroking my hair with her thick fingers and gentle way. I've known her since I was born. Mamma's known her since *she* was born.

I regret yelling at Mamma, but I don't turn back to apologize. I just want to crawl into a hole myself like she always does.

"Any better?" Miz Landry says.

"I'm okay," I mumble, my hair falling over my face, not wanting to look at her.

"Think you got yourself a goose egg on that noggin of yours." Miz Landry shuffles me down to the hall bathroom and gets a cold cloth to press against my forehead. When she opens the cupboard door, it falls off its hinges and clatters to the floor. "Tsk, tsk," she clicks her tongue. "This house fallin' down 'round our heads. One day you gonna wake up to rubble and dust surrounding your beds and nothin' in the pantry to eat."

I stare at her. "Really? Are we actually poor?"

She gives a snort. "Now I don't know nothin', but I know your mamma's hidin' here in this house thinking all her problems gonna go away. And they ain't. That trust fund has gone and disappeared over the years. Shoulda sold out long ago, got rid of all them antiques while they was worth something. Sold off some property."

"Maybe my daddy can give us some money."

Miz Landry blinks her big brown eyes. She snorts again and rolls her eyes like Riley. "Oh, Miss Tara, when that happens it'll be the Second Coming!"

A slow heat crawls up my neck. "But he does! Child support or something, right?"

"I suppose so, child, I suppose. Maybe buys a bag or two of groceries at the Piggly Wiggly once in a blue moon." She tsks her tongue again and lets out a mighty sigh. "Listen to me talkin' 'bout your family like this. It's wrong of me. Sinful. He's your daddy, and I suppose he's got some qualities. After all, he's got two beautiful daughters, right? The prettiest in all of Bayou Bridge and beyond."

I allow myself a tiny smile, but all my worries rush right over again like a Gulf wave sucking me out to sea. "Oh, Miz Landry, what if Mamma has to let you go? What will we do without you? I can't leave with that butler if Mamma is gonna be here all alone!"

"I ain't goin' nowhere, child. You can count on that. Me and my mamma — bless her soul — been watching over this family of girls for three generations now."

Miz Landry squares my shoulders and looks me in the eye. "So I don't want you worrying 'bout anything. You mind me, Miss Tara? You hearin' what I'm tellin' you?"

Slowly, I nod, realization washing over me. "Mamma isn't paying you, is she? Hasn't been for a while. Am I right?"

Miz Landry stares into my eyes, shrugs her big shoulders, then briskly rubs her warm hands up and down my arms. "Gotta check on Miz Becca and get some food down her and then give her a bath and make sure she sleeps tonight."

I'm right, but she won't admit it. Miz Landry been coming here helping my mamma for a long time, and doing it all for free. "You really do love my crazy mamma," I say softly.

She laughs and her belly shakes a little under her girdle. "That I do. And I loved your Grammy Claire with all my heart, too. And I love you, Tara. Love all my crazy, wonderful Doucet women."

I have to admit that I kind of like being called a Doucet woman.

"If I have to bar the doors and man the battle front with pistols in both hands to keep this house from being lost to your mamma and you girls, I'll do it without blinking twice." Miz Landry takes my cold hands in both of her strong, chapped ones. She leans in real close and whispers, "Can't help worryin' 'bout you and Riley going off now. Even if I do trust your Grammy Claire with all my heart and soul. Just remember, Miss Tara, if you need me, I'll be there in a jiffy. You can count on it."

I look into her eyes. "Make Mamma get out of bed and sit on the porch every day. And watch out for blue butterflies."

Miz Landry's eyebrows jump into her hairline.

I shrug. "Trust me."

"I'll do that, Miss Tara."

Chapter Six

Butterflies are invisible fairies, creating flowers wherever they dance.
~MIRELLA MILYSSA RIVERA LITTLE~

When I get back to my bedroom my luggage has disappeared. Butler Reginald stands on the landing. Gently, he says, "We've loaded your belongings into the truck. Are you ready to go, Miss Tara?"

I give a tight, jerky nod and he turns around, leaving me to do whatever I need to do to say good-bye.

I wonder how long I'll be gone. What's gonna happen to me at Grammy Claire's house? My grandmother hasn't lived there regularly for five years.

I remember hearing Daddy and Grammy Claire argue about her old, drafty house. Daddy said they should bulldoze the house, build a set of condominiums, and split the profits. Grammy Claire just pursed her lips and gave him the evil eye. Then Daddy started flying off to Hollywood to meet with producers and directors. Pitching ideas. Writing screenplays. On the phone constantly. Wanting to move to California permanently.

Mamma wailed that she could never leave her Southern life and all her friends and survive in a sterile suburb and have to fight a traffic jam just to pick up a chicken for supper. Mamma was Becca Doucet, sixth-generation princess of Bayou Bridge when she married Daddy. She was born to that. And she was gonna die as that. "What could be more grand than throwing garden parties, living in the biggest house, and running all the clubs in town?"

Then Daddy met Crystal over there in Hollywood, and nothing was ever the same again.

I take a sudden gulp and it hurts my throat. After smoothing the bedspread, I straighten the pictures on my dresser and make sure the closet doors are lined up. "Good-bye, bedroom."

What if I never see all my books and clothes again because the Doucet Mansion gets foreclosed while we're gone? What if Miz Landry can't stop it? What if they take Mamma to a mental hospital and I can't find her again?

I think I may need a lawyer.

Guilt throws darts at my conscience. I yelled horrible words to my mother. I picture her sitting in a wheelchair wearing a straitjacket when I see her again. My whole life is crumbling around me. And Grammy Claire wants me to leave. Why? Doesn't make sense.

I'm stumbling around on a sinking boat. Do I trust my Grammy Claire? Guess I have to go on trusting her, even if she's gone.

Locking the window, I peek out over the roofline once more, hoping to see the purple or the transparent butterfly. They're nowhere in sight. "Good-bye, window," I whisper.

The brass key in my pocket bumps against my thigh as I shut the door to my bedroom and walk downstairs. The house is so quiet, it's almost like nobody lives here.

Outside, Butler Reginald is standing in front of a bronze, sparkly Lincoln Town Car. He's got the rear door open, waiting for me. I catch sight of Riley climbing into a yellow taxicab, her derriere hanging out the backseat for a split second before the door slams shut.

"Riley!" I scream. The taxi rolls forward and I bang on the tinted glass, hollering.

She rolls down the window. "Darn!" she says. "You caught me."

"What the heck are you *doing*?" I'm sweating. I'm panicked. She's leaving me. And I am not a girl who sweats or panics. Or entertains the notion. "We're going to Grammy Claire's house! With Butler Reginald!"

"No, *you* are going to Grammy Claire's house. Daddy wired me a ticket for the six o'clock flight to Los Angeles. I'm gonna go soak up some California sunshine and beaches and surfer dudes."

"But you can't go without me! And what about your boy-friend, Brad?"

She smiles prettily behind a pair of sunglasses, which don't really work with spiky blue hair. "I'm not going to touch, just look. Listen, Tara, *you* got those letters from Grammy Claire, not me. And you're gonna have a great time getting out of suf-focating Bayou Bridge. Let Mamma get her crying jags out of the way and pull herself together. I'll call you every day — deal? You got your cell phone? Charger?"

"Um, yeah. I think so." I place my hands on the edge of the window, as if I can keep her here, even though the metal trim is boiling hot and I have to yank my hands back before it burns my skin. "I don't want to be alone!"

"Believe me, I'll just complain and get bored. We'll both have more fun where we're going. Right?"

I try to read her eyes. Why does everybody wear dark glasses so I can't see what they're not telling me?

"You got Butler Dude at your command. Make him take you shopping, to the movies. Eat gourmet food, watch TV all day, sleep in. Go crazy — it's summer vacation."

"We could do all those things together. Please?"

"Come here," Riley says suddenly.

"What?" I ask, suspicious.

She rolls her eyes. "Just come closer and lean in the window."

I obey, moving stiffly. The taxi smells like cigarettes and burnt coffee. My eyes dart to the taxi driver, then back to Riley's face, stormy and stubborn.

She kisses my cheek, then begins to roll up the window. "Feel better?"

No, I do not feel better. I'm all-over numb. I think I'm gonna puke.

"See you in a few weeks!" she calls through the window crack.

The taxi guns it down the oak-lined street and disappears around the bend. The neighborhood is silent. Not even the trees shake their leaves. No squirrels or birds or traffic. I feel completely, utterly alone. I want to run to the cemetery to visit Grammy Claire's grave. But hanging out in graveyards is the sort of thing kids like Shelby Jayne Allemond do.

My throat lets out an embarrassing sob, but I suck it in fast. After all, I'm a daughter of the Doucet family. Seventh genera-tion of the South and the Old Confederacy. Drilled into me since birth. Too bad it skipped Riley. She doesn't care at all what people think. What would it be like to be her? I shudder at the thought. But part of me secretly wishes I could be a rebel, too.

Butler Reginald is standing patiently, waiting to open the rear door. Grammy Claire said she trusted him, and I look into his ocean-blue eyes, feeling a tiny bit free from worry since I don't have to take care of Mamma or fix my own meals now.

"Think I could bring my best friend, Alyson, with me?"

"I'm sorry," the butler says, sounding genuine. "Inviting a friend isn't in my instructions."

My eyes sting in the bright sunshine. "Where's the truck guy with all my stuff?"

"He went on ahead. Your luggage will be at the house when we arrive."

"Okay." I pause. "What about my mamma?"

"I assure you, Miss Tara, she will be well taken care of. She's in no condition to travel," he adds softly. "Your grandmother gave me instructions to help Miz Landry care for her while we're gone."

That makes me feel better, even as I chew my lips and stare down the empty road. Finally, I slide into the backseat. Even with the air-conditioning going full blast the leather is sticky on my sweaty legs.

Putting my hand into my pocket, I feel the cool brass key Grammy Claire sent me. Ever since the horrible car accident, I feel like I've been floating in space, or drifting out at sea without a map, but now I have a little piece of my grandmother with me.

Butler Reginald drives like he's my very own chauffeur. I smell the scent of his aftershave as he spins the steering wheel. Classical music pipes softly through the car.

Twisting around in my seat, I let out a gasp when I spot a black car with government plates pulling around the bend of the street and heading straight for my house, perfect on the outside, crumbling on the inside. What if it's the bank with foreclosure papers, ready to kick Mamma out?

I picture us being thrown out of our house, homeless. Mamma wandering the streets. Never seeing Riley again because she's either a beach bum or an extra in one of Daddy's movies. Or a backup singer — I mean screecher — for Kittie.

I pray Miz Landry will bar the doors, shove furniture under the knobs, and not let anybody inside. Not without a search warrant and the police and a SWAT team.

I'm grateful for tinted window glass. Relief that I'm zooming away fills my chest — followed by a steady drip of guilt for leaving Mamma behind, glued to that dern bed.

"That black car going to my house?" I ask Butler Reginald with a gulp.

"No, Miss Tara. Please don't worry. Everything will be well."

I'm still on my knees, staring out the back window, when I spot a large monarch butterfly flying wildly down the white center line of the road. Darting, zooming, batting its wings at the air.

I can hardly believe my eyes.

A fourth butterfly is now following us.

Chapter Seven

The butterfly counts not months but moments, and has time enough.

~RABINDRANATH TAGORE~

I twist back around, secretly sucking on the soft strands of my hair and hoping Butler Reginald isn't peeking at me through the rearview mirror.

Mamma hates when I chew on my hair, but it can be very comforting. I say a prayer that Miz Landry will turn out all the lights and not answer the door. I curse Riley for deserting me. And when I think about Daddy and Mamma I feel so angry I want to spit, but I can't even throw a temper tantrum. I have to pretend I'm fine. Because a girl like me never spits or pitches temper tantrums.

There's a new girl at school — Shelby Jayne — who calls me Pantene Princess. When she said it the first time, it was all I could do to freeze-smile at her because it actually hurt my feelings. She probably thought I was rich and stuck-up, but believe me, living in the Doucet Mansion is often not worth the trouble.

Jett Dupuis told me that my hair looks like a waterfall when it hangs over my school desk. Which is the nicest thing anybody's ever said to me. Girls never give you a real compliment.

Settling back against the seat, I turn the air-conditioning vents toward me and let out a sigh. I want to eat Grammy Claire's homemade pecan pie with globs of whipped cream and feel stuffed and satisfied, but I only got a hollowed-out feeling. Daddy will spend money on Riley at the fancy-schmancy shopping malls and introduce her to all the Hollywood stars. I hate my sister right now. And Daddy for not rescuing me.

An hour later when I wake up, the leather seat is stuck to my cheek. After peeling myself off, I roll down the window and let the wind whip my hair as we cruise through winding roads sheltered by giant oaks. I can feel a funny web of creases on my face from sleeping, and I got a crick in my neck.

Glancing in the rearview mirror, I catch sight of Butler Reginald's eyes and then turn away, not wanting him to know that I was watching him. He steers impassively, nods politely, and puts his own eyes back on the road.

"We're almost there, Miss Tara."

"Um, okay." Actually, I barely remember this road that leads to my grandmother's house. It's outside of some other small town, and it's been three years since I visited the place. She always stayed with us when she came home for her vacation.

Patches of water sparkle through stands of cypresses, sun reflecting off the surface, making me squint. The Lincoln slows, makes a turn onto a dirt road, and my stomach jumps over the potholes along with the tires.

I see the roof of the house peeking through the trees, along with a series of chimneys. I do remember lots of rooms and hallways and staircases. Smoke curls out of one of the chimneys. Someone is inside. Are they cooking dinner? Building a fire? Last time I checked it was July, not December.

Shooting around a circular driveway, the Lincoln glides up to the front porch and the butler presses the brakes real smooth and easy like he's done it a million times.

I stab the unlock button on the car door and jump out.

Grammy Claire's house is an old Victorian. It needs a paint job, the yard is overgrown, but the front door has been polished and the porch swept. There's even a swing rocking back and forth in the breeze at one end of the front porch.

I remember that swing. I remember my grandmother rocking me in her arms when we watched fireflies at night in the woods. "She helped me catch 'em in a jar once," I say, the memory zinging right out my mouth.

Butler Reginald raises an eyebrow as he lifts a suitcase from the trunk.

"Fireflies," I add, and turn away so he can't see my face turning red from talking to myself.

An old water pump sits next to the dilapidated barn, red paint peeling up in curls like ribbons on a birthday gift. The biggest oak tree used to have a swing, but now there's only a frayed rope dangling from one of the limbs.

"I believe Madame See has already arrived," the butler tells me, hauling the last suitcase to the front door.

I blink at him. "*Who* is that?"

"Our cook. And housekeeper of sorts, although I do believe we'll need to help with the washing up and dusting."

"Oh. You never mentioned her before."

He smiles at me, the skin around his eyes crinkling up like a grandfather's even though I never knew my grandfathers. "I didn't think you usually concerned yourself with the help before."

"Oh," I say again, not sure if he's just making a statement or making fun of me. "I guess so." Then I remember Grammy Claire's letter. I'd forgotten that she'd mentioned someone named Madame Erial See would be cooking for us. And that she was a darn good cook. My stomach suddenly growls, empty and hungry. It's all part of the peculiar plan Grammy Claire arranged for After Her Death.

"Shall we?" Butler Reginald says, beckoning for me to climb the porch steps.

"Well — I — you go on ahead. That letter. Grammy Claire —" I stop, not wanting to explain Secret Key Number One. "Don't worry, Mister Butler, I know my way around." I'm sorta lying, but sorta not. I don't gotta tell him that my memory is fuzzy.

"You may call me Reginald."

"Okay. See you at dinner!" I pause and take a breath. "Butler Reginald."

Then I disappear into the shrubbery around the side of the house. Oak trees loom over the yard, sunlight painting the ground in yellow strokes between the dark, shaded spots.

I pull out the brass key with the dangling tag. When I see it, I know deep in my heart that Grammy Claire is watching out for me, even if she is in heaven.

She'd sent me the secret key to the secret door.

Memories flood over me, snatches of conversation I'd forgotten. My grandmother had once told me that if anything ever happened to her, she was going to send me to her old house with her laboratory and books and that I'd inherit it all.

Five years ago when she moved to that island, those words didn't mean much. I was only seven. But now it does mean something. Something very much.

As I tramp through a pile of old crunchy leaves, I glance up at the wooden slats of the house, turrets and angles sharp against the blue sky. I also spot the bay window, lace curtains hanging across shadowed glass.

Grammy Claire's house can be my secret hideout. A place to get away from Riley and Mamma and Daddy and all that depression and divorce stuff. I wonder how long I get to keep Butler Reginald and his services. Maybe he's a gift from Grammy Claire, too.

I start running until I reach a yellow-painted lattice arch. A mass of tangled green vines weaves through the slats like snakes. It's cooler back here, mysterious, and chills run down my neck as I stick the key into the lock.

Grammy Claire and I always called it our secret door — even if it wasn't really secret. It was our secret entrance because it wasn't the *front* door. The door opened into the back of the house so we could come and go as we pleased without anybody else knowing what we were up to. Especially when Mamma and Riley and Daddy were here, too.

Pressing against the dark green door, I suddenly remember those times Grammy Claire held my hand as we walked down to the bayou and caught dragonflies and frogs and fished off the dock. We had picnics with strawberry jam sandwiches and cold lemonade. Crunchy dill pickles and cupcakes with candy sprinkles.

Emotion burns my eyes, makes my throat close up hard and tight.

When the knob doesn't turn, my stomach drops all the way to my toes. Then I realize that I haven't turned the key in the right direction. Using both hands, I jiggle the key in the lock, and hear a wonderful, distinct *click*.

The door gives a creak as I push it open and enter a long, dim hallway.

This door actually enters on the second floor. The house is built on a sloping hill so the kitchen and dining room and great room are on the lower part of the hill. Our secret back door enters a different part altogether, right into the middle of the house.

Guest rooms and bathrooms occupy the second floor, as well as a small sitting room. The hallway ends right smack on a brick wall. Next to the wall is a door that looks like a closet, but when I open it, a winding set of stairs leads to the ground floor. I tiptoe down to the first landing and peek through empty space to the foyer below. I hear shuffling feet as Butler Reginald comes in with the luggage. I see my backpack sitting in the middle of the pile as well as a raincoat and briefcase and assorted boxes filled with groceries.

I run back up the staircase so he won't see me. There's a closed door at the other end of the hallway, which hides another set of stairs leading to the third floor.

When I pound up the carpeted steps, the air is thick and motionless and steaming hot. Sweat dribbles into my eyes, but memories are coming back, faster and faster.

On the third floor is a library with tables and rugs and so many books I stand stock-still in shock. The library is cool and

shaded by one of the oak trees. There's even a set of doors leading to a balcony for reading outside. I hug myself, thinking
about how this library is mine now.

More doors on the third floor open up to linen closets and
storage closets filled with boxes and junk and old furniture,
bird cages and trunks. When I throw open the last door on the
east side of the house I let out a squeal of delight. "It's here, it's
still here!"

Grammy Claire always called this the morning room. Wide-
paned windows stretch across the east and south walls, so big
they are almost ceiling high. The windows give a panoramic view
of the dark oaks, magnolias, and cypresses — the bayou running like a milky brown thread just a few hundred yards away.

The first sunlight of the day pokes its rays into this room. We
used to have breakfast here before my grandmother went to
work — or before we took hikes or went picnicking.

When I was eight, nine, and ten years old, I got to spend a
week here during summer vacation, but I never remember
Riley being here. Only me. Did Riley not want to come? I don't
know and don't remember.

I'm so glad to be here I want to dance and shout, but part of
me wishes that I wasn't alone. Just me and Butler Reginald.
And some lady called Madame See — a very strange name.
Why not Miss or Miz? I wonder how long she's worked for
Grammy Claire. Maybe they met while she was researching in
Africa or India or China. I could never keep track.

There's still one more floor at the top of the house, and I practically race up the narrow steps, my sundress swishing against my legs, the brass key bouncing in my pocket. I'd buttoned the pocket just in case, so I wouldn't accidentally lose the key.

The fourth floor only has one fat, heavy door, and I've never been inside. Grammy Claire never let me up here — and the small, crooked steps in the dark, windowless passage are creepy.

She told me there were delicate and complicated science experiments going on in this room and I was not to disturb them. Ever.

I wonder what will happen to her laboratory equipment now that she's gone. Maybe Butler Reginald's instructions are to clean out the fourth-floor laboratory while I have a little vacation and Mamma has time to recuperate. I try not to think about how lonely I'll be the next week without Riley. Instead, I've got the freedom to do whatever I want every single day.

I pull the hallway light switch and as soon as the bulb glows, the faint sound of music wafts through the floorboards and oozes out the walls. Shimmery music, like an angel choir. *Where is it coming from?*

A moment later, Butler Reginald calls my name from the bottom of the house.

My stomach growls again, empty. Looks like my appetite is coming back. I hope Madame See fixes real food and not just rice with chopsticks and soy sauce.

"Miss Tara! Where are you?"

I run to the stairwell and yell, "Coming!" Then hurry back to Grammy Claire's laboratory to check the doorknob, but it is truly locked. And I have no key.

In the dim light, I see a note clipped to a nail on the door. Just a small square of cardstock hanging silent as a mouse. And written in my grandmother's beautiful, familiar handwriting are the words, *Not yet, Tara. Not yet. All my love forever, G. C.*

Chapter Eight

If nothing ever changed, there'd be no butterflies.

~ U N K N O W N ~

Dinner is fried catfish and hush puppies and coleslaw with sherbet for dessert and fresh sliced strawberries spooned on top.

I eat until I'm stuffed. Then I feel a bit sick when Butler Reginald shows me to my room. "I think my stomach shrank," I whimper.

"Madame See *is* an excellent cook. A warm bath will do you a world of good," he tells me in his comforting accent. "Your private bath is right next door."

"Um, where is your room?"

"I have arranged my belongings in the downstairs guest room. So the second floor is yours alone, Miss Tara."

I chew on some of my hair and nod. "So where is Madame See?"

"She's in a bedroom right by the kitchen. It was a servant's room when the house was first built. She prefers it that way. Her English is only passable and she'll only be with us for a few weeks before she returns to the island. Then you go home and so do I. Very simple."

"Did Grammy Claire know her from that island?"

"I believe so. I've never met her myself until today. Your grandmother arranged all of this in case of an untimely death. She knew you would need quiet and privacy. There's an open-ended airline ticket for myself and Madame See in case of an unexpected, um, situation such as her sudden demise. Your grandmother took precautions, planned ahead, and always thought of you and your sister." He says this last part in a tight voice and I realize that he's grieving a bit, too.

During dinner, I'd caught glimpses of a round, short woman with thick black hair piled on top of her head. I'd figured she was from China or somewhere near it, but now that I think about it, she looks more like some sort of islander. From World Geography, I know that the Pacific Ocean is filled with thousands of islands. Grammy Claire had once shown me a map, but I know I won't be able to find the right island again without someone pointing it out to me.

When I'd dragged my suitcase and stuff upstairs, I'd heard the sounds of pots and pans and crackling hot oil coming from the kitchen. The smells had been heavenly. The food even better.

"Where'd Madame See learn to cook like a Southern gramma?"

Butler Reginald retrieves a set of bath towels from the linen closet. "The kitchen is well stocked with recipes and cookbooks. A professional cook learns how to make just about everything. Dinner reminded me of fish and chips as a boy in Leeds. Your grandmother wanted familiar, home-cooked food for you these first few days. She thought of everything. Even the menu."

I'm overwhelmed by Grammy Claire's detailed instructions as I take the stack of towels and yawn, anxious to get a bath and unpack.

Grammy Claire had also chosen my room for me, but it turned out to be the same room I'd used in the past, a bedroom overlooking the flower garden on the west side of the house.

The walls are pale pink with green trim, the floorboards so old they creak. The closet is one of those old-fashioned wardrobes. I hang up my clothes and then grab my nightgown and clean underwear and head for the bathroom.

After I'm done bathing, I'm even sleepier. I close the curtains and notice that someone brought my pillow from home.

I'm so tired and grateful to Butler Reginald, I almost break down crying again.

While I comb out my wet hair, I put shirts and socks into the drawers inside the wardrobe. When I open the second to last drawer, it's jammed shut. Some sort of tall wooden box inside is preventing the drawer from opening. Wiggling and tilting, I finally yank it open.

An envelope slides out, too — and my name is on the front!

The box is about the size of a jewelry box. On the lid there's a swirl of knots and loops, inlaid with black onyx and amethyst. *Wow.* I've never seen this box before. It's so gorgeous I just stare at it, running my hand over the purple stones. It's also locked — with a big, fat, ugly padlock.

I dig into the letter, dying to read what Grammy Claire is going to tell me next!

Once again, the envelope is sealed, and the letters *C.T.C.* pressed into the wax while it was hot. Grammy Claire's initials. The wax makes a hardened puddle, covering most of the envelope's flap. If somebody else opened it up before I did, I'd know it for sure.

Inside the new envelope are three notes numbered *1, 2,* and *3.* The first note is made of a cream-colored cardstock that's been folded in thirds and taped shut. When I slit the tape and unfold it, a small silver key is fastened to the cardstock. A key tagged with the words *Number Two.*

This key will probably open the jewelry box!

When I stick the silver key into the padlock, it makes a popping noise. I jerk out the bolt and pull it apart to lift the lid. Inside the box is a huge assortment of keys, in all sizes and shapes. Modern keys and old-fashioned keys and skeleton keys. Every single key has a tag attached to it, looped with a thin gold thread — just like the key still sitting in my sundress pocket.

I set the keys across the yellow embroidered coverlet, putting them in order. Number Three, Number Four, Number Five, Number Six, Number Seven, Number Eight, Number Nine, and finally Number Ten.

Grabbing Key Number One that opened the back door to the house, I add it to its correct spot, as well as the key to the padlock, which is Key Number Two. I stare at all those keys until my eyes bug out of their sockets. Ten keys. Ten locks.

Hurriedly, I open Note #2.

Dearest Tara,

What a treasure, eh? The keys in this beautiful box all belonged to me and now they belong to you. Guard them with your life. If I told you right now what they opened nothing would make sense, but all in good time, darling child. When the time is right, you will know the answers to all your questions. You may have to figure out a

few mysteries and puzzles along the way, but I
know you can do it. If you need Riley's help, know
that you can trust her.

I stop reading and frown. Now that Riley's gone, she's no use at all. I'm angry at her for leaving, but she misses Daddy more than I do. She's got more memories of him.

And now I realize that I miss *her* — even if she yells a lot. This house is so very quiet, but I keep reading, shivers dancing along my arms.

Remember what I said from the first letter
earlier today.
All my love forever,
Your Grammy Claire

P.S. If you're wondering where the unique box
came from, I received it as a wedding gift from
your old romantic granddaddy. He got it
from Miz Annie Chaisson, a woman who lived
in the swamp and one of my dearest friends
before she passed two years ago. She was also a
healer, a <u>traiteur</u>, which is a Cajun French word
for someone who treats and heals sick folks. Miz
Annie had a special knowledge of herbs, too.

*Your mamma has suffered from "melancholy,"
ever since she was a teenager, but don't hold it
against her. When I took your mamma to visit
her, Miz Annie always knew what concoction to
give Becca, plus all those prayers and love Miz
Annie blessed her with. Your mamma — she really
does need you. Forgive her and love her. And
Riley, too!*

My mind whirls as I run a finger over the paper and chills run down my neck.

"I'll bet Grammy Claire's talking about the mother of Miz Mirage, the woman who lives in the swamp," I say out loud. "The one all the kids at school call a swamp witch." I'd always heard she was spooky and might put a spell on you. Now I wonder. "Maybe what she does ain't bad magic at all."

Words dance in front of my eyes. *Herbs. Healing. Prayers. Love.*

Swallowing hard, I think about that new girl last year at school, Shelby Jayne, the daughter of Miz Mirage. I think about how I teased her and dared her to jump off the old broken pier into the bayou where the alligators swim.

I feel myself go hot as I realize that since my Grammy Claire used to take my mamma to get healed by Miz Annie, she must also know Shelby Jayne's mamma, Miz Mirage. How peculiar. I also notice that Miz Annie has the same last name Grammy Claire does. Were they related? Or is it just coincidence?

Another thought races into my head. A good one. Miz Mirage is a *traiteur* — and she's still alive. Maybe she can help my mamma now, just as Miz Annie did all those years ago. I can't stand the thought of Mamma rotting away in that South Wing for the rest of her life, and now me and Mamma and Riley are all in different spots around the country. Separated. Alone. Doesn't feel right at all.

I take a shaky breath and open Note #3, written on the same paper as the first two.

> *Key Number Three is next, Tara. You'll find it will work in my bedroom, but more details than that I cannot give you. It's a matter of security. You're a smart girl and I have no worries about you. As long as you know that the nipwisipwis is the most important thing in the world right now. Above anything else! Even your very life!*
>
> *IMPORTANT: Destroy Note #3 about the key ASAP!*

My heart is beating so fast I can barely hear myself think. Destroy this note? What is my grandmother afraid of? Cold chills run along my arms and legs. And what the heck does *nipwisipwis* mean? How can *nipwisipwis* be more important than my own life? Is someone gonna kill me over some freaky-sounding word like *nipwisipwis*?

I hold Grammy Claire's new letter with all its words and stories tight to my chest, wanting to hug it, wanting to kiss it, wishing so bad I could hug *her* one more time.

The letters are more of a treasure than the box or the keys. I read every word ten times over, soaking it up, laughing because I can hear her voice in my head, like she's talking to me.

Except for that whole *nipwisipwis* thing . . . which is giving me the heebie-jeebies.

I scoop up the ten keys in my hands, cupping my palms to hold them all together. Ten mysterious keys straight from Grammy Claire. Ten keys that unlock what?

I pour the jumble of silver and gold and brass through my fingers like the keys are jewels, the tags fluttering like wings as they fall on the bedspread.

I feel like I've got ten secrets.

With a start, I notice that my yellow bedspread is embroidered in butterflies, and that every one of them is outlined in gold thread. The bedspread is like an omen, and I can't shake off the memory of the four butterflies I saw today. Two flying right into my window, the blue butterfly and Mamma, and the orange-and-black monarch fluttering behind our car. What do those butterflies mean? Probably nothing. I'm probably turning as loony as Mamma. But I get chills when I remember the purple butterfly looking into my eyes, like it was reading my thoughts. The way it clung to my finger, then landed on my heart for that single, magical moment. I get shivers all over again.

No, there were *five* butterflies today. A butterfly had died a dreadful death on Riley's dresser. I can still picture the smashed wings, the broken body. I wish I could have saved it.

A butterfly had come to Riley, too. It was a sign. And she wasn't here.

I'm so tired I'm about to fall over, but now I *have* to go to Grammy Claire's bedroom.

First, I have to destroy the note as instructed, but I can't just tear it into pieces. Someone could come along and tape it back together. I decide to burn it and then flush it down the toilet.

As I tiptoe down the main staircase to find a box of matches in the dark kitchen, the front door crashes wide open. And someone starts yelling at the top of their lungs.

Chapter Nine

There is nothing in a caterpillar that tells you it's going to be
a butterfly.

~RICHARD BUCKMINSTER FULLER~

I leap off the bottom step, slip, and slide on the polished floor. And crash-land right into Riley.

She's like a ghost come back from the dead. Or, rather, from Hollywood.

"What are *you* doing here?" I ask her, completely shocked to see her.

"I don't want to talk about it."

She dumps two suitcases, a duffel bag, a backpack, and a couple of black hoodie sweatshirts onto the floor of Grammy Claire's foyer.

"What happened to the flight? Did you already go and come back again?" I'm puzzling out how she could have flown there and returned so fast. My brain isn't working.

"I don't want to talk about it."

"You said that already."

"What part of, 'I don't want to talk about it,' don't you understand?" Her eyes are wild in the dim light. Her skin looks pasty white like she hasn't eaten or slept in a week.

"But Daddy sent you a ticket! I didn't think I'd see you until school starts again — if you didn't desert me and never come home again." That scenario had actually crossed my mind.

"That makes two of us." Her voice is edged in broken glass, and she looks like she wants to claw someone — anyone.

But I feel strangely relieved to see her. I want to hug her, but I don't dare. She might draw blood.

"Was the flight canceled?"

"No!"

Sarcasm oozes out of my mouth like molten lava. "Did you get kicked off the plane for too much luggage? Too much Kittie blasting out your ears? Punching your seatmate?"

"No, no, and *no*!" Riley kicks at her duffel bag, then paces up and down the hall, peeking into the kitchen where a night-light is plugged into the wall by the stove. She goes in and out of the dining room, its table and chairs shrouded in shadows.

"Tell me what happened!" I demand, following her.

Her eyes are dark and fiery as she *clomp, clomp, clomps* back and forth across the entry hall in her boots. A moment later I hear that shiver of music again, trembling in the distance, wafting through the air. Where's it coming from? Seems like I should know.

"Tell me," I say once more, slumping onto the bottom step of the staircase. She's going to wake the dead with all that noise, but maybe Butler Reginald and Madame See are cowering behind their doors, figuring it's safer not to get in Riley's way.

She finally stops clomping, sticks her hands on her hips, and says in a hard, mean voice, "If you simply *have* to know, Tara, there was no ticket waiting for me at the airline counter."

"But Daddy said he'd call ahead and purchase it for you."

"News flash: Daddy is a liar. I drove two hours all the way to New Orleans and two hours all the way back for a pack of lies."

I gulped. "Did you call him?"

She gives me her famous eye roll. "Of course I called him."

"What did he say?"

She's tall and tough standing in front of me, and I'm almost afraid of her. "He said he had to go somewhere on location out in the Mojave Desert to shoot some scenes for a couple of weeks and I'd — I'd just be in the way."

"Maybe you could stay with the new wife until he gets back."

She fixes me with a cold stare. "He took her with him."

I'm so shocked, outrage rises up in my throat. "I'm sorry," I whisper, hoping she won't yell at me for saying it.

Riley's voice goes deadly quiet. "I'll never believe him again as long as I live. There was never any ticket. There was no real trip for me to see him. He just strings us along, thinking we'll buy it hook, line, and sinker."

"He didn't even come to the funeral," I add, and I can feel my lips begin to tremble.

"We're not going to be suckers anymore, Tara. I won't see him again until he comes crawling back on his knees all the way from Sunset Boulevard."

My eyebrows shoot up. That's impressive. Sometimes I wish I was more like my big sister. She's so stubborn. Obstinate, Mamma always says.

Riley rolls the strap of her giant black purse off her shoulder where it lands on the floor with a thud. I wonder if she packed her entire room. Maybe she brought that blistering speaker system with her, hidden under her collection of obnoxious combat boots.

"It's just you and me, kid," she finally says, and it sounds like a line from some old movie.

Two seconds later, my callous and dangerous sister — who was born without a real heart — and who actually got herself a tattoo of a snake on her hip during Mardi Gras — bursts into tears.

Later, we sit in the empty great room, drinking hot chocolate from packets I dug out of one of the kitchen cupboards while Riley boiled water in a teapot.

I don't like sitting in a house full of shadows so I turn on every single light and pretend it's afternoon on a bright, sunny day.

The great room or parlor or front room or whatever it's called is big and open and drafty. Parquet floors run the entire length and there's a majestic grand piano taking up one whole end. The velvet red drapes on the picture windows are closed for the night.

Two grandfather clocks sit, one on either end, and several ornate European clocks hang all over the walls. Every fifteen minutes, one of them chimes out a different melody.

Riley sprawls over one end of a Victorian fainting couch. I sit on another sofa and listen to the whispering music I've been hearing all day. Turns out the music is coming from an ancient pipe organ sitting in a corner.

Riley sips her cocoa as we listen to the shivery music floating above us. "I'm pretty sure the pipes on that organ are broken. Got holes or something."

I nod and try not to burn my tongue on my drink. "It's like a ghost is playing that organ."

"The air must be passing through the broken pipes and humming through the whole house."

I give her a cautious smile. "I kind of like it. As if the house is talking to us — or singing to us."

Riley lifts her eyebrows and actually returns the smile for a whole three seconds. Streaks of dirt run down her cheeks, like she walked all the way back from the airport crying.

The great room has an open columned archway all the way around it. Crumbling Italian columns with peeling paint. It always feels like I'm sitting inside a Roman swimming pool without any water.

Inside the hallway of columns is a picture gallery. Paintings of Victorian residents sitting in cafés and gardens. A couple of stone turreted castles with moats and fog lacing the air.

There's a mildew smell inside the house, even though I have my nose inside my mug of chocolate. Luckily, I'd found marshmallows in the pantry, too, and I dunk them with my spoon, slurping up bites like I'm eating cereal.

I remember this room, but seems like we spent most of our time outdoors or in the kitchen. Or I read a stack of books in the swing while Grammy Claire worked in her study. The house has been shut up too long. The sweltering humidity has wormed its way into the linens and draperies, creating the strange smell.

"This is a weird house," Riley says, staring at the ceiling. "Did Grammy Claire furnish it like this or did it come already done up?"

"I'm not sure. She didn't spend much time here."

"She was tied to that dumb island for some reason," Riley adds.

Even though Grammy Claire telephoned, sent packages, and we Skyped every Sunday, I missed her all the time. I'd ask her what was so great about that island, and she'd say, "Secret research, darling girl. One day I can show you. Soon, now. Very soon."

Now I'll never know what she loved so much that took her away from us. Anger stabs my heart. Seems like she loved that island more than us. I want to hug her and yell at her both. And I can't do neither.

I blurt out, "Maybe Grammy Claire brought us here so she can *give* us this house. In case we really do lose the Doucet Mansion."

"The Doucet Mansion is a dump. Daddy should have sold it to the state and turned it into a historical site with tours and a gift shop. Then Mamma wouldn't have lost the entire inheritance."

The fear of foreclosure looms again and my stomach knots up. "Can't imagine not living there. After seven generations."

Riley snorts. "You're so funny, Tara. Don't get so hung up on 'seven generations.' You sound like Mamma. She's brain-washed you good. What do you care? It's just a house. An old, creaky, falling-apart one. Most families eventually lose them. Or bulldoze 'em."

"But it's still our house! And this one's old, too! Mamma will just die if the bank takes our house from her. They'll have to carry her out of the South Wing. What will the neighbors think? Or the Parish Ladies Club? It's positively mortifying."

Riley swings her legs around and gives me a piercing gaze that makes me flinch. "Don't go all Scarlett O'Hara on me, okay? Mamma will have to just get over it."

"But I don't want to live all the way out here, especially without Grammy Claire."

"Maybe we can sell it and get an apartment or a condo."

"I refuse to live in an apartment! I'd rather die myself."

Riley giggles, and then begins seriously laughing, holding her stomach. I'm offended. For me and Mamma both. Doesn't she care about our long-held family name?

"You are hilarious, Tara. Absolutely hilarious. You should have been born a hundred years ago."

I let out a loud harrumph, but it's not as good as hers. Tentatively, I ask, "You think Mamma's okay?"

Riley goes back to swinging her feet, lying back on the arm of the couch, face staring at the ceiling. "Yeah, she'll be okay. Same as usual."

"I want her to be *better* than same as usual." I slurp the last of my cocoa and set the mug on a coaster. "Riley," I start again, real soft. "I'm glad you came back from the airport. I'm glad you're here."

She jerks her chin up and I know I've surprised her. I have never said that to my sister in our entire lives.

"I didn't want to be alone. Even if Butler Reginald and Madame See are here."

She shrugs again. "Um, okay."

"Grammy Claire says I can trust you."

Riley's eyes get a funny look. "When did she say something like that?"

"Today — in her letters."

"You're getting more letters? That's weird. How come I'm not getting any letters?"

"Maybe *you* haven't been in the right place at the right time yet."

I watch her smile again, and she looks like a grown-up, amused at what I just said. Strangely, I feel comforted. I straighten the doily under my mug and line up the table with the couch so the furniture is square and perfectly straight.

I suppress the urge to fix the rug fringe laid out over all those yards and yards of floor.

"Relax, Tara, you can fix it in the morning. Let's go to bed. I can't think straight any longer."

Then I remember the strange word from Grammy Claire's letter. "Can I borrow your phone? Mine doesn't have Internet and I have to look something up."

She doesn't move at first, and she really does look exhausted after going to New Orleans and back. Finally, she digs inside her bra strap where she keeps her cell phone and moves her fingers over the screen. "What do you have to look up?"

I roll my eyes just like she does. "Can I do it? I'm not going to break your phone."

"Nope, I can type faster than you. Tell me what I should search for."

I relent. "The word *nipwisipwis*."

"Huh?"

I spell it for her, closing my eyes as I see the word from Grammy Claire's letter in my mind.

Riley taps at the screen, and then waits a couple seconds. Finally, she looks up at me, a strange expression on her face.

"So what is it?" I *really, really* wish I knew what the word meant before my sister did.

"*Nipwisipwis* is from some bizarre language I never heard of before. Where'd you say you saw it?"

"I didn't." I don't want to tell her, but if I don't, she probably won't help me. "Grammy Claire's letter."

"Aah," Riley says. "I get it now. It's a language from an island in the South Pacific. It must be from the island Grammy Claire was living on. The language is Chuukese." She tries to pronounce it and gets her letters so twisted it sounds hilarious.

We start giggling, but I stop. "So what's the word? What does *nipwisipwis mean*?"

Riley extends the phone and I leap up, holding the screen

83

close. An odd ringing starts up in my ears, but maybe that's the old pipe organ letting loose again.

"You look strange, Tara."

My throat tightens. "I should have known already."

Riley's dark eyes look hollow in the lamplight. "Known what?"

I can barely choke out the words. "*Nipwisipwis* means *butterfly*!"

Chapter Ten

Divine creation can be seen painted on the canvas of a butterfly's wing.

~ K . D ' A N G E L O ~

Sitting on the couch, I know that I've just had the most peculiar day of my whole life.... Are butterflies actually following me? Do butterflies have a brain that can think and follow directions? Maybe they do in an alternate reality — or another universe, but not on this planet.

Why did my grandmother use the word *nipwisipwis* — from the very island where she's been living all these years? Why didn't she just say *butterfly* — why all the secrecy?

As long as you know that the <u>nipwisipwis</u> is the

*most important thing in the world right now.
Above anything else! Even your very life!*

Nipwisipwis are more important than my own life? Crazy!
Chills race down my neck and buzz my toes and the tips of my
fingers.

Maybe *nipwisipwis* — or *butterfly* — is some sort of code word.

Riley's practically falling asleep on the fainting couch and
I'm yawning so deeply my jaw cracks. We stick our mugs in the
kitchen sink, and I run water to soak. We drag ourselves
upstairs, and I find a bedroom made up for Riley just down the
hall from my room — which obviously means she's *supposed* to
be here with me.

Riley flops on her bed, still fully dressed. "Tara, would you
please help me take off my boots?"

"Oh, you big baby!"

"Pretty please? I'm so tired I can't move."

I glare at her, but the "please" gets to me. I unwind the
laces around the metal hooks and pull hard. The boots
come off with a popping sound and I practically fall on the
floor.

"You need to do laundry," I say, holding my nose.

"Yeah, yeah," Riley says with her eyes closed (but I swear
she's doing an eye roll in her sleep) and she's gone. Snoring.
Spread-eagled on her stomach, toes hanging off the end of the

mattress, hair gel glittering on the pillow, mascara smeared down her cheek.

I throw an extra pillow at her and shut the door.

Then I memorize how to spell *nipwisipwis*, take a match to the note sitting in the sink, and watch the yellow flame eat up the paper until it's nothing but charred-up ashes. The worst part is watching Grammy Claire's handwriting go up in flames. I'm so glad I have the letters.

After I flush the ashes down the toilet, I try to go to sleep, but I can't. It's almost midnight — I can hear the clocks chiming from the great room below me — and my eyes are burning just like that note.

I roll back and forth under the butterfly quilt and suddenly I hear Riley stumbling around. Her music comes on, soft, but it's a dull *thud, thud, thud*. Like a pulse under my skin. Maybe she can't sleep without Kittie. They say you can go deaf wearing earphones twenty-four seven, so I'd decided a long time ago that I would never do that. Besides, how do you properly clean earbuds?

Finally, I stumble out of my bed myself. I can't sleep until I try that third mysterious key.

The house is still warm from the heat of the day and I'm only wearing my shorts and tank-top pajamas. I grab a robe in case I run into Butler Reginald or Madame See headed to the bathroom, and tiptoe into the hallway.

Grammy Claire's bedroom is the farthest one down the hall, tucked in the corner. The door is closed — and locked. Grammy Claire told me in the letter — specifically — that Key Number Three is supposed to open something *inside* her bedroom. But if it's inside, how am I supposed to get to it?

I stand there in the dark hall, stumped. And depressed. And alone.

I peer into the keyhole, but I can't see anything, it's just too small and dark.

The next instant, a creepy prickling oozes up my neck.

Someone has been tampering with Grammy Claire's door-knob. The outside edges where the key goes are jagged and rough, like someone tried to stick something inside and jiggle it open without having the actual key.

Who would have done that? And when?

My heart races. My mind goes wild. It was probably a burglar sneaking into an uninhabited house to rob the place sometime over the past year. Or kids sneaking in on a dare. My grandmother paid a caretaker to check on the house while she was gone. Someone to mow the lawn, check the gas, throw away the junk mail.

I suck on my hair, tasting the green-apple scent. I run a finger over the lock. Someone tried to get in here without a key, and the thought of that makes me nervous.

Butler Reginald told me that he checked out the house when

we got here so there shouldn't be someone hiding behind the door.

I finger the Number Three Key and listen to the house creak and settle and sigh. Faint organ music whispers through the air ducts.

Grammy Claire wants me to do this. I have to find a way inside. Something important is going on and my grandmother has entrusted me with it. Me! She practically said it was a matter of life and death. Goose bumps race along my legs and arms.

Then I let out a snort and drop my piece of wet, sucked-on hair, feeling very stupid. I must *really* be tired! I'm holding the answer in my fist. I thought Key Number Three opened something *inside* the room, but it must be for the door, and I'm standing here like an idiot! Still, I hope nobody is inside ready to smash a bottle over my head.

Bending over, I stick the end of the key into the lock. It's tricky since the tumblers are bent, but I jiggle a lot, twist the knob, and push the door open.

For a moment, I stand in the doorway and just look.

Moonlight flutters across the polished oak floors. The light creates silver ribbons on the braided rugs and along Grammy Claire's old-fashioned headboard.

I let out a sigh of relief. I'm in. And the room looks just like I remember. It's tidy, too, which always gives my brain a sense of relief. After closing and locking the door, I straighten the doily under the nightstand lamp, but that's all that needs doing.

The air is musty and damp so I push aside the floor-length drapes to open the window. Cooler air rushes in, bathing my face. Crickets hum and a distant bird calls somewhere over the trees, but it's too dark to see more than the shadows of the cypress standing at the edge of the bayou waters.

"Okay, Grammy Claire," I whisper. "I'm here. Now what?"

There aren't any secrets sitting on the bed. Or in the wardrobe, which is empty, except for a couple of cotton gardening shirts and a pair of work boots lying on their side on the cedar flooring. I peek inside the boots anyway. Nothin' but dust.

I know what I have to do, but my stomach jumps into my throat. "I hate snooping, Grammy Claire, but I don't got no choice."

I start peeking into every drawer — which are all empty. A couple of expired roly-polies sit in one corner and a curled-up dead spider in another. I turn *over* the drawers and there's nothing underneath them, either.

I look behind the curtains, run my hands along the ledges, check the closet shelves, and pry behind all the scientific books sitting in a case along the wall.

Next, I perch on the edge of a stuffed chair with flowered print and think. Then I go back and open every single one of the books. Nope. No hidden interiors with the pages cut out.

Finally, I check the bathroom, which is also empty, except for some cleanser and sponges and a toilet brush under the sink. Nothing in the shower except a few more dead bugs, which I for sure am not going to pick up and throw out!

"You got me," I say, throwing myself across the bed. I spot sheets under Grammy Claire's bedspread, patterned in the same flowers as the stuffed reading chair.

I pull back the covers and run my hand along the linen. They don't feel dusty, just musty like they've been on the mattress a long time, but the faint scent of Grammy Claire's perfume rises. The smell is woodsy and homey and screams Grammy Claire. Feels almost like she's hugging me as I press my face into the pillow and try not to let fresh tears get everything wet.

I crawl under the comforter and close my eyes. I think I could sleep for a week.

I really gotta get back to my own room and get to bed. . . . I gotta figure out the puzzle of all those keys in the box. . . .

When I wake up, it's the middle of the morning. Bright sunshine streams onto my face. I slept here all night!

I'd left the window open and the bayou has woken up, too. Birds are chattering, cicadas are buzzing in the trees, and there's the soft shush of water down at the dock.

I look for a clock and find one actually plugged in sitting on the nightstand. And ticking. It's almost ten o'clock, but the house beyond the door feels so quiet. No screaming sister. No calls for breakfast. No pounding from Butler Reginald looking for me. Where is everybody?

Lying on my back, I close my eyes, wishing I could sleep for another two hours. But the quiet is bugging me. When I roll over to get up, a butterfly flits through the window. Another butterfly!

I suck in my breath, trying not to move. How'd a butterfly find me here? Heck, how did they find me back home in Bayou Bridge? Double heck, how do they even know who I am to keep finding me in the first place?

The butterfly dances around the furniture, and then peeks into the empty closet before hovering over my head. Staring down at me, its wings softly open and close.

This butterfly is enormous. Twice the size of a regular butterfly, like a giant species. It's got the softest, prettiest shade of pink, ribbons of green along the edges, and brown spots right in the middle of each wing.

"*Nipwisipwis,*" I whisper, and as soon as I speak the word, I swear the butterfly stops to listen, like it recognizes its name. Its antennae waggle back and forth like it's excited. "*Nipwisipwis!*" I say again, louder this time.

The butterfly begins to circle my head. I hear the soft shush of its wings as it flies past my ears. Slowly, it circles and lands on the ribbon edging of my tank top, close to my heart. The giant wings are like brushed velvet, the pink and green colors like the most delicate weaving ever created. "Oh, I wish you were here, Grammy Claire, so you could see this!"

Three breaths later, the pink butterfly lifts off again.

Untangling my bare legs from the sheets, I leap out of bed. I know what I'm supposed to be looking for! Well, I know *where* I should look now. Did the butterfly tell me — or did a good night's sleep make my brain coherent again?

Dropping to the floor, I look under the bed. Then I get the lamp, turn on the switch, and set it on the floor so I can see better. Scooting under the bed, I try not to let the squirmy feeling of dust clumps and more dead spiders freak me out. Then I see it. Something is clinging to the box springs right in the middle of the bed!

I reach out and discover that the lump is a thick bubble envelope taped to the frame — taped a *lot* so it won't fall. There's a ripping sound as I yank it off.

Sliding back out, I sit up and stare at the envelope. My name is written on the front — underneath all the packing tape — in Grammy Claire's handwriting. I'm shaking I'm so excited, and it's painstaking to get all the tape peeled off. Finally, I rip my finger under the flap of the envelope and slide out a small photo album. With a sturdy lock.

Whoever heard of a locked photo album?

Finding the bedroom key lying on the nightstand where I'd left it, I stick it into the lock. It won't fit. The key has the wrong-shaped teeth. I need Key Number Four!

I gallop to the door and peek into the hallway. The coast is clear, and I can't hear anybody moving around. Not even Riley's music. Still, I feel funny. Like I'm being watched.

I go back inside, close and lock the windows, and realize that the giant pink butterfly disappeared while I was under the bed. I can't see it anywhere outside, either. Those butterflies sure know how to disappear.

After relocking the bedroom door, I run back to my own room. I'd hidden the pile of keys between the two mattresses on my bed, all the way in the center. After I find Key Number Four, I shove the rest back in and hurry down the hall.

Once I've locked myself inside again, I stick the key into the photo album and it clicks open perfectly. Breathing hard, I see page after page of photographs. Me and Grammy Claire over the years. Birthdays when I was smashing cake into my face, holidays at the beach, picnics in the backyard, me rowing a pirogue in the water, a photo of me and Grammy Claire laughing hard over something, I can't even remember what. I wonder who took that picture, Mamma or Riley? Or maybe even Daddy? In the center of the album, there's another envelope sealed with that familiar purple wax and the initials G.C.

Dearest Tara,

Good girl! You found it and figured out the keys. The pictures in the album are some of my favorites of you and me over the years, of our life together. I treasure you and I hope you will always treasure these beautiful memories, too. I hope I'll be a part of future memories, but if you're reading this letter, I'm not sure. I'm not sure at all. But we're on our way now, my dear! There is so much more ahead of you — possibly dangerous for us both, but I have confidence that all will be well. I have faith in you and in the <u>nipwisipwis</u>.

Did Angelina visit you this morning, my Giant Pink? I hope so! Isn't she beautiful? She is the reason I gave you Key Number Three to my personal bedroom. You needed to see her. And she needed to meet you. Try to keep her safe. Try to keep them all safe. That is your mission. Guard <u>all</u> that I give you. Tell no one!

All my love forever,
Grammy Claire

Inside the letter is a smaller slip of paper folded into thirds. I open it with a tiny feeling of dread, wondering what's coming next.

Key Number Five is next, Tara. You'll find that this key will work in the most important room of my house. The room with answers. And more questions. And much, much more danger.

IMPORTANT: Destroy this note ASAP!

Chapter Eleven

They say, "Only in dreams men are truly free,
What does a butterfly dream about? — It's already free!"

~SCHOLASTICUS K~

chew on the ends of my hair furiously. Danger? Answers?
Questions? Why is Grammy Claire talking in riddles!

My stomach starts to hurt, but maybe I'm just hungry. The
smell of bacon spirals up to the second landing. Madame
See must be finally cooking, or maybe I finally noticed that I
need food.

I hold the photograph album tight to my chest, lock up
Grammy Claire's bedroom as fast as possible, and race back to
my own room.

Sweat dribbles down my forehead as I scan the room, wondering where I can hide the album. Not that I really need to; the album's purpose was just to hide the new letter. Still, I stuff it into the lining of my suitcase and zip it up and stash it in the closet.

Danger. What kind of danger? Like getting hurt danger? My stomach clenches up even more.

I hear a door slam next to mine and Riley comes out of the bathroom, her feet stomping. I'd recognize her footsteps anywhere. I guess everybody slept in this morning. Sleeping in Grammy Claire's bed was the best night's sleep I've had since she died.

I think about Butler Reginald and Madame See, who just traveled about ten thousand miles to help us while Mamma's locked away in the South Wing. They're probably jet-lagged bad. It's tempting to crawl back into bed myself, but I'm so hungry, I could eat my arm.

Rubbing the toes of my right foot against my left leg, I feel stuck. Too many things to do, too many things to think about.

Shower first. Get rid of the sticky sweat. Clothes. Breakfast. Then Key Number Five.

Fast as I can, I dig out the keys from under the mattress, stick them in the box, then hide the box inside the clean clothes I take with me to the shower. I feel better having them with me. Someone is lurking out there, watching and waiting.

Somebody tried to force Grammy Claire's bedroom door open. For all I know, they succeeded and locked the door again behind them. Maybe there's stuff missing that I don't even know about! The room *is* pretty empty. But whoever it was did not find the package hidden under the bed. The space underneath is pretty narrow and low. I'll bet I'm the only one who could slide under. Even Riley's probably too big.

'Course, that tells me absolutely nothing. Just more puzzles.

While I wait for the water to get warm, I light another match and burn the second folded-up note. Then I run water in the sink to cool off the ashes and flush them down the toilet again. After putting the box of keys inside a towel, I place it on the ledge of the tub so I can see it.

As I shampoo my hair, I frown at the lumpy towel. There is no way I can carry the box with me all the time. I'll have to memorize the shape and color of each key as well as their numbers, and keep them in my pockets when I go out. After I'm dressed I leave the empty box underneath my stack of underwear while I run down for breakfast.

Butler Reginald has already eaten and is outside washing the car. A lawn mower stands ready, oil and gas cans on the ground.

I catch a glimpse of Madame See through the swinging doors, squirting soap into the sink. The smell of fried food hangs on the air and the radio is squawking some talk show. I wonder if she understands much English. As if in answer to my unspoken question, she turns the station to classical music just as a pan clatters to the floor.

"Think we're supposed to do dishes and chores?" I ask Riley as I enter the dining room.

My sister is eating bacon with her fingers and pouring Tabasco sauce on a pile of scrambled eggs.

"Don't know," Riley tells me with her mouth full. My sister is not one of those girls who eats lettuce three times a day and reads diet magazines. She burns food off fast. High metabolism. "No one's said anything about a chore list, but isn't that why we have a cook and a butler?"

"It's strange to be here without Grammy Claire," I say, feeling guilty that I'm stuffing my mouth so fast, too. Madame See also made *pain perdu*, my favorite. Thick pieces of French bread fried in oil. And a big pitcher of warm cane syrup. I pour a big puddle and start dipping squares with my fork. I can't believe Grammy Claire left Madame See a menu and shopping list like she's leaving me those letters. But I'm not surprised.

My grammy was very organized. Maybe I take after her. I wish I could ask her how she suppressed the urge to comb carpet fringe. Thank goodness most of this house has hardwood floors. And thick bath carpet without any fringe at all.

"I'm bored already," Riley says, yawning. "Bayou Bridge has absolutely nothing to do, but out here, there's *really* nothing to do. Maybe I'll steal Reginald's Town Car and cruise into the nearest village. 'Course, Lafayette's only a couple hours. I could go to the mall."

"Butler Reginald ain't gonna let you go shopping all day with his car."

"But if Grammy Claire's estate is paying for that car, I have privileges," Riley says, lifting her eyebrows meaningfully.

"How you gonna buy anything?"

"Mamma gave me her credit card for emergencies."

I stop chewing. "So you were gonna go to California with that credit card and leave me with nothing?"

"You're only twelve; you don't need anything. And besides, you got household *staff.*"

"You're so selfish."

"And you got letters from Grammy Claire in that antique box."

I drop my fork. My sister sounds jealous. "You mean the box in my — ?"

"The one and only." Riley stands up and scrapes back her chair.

"You went snooping in my room?"

"Just looking for my earphones."

"I don't have your earphones — and stay out of my room!"

"Fine," she says airily, like she couldn't care less.

I grab a clump of my freshly washed hair and suck the last of the water. I taste apple blossoms and the tang of conditioner.

Thinking about Riley barging into my bedroom and going through my things makes me want to start throwing furniture — which would practically be against my religion. Even the bit of dust on the sideboard is driving me a teensy bit crazy.

Riley sees me eyeing the furniture. "Clear the table instead, Tara."

"It's your mess on the table! And stay out of my room!"

She smiles, completely composed. "You already said that."

Riley starts to leave the dining room and I touch Key Number Five in my pocket, rubbing my finger along its sharp teeth. "So Grammy Claire's box might be worth something?"

"I always thought —" She stops. "Always thought she'd give it to me."

With that, Riley spins on her heel and walks out.

My throat closes up. I think my sister is hiding tears. I think she's hurt. I wonder if she wishes she was getting the notes and the keys. I haven't even shown them to her. The letters and the keys make me feel special. I want to keep them to myself, but I know it's selfish. Reluctantly, I remember Grammy Claire's words: "If you need Riley's help, know that you can trust her."

I don't know why she didn't send Riley all those keys. I'm barely out of elementary school, but maybe I *am* supposed to trust her — maybe even confide in her. Besides, Riley has a driver's license, and if the bad guys — whoever they are — show up, she can help us escape.

Bad guys. I can't deny it any longer. Grammy Claire *said* there was danger, and she wanted me to guard the *nipwisipwis* with my life. But how do I guard a bunch of butterflies that come and go whenever they want? I can't catch them or pin them down. *If* Grammy Claire is talking about the butterflies I've seen so far. But how could she know about them? Aren't the butterflies just some random thing, a sign of summer? Or because I left the windows open!

Still . . . those words in Grammy Claire's letter wondering if I'd see *Angelina, her Giant Pink. . . .* My grandmother personally knew the butterfly I saw an hour ago.

"Hey, Riley," I call out, jumping up from the table.

"What? I got stuff to do."

"Will you come with me?"

Her bangs hide her brown eyes this morning. She'd forgotten to gel them into black and blue spikes. "What do you want now?"

I glance at the kitchen door where Madame See sits at the table eating her own breakfast. She catches me looking at her and quickly covers her face with her palms, mortified. As though we're living two hundred years ago in a castle and servants are supposed to stay out of sight by using secret passageways. When she ducks her head, her black hair falls like a sheet across her eyes. "No see, no see," she babbles. "I do dishes. Clean up."

We both jump as someone knocks on the back door. "Delivery!" she calls out. "Food store make house calls," she says in her stilted accent. A cross between a Pacific Islander and somewhere else in Asia. "You go. Do fun."

The door closes on us and the house returns to its former quiet.

"Where's Butler Reginald?" I ask.

"He hasn't come in yet. Later, gator." Riley heads upstairs, probably to a day of computer games, phone calls to Brad, and earphones planted permanently in her head.

I hear the start of the lawn mower through the screens of the dining room that face the front of the house, but the rooms and hallways in the back still lie in shadows. No point in opening up three stories of blinds and curtains. Besides, it's gonna be another scorcher.

"Riley," I call again, pounding up the stairs after her. "Will you come with me?"

"I'm busy."

"No, you're not."

"Go align some rug fringe."

It's beyond comprehension that one minute my sister is potentially vulnerable and hiding tears, and the next she can be just plain mean.

I start to reach for a lock of hair to chew, and then drop my hand, using every bit of willpower I have. "I'm going to open up the lock for Key Number Five."

I'm graced by the famous Riley eye roll. "What are you talking about?"

I bring the key from my pocket and dangle it in front of her. "Upstairs. At the very top of the house. I'll explain on the way."

"I'm not in the mood for stupid games. I have a phone appointment with Brad."

I experiment with my new Tara eye roll and end up feeling ridiculous. "Bo-ring."

"Maybe to you, but not to me. I guess you gotta be older to understand."

Jett Dupuis's face flashes across my mind. The cutest boy in sixth grade. I think I understand better than she thinks, but Jett and I don't make appointments or dates, we just meet up and do stuff.

"Follow me," I tell my sister, giving her an order like I never have before.

Astonishingly enough, she obeys.

At the first landing, I run to get Grammy Claire's letters from my bedroom.

The house is quiet, quiet, quiet, and since nobody's around I tell Riley to read the letters quick while we walk upstairs. "But be careful, don't drop them! And don't lose them!"

"Sheesh! I won't!"

I lead the way up to the third floor and then down the hallway until we get to the narrow steps that go up to the fourth floor. The walls close in together, tight and enfolding. The creaky steps are *still* creepy, but not as much during daylight hours — or with a companion.

"The room up here is Grammy Claire's laboratory, isn't it?" Riley asks. The narrow space is hot and airless. Sweat trickles like spider legs down my face. "Tara, you're not supposed to go in there."

"She's — she's — gone now. It doesn't matter anymore."

"Of course it matters. The laboratory is for the grown-ups to clean out and pack up. All that scientific stuff. Maybe they'll donate her research to the university in Lafayette. Hey, maybe that's why Butler Reginald is here. To clean up the house and yard and get it ready to sell."

"Sell this house?" The thought freezes me to the floor. "But we can't do that!"

"What are we gonna do with it? Mamma ain't gonna take care of it. And the money will help keep up our own Civil War relic back in Bayou Bridge."

She's so heartless. So cold-blooded cruel. "But — but — *we're* supposed to go inside first," I tell Riley, and she gives me a peculiar look.

"Why?" she asks.

I shrug and keep climbing. My heart stutters inside my chest as I reach the thick oak door. Behind me, Riley flips the hall light and a yellowish light glows. Once again, the faint sound of music wafts through the floorboards, making me jump. *"Whoa. Is that the organ?"*

"Yep, all the way from the great room three stories below."

Air wheezes through the hollow pipes, filling the house from top to bottom like a ghost.

Riley pinches my arm, trying to make me scream. "Sounds like a haunted house, huh?"

"Cut it out!" I hiss. "Look! See that note?"

We stare at the note I'd seen yesterday, the one in Grammy Claire's handwriting.

Not yet, Tara. Not yet.

"What does that mean?" Riley demands.

"Just what it says. That I can't go in until it's time."

"And is it?"

"Yep, it's time." I hold up Key Number Five as proof, and smile. But there's a part of me that's holding my breath, hoping I'm right. And an even bigger, scared-er part of me that is afraid to walk inside. But the biggest part of me — the one dying of curiosity — can't wait to open that door. "I got the clue in the last letter."

Riley pins her eyes on mine. I can't tell if she believes me or not. "Where was that letter?"

"Underneath the —" I start, and then stop. I don't want her

to know Grammy Claire's hiding places. Just in case . . . of what, I don't know. But Grammy Claire is leaking the letters and notes and keys in slow dribbles, emphasizing the secrecy and danger. There must be a reason.

"Oh, sheesh, will you cut that out?"

"What?"

"You're sucking your hair again. It's sickening."

Quickly, I drop the lump of hair, then wipe my mouth with the back of my hand. I don't even realize I'm doing it anymore.

Riley lowers her voice, eyes glittering in the dim light. "You ever think that maybe Grammy Claire went a little crazy the last couple of years?"

My skin starts to crawl.

"Maybe while she was living out there on that island she got some nasty gigantic African insect bite. Made her delirious, and she hasn't been right in the head ever since."

"For your information, the islands of Chuuk ain't nowhere near Africa! And Grammy Claire didn't get bit by some crazy bug!"

"Don't take it personally, Tara. Coming here because Grammy Claire sent you a telegram — from beyond the grave — just feels dumb. Like there's some big secret — but there isn't. Our grandmother went nuts with her science experiments on some island thousands of miles from civilization. That butler dude probably just wanted a free ticket back to the

States, and Madame See is trying to make a buck off of us because they think we've got money. But you do know that the family fortune is pretty much gone, right? We might lose the house if we can't pay the taxes and insurance, and Mamma can't face it. The family fortune has disappeared over the years, and Daddy keeps his own cash tight in his fist and won't help us. And did you *also* notice, dear stupid sister, that we didn't stay at the Doucet Mansion, we came *here* — probably to help clean out this place and help them find some hidden stash of money?"

"There ain't no hidden stash of money!"

"*We* know that, but they don't. And we already *got* Miz Landry back home so we wouldn't need them."

"Sometimes I just hate you, Riley Doucet! Grammy Claire sent the letters, not them! It's *her* handwriting!" Tears prick behind my eyes. "You honestly think Mamma is pretending?"

"No, Mamma does need help. But I'm tired of living in that stuffy old plantation watching her lose her mind."

"Stop saying that!" I hate to hear it, even if I think it myself.

"Okay, I'm exaggerating a *little*, but Grammy Claire knew Mamma would go off the deep end again if she died so she brought us here to stay out of the way, and Butler Dude and Madame See came along for the ride and a bit of cash. We'll probably be home by next week. Maybe we can still go to California for summer vacation."

My fists are tight against my legs. "No way Mamma will go to California."

Riley uses the wall for a prop as she rubs her right foot against her left leg. I feel comforted just watching her. Like I'm suddenly watching a younger version of Grammy Claire. "Maybe she'll meet some rich director. With lots of annuities."

"Mamma is not a gold digger!" I start to shout, then wonder if they can hear us downstairs.

"You're so dramatic! I didn't say she was, but sometimes a woman needs money, especially if she can't work herself. That's just life, Tara, face it. Our family is broken up, and with Grammy Claire gone, Mamma needs options."

"Then I hate real life — and our family is not broken!" Angry, I brush at the tears running down my cheek. But deep in my heart I know it is broken. Daddy's off with a new wife and his Hollywood deals, Mamma's nursing her grief in the South Wing, and Grammy Claire, the only light I had left, is dead. So sudden, so quick. So final.

"Can I see those keys?"

"No!" I turn away, the key digging into my palm. After all the terrible things Riley just said I never want to show her anything again! "Later," I tell her. "Right now I'm gonna look for the next clue."

Key Number Five slips into the keyhole and the door clicks open.

Riley and I stare at each other. My ears start to drone like a bumblebee.

"You're scared," she tells me in a loud stage whisper.

"No, I'm not."

"Yes, you are, I can see it in your jiggly eyes. And you want to chew on your hair so bad you're ready to chomp a whole chunk of it."

"You're a brat!"

She smiles like she knows it and doesn't care a whit. Why were big sisters ever invented?

As I turn the knob, the oak door swings inward. With the very first step inside, my eyes are drawn to the ceiling.

The room is one huge circular shape, and the ceiling is a dome of windows staring straight up at the blue sky. White clouds float past the dusty panes. Two of the windows are propped open a few inches, and three seconds later, a cluster of butterflies swoops down through the window and heads straight for us.

Chapter Twelve

I do not know whether I was then a girl dreaming I was a butterfly, or whether I am now a butterfly dreaming I am a girl.

~ZHUANG ZHOU~

Fast as she can, Riley retreats, arms flailing, eyes bugging out. She collides into a table holding a stack of petri dishes and they all crash together, seconds away from dashing into pieces on the floor. The sound of cracking glass hurts my ears and I close my eyes, waiting to be drenched in thousands of glass shards. But the petri dishes right themselves again and the worst is averted. I peek open one eye and breathe a sigh of relief.

"Why are those things coming in *here*?" Riley yells, sticking her hands in front of her face.

I hide a smile. Never seen my sister react so scared. I thought she only had irrational aversions to cockroaches, centipedes, and snakes.

Instantly, I shoot out my arm and slam the laboratory door closed so the butterflies can't escape. This room is obviously their home. This is where the butterflies came from. I know it down deep in my gut.

All three butterflies flutter around me, circling wildly as if they're excited to see a real, live human. The purple-and-yellow butterfly as well as the translucent one alight on my arms. The Giant Pink latches on to a button of my shirt.

"Oh my gosh!" I whisper to Riley, holding as still as I can. The velvety wings brush my skin, soft as a kiss, gentle as a quiet sigh. *"Look!"*

"Believe me, I'm looking," she croaks. "Just keep them away from me! Bugs flying around my face is the worst!"

I think about the times Riley screams when there are spiders scurrying along the bathroom tile. Cockroaches darting around the kitchen late at night.

A new thought comes to me, stronger than ever. *This is why Grammy Claire chose me.*

The butterflies open and close their wings, their little eyes staring at me, their feet so tiny it's like a breath of air stirring the hairs of my arms. "Don't you wish you knew what they were thinking, Riley?"

"Butterflies don't have a brain."

"I think they know who I am!" I whisper.

She snorts, moving away from the door to explore the room. "You just happen to be in the way of their flight pattern."

"They came through the skylight like they knew where they were going."

Now that I look more carefully, I realize that the room isn't much of a true laboratory at all. The space does contain tables with lab paraphernalia, trays and test tubes and built-in sinks and faucets, but most of the room is a tangle of trees and vines. Shrubbery and flowers. Like a garden. As if my grandmother had landscaped this upper floor so she wouldn't have to go outside to enjoy nature. Which is very odd. Grammy Claire loved the outdoors. That's why she was a botanist. Why not enjoy the butterflies in a private flower garden outside?

Just then the three butterflies shoot off my arms, fluttering toward the sunshine flooding the windows, even though the glass is rain-spattered. "Must be hard to clean," Riley mutters.

A path of blue tiles meanders through an arch of vines, disappearing into the center of a messy, overgrown garden. No pruning's been done for at least a year. The place is wild. Trees reach skyward, but it's like I've been transported inside a dark jungle island.

Then I notice splashes of color between the shades of green. As I step deeper into the foliage, I realize that the colors are actually butterflies. More butterflies!

Riley has left the blue-tile path completely. She checks out the tables and pokes around on Grammy Claire's shelves. I hear glass moving and papers shuffling.

No more butterflies come to me, and the room goes still. Then I halt.

The butterflies aren't hovering or darting among the flowers at all. Actually, there aren't many flowers, period. Empty bushes and plants surround me where flowers should be blooming. The plants are dry, withering away. This whole place has been left alone for too long.

With a feeling of dread, I walk up to a spray of dry leaves. A small blue butterfly is perched on the leaf, horribly motionless. Because it's dead. And then I see another one, and another, a whole pile of delicate blue butterflies.

My hands begin to sweat. I reach out to touch the tiny wings and they turn to dust between my fingers. Small blue butterflies, exactly like the one that danced around Mamma's chair on the upstairs balcony. The butterfly that made her smile just a little bit.

Feeling sick, I weave through the garden like I'm dizzy. There are splashes of color everywhere, and every time I reach out to touch the yellow or orange or red or purple wings, they fall to powder in my fingers.

Every single butterfly is dead. This is a room full of corpses.

I stand on the blue tiles in the center of that dead garden, unable to believe my own eyes. Then I burst into tears.

"Tara!" Riley calls out. "Are you okay?"

I can hear her bumping into things, trying to find me from the other side of the thick shrubbery. When her arm grabs mine, I whirl around. "They're dead!" I sob. "How can they all be dead? Every single one! Who killed them?"

I know my sister can't stand doing what she does next, but she does it anyway. After hating her so frequently over the last five years, I start to love her again. She actually holds my hand tightly in hers and walks with me around the path, pulling me away from the terrible sight.

"You're right, Tara, but I'm not sure *some person* killed them. They've been here a long time. Probably ran out of food or water," she goes on. "This place *feels* like a tomb. No one's been in here for ages."

"But why didn't they just fly through the windows like the other three did?"

She gives me a sympathetic look. "I have no idea."

My eyes swim with tears until I can hardly see straight. Finally, I take a bunch of deep breaths, purposely not looking at so many butterflies sitting frozen on the shrubbery as we push through the tangle of branches and leaves until we reach the back wall.

"Let's get out of here, Tara," Riley finally says. "You're just getting more upset."

"But — it's just so awful."

"Hey, butterflies don't last that long anyway. They all die after a season, right? Or a few weeks? Days at the most."

She has a point, but these butterflies are different; I know it deep in my gut. The way they move, the way they look at me and aren't afraid. Butterflies don't just zoom up and land on your heart as a conversation-starter!

A gust of wind comes through the skylight and rustles the room. Grammy Claire must have some wind chimes because I can hear them tinkling like fairy bells. That's when I see a small table sitting underneath a line of rosebushes without any blooms. On the table is an envelope with my name on it: *Tara*.

My hands start to shake. There's the same puddle of purple sealing wax covering the flap.

I glance up, noticing that Riley has disappeared. "Hey, where'd you go?"

"Over here, going through a filing cabinet," she calls back. "It's pretty obvious this whole fourth floor used to be Grammy Claire's laboratory, but the last dates on anything are from about five years ago. I wonder what she was researching about butterflies."

"Five years ago? That's when she started living on the islands of Chuuk."

"Guess she moved all of her current research over there and left all this junk."

"She was too busy doing amazing things to clean," I say softly, clutching the new envelope. Shivers of suspense tingle up my spine. "Grammy Claire said she'd dust when she retired."

Keeping an eye on Riley through the branches, I carefully split the wax seal. Quiet as I can, I unfold the letter with its second, smaller note, my heart beating like a hummingbird's wings.

Dearest Tara,

How do you like my Secret Butterfly Garden? Isn't it spectacular? I can only picture in my mind how much you will love it, and I wish I was there to share its beauty and wonder and secrets. Unfortunately, I'm sure the place is dying, but if you can imagine a thousand butterflies in that small space, you can also begin to imagine the excitement of my life's work. More on that later, but I'm so grateful you're a smart girl, a girl with a steady head on her shoulders — and a girl who can keep secrets.

Now comes a warning: There are those who would destroy my butterflies, suck the life out of them, and use their power to make themselves wealthy beyond imagination. Yes, I'm talking in riddles — but I can't reveal any more within a letter that may or may not reach your hands. I

can only hope and pray . . . and once I'm gone,
I can only look down from heaven and wring
my hands. I'm afraid I'm already in my hand-
wringing phase just writing these letters . . . and it
hurts beyond belief to keep writing these words.
Because I want to be with you. To share the beauty
and joy and love and magic.

There . . . I've already said too much. . . . If the
Butterfly Garden is dead, probably so much
the better. The butterflies can escape through the
windows and will hopefully die peacefully within
their appointed life span. Unless . . . there! I just
threw my pen across the room! I must smack myself
for revealing more than I should.

I feel as though someone is reading over my
shoulder. . . .

Stay on course, darling girl. All will be well. I
must have faith myself.

Follow the next instructions and don't let
anyone become aware of your actions.

All my love,
Your Grammy Claire

When I finish reading, I'm shaking so bad I slump against
the table. My chin jerks up. Riley isn't paying any attention.
She's reading some old files or ledgers in the far corner. The

humming of the pipe organ swirls around the room as I slip the letter back into the envelope.

Quickly, I open the second note. Will someone try to steal it before I have a chance to find matches? The danger level has suddenly raised another notch.

The Secret Butterfly Garden did have answers. At least a few. *Nipwisipwis* is not a code word — there *really are* butterflies! And Grammy Claire was keeping them a secret! But why? She said I would have more questions, and she sure as heck got that right.

We're moving onward! Key Number Six is up and you'll be undertaking a secret journey, which this key will reveal. Just use your head, Tara.

IMPORTANT: Destroy this note ASAP!

Chapter Thirteen

No garden truly blooms until butterflies have danced upon it.

~K. D'ANGELO~

The new clue practically sizzles my fingers, and yet I have to destroy it this very moment — without matches. It's too dangerous to take it with me. What if I accidentally drop it? What if someone is waiting on the stairs ready to steal it from me?

Who is Grammy Claire afraid of? Why is she so secretive? What is so dangerous? Butterflies are beautiful and gentle, not deadly. Harmless, not a matter of life and death.

Across the room, Riley yawns and sticks a folder back into one of the filing cabinets. "Boring scientific mumbo jumbo!" I hear her say. "Hey, Tara, where you got to? Let's go."

Without thinking, I tear the note into four pieces and stuff them into my mouth. I start chewing, pretending it's bubble gum. I read about this tactic in a book. There was a Southern lady who became a Confederate spy during the Civil War. She was carrying a piece of crucial information, and when she got home, Union soldiers were swarming her house. So she *ate* the note! How daring! I always wondered if it made her sick later. Guess I'm gonna find out.

Acting real casual, I keep chewing, tasting the bland mush of paper, the tang of the ink, and try not to make a face. Tiny spit-soaked bits stick between my teeth.

"What are you doing?" Riley asks.

"Nothing," I mumble. I try to swallow, but can't bring myself to. Chewing paper is really yucky. I think I'll throw up if it goes down my throat. Turning away, I try not to gag.

Riley stares at me. "You're trying to swallow a piece of gum, aren't you? How juvenile. You're not two years old."

I shake my head, not facing her so she can't see that I don't have gum at all.

"Don't swallow! Your stomach can't digest it. You'll have a pile of old, tasteless gum sitting there for the rest of your life. That's disgusting."

"That's not true!"

"I saw it on a television show." She pauses. "I'm off to steal Butler Dude's wheels and go for a drive. What are you going to do?"

I notice that she doesn't invite me. Bet she's gonna go meet her boyfriend.

I shrug, knowing exactly what I'm going to do. "Make cookies?" I manage to say around the wad of soggy paper. I wonder if Madame See will let me into her kitchen. I wonder if there are any chocolate chips in the house.

I need to go lie down. Try to decipher Grammy Claire's latest clue that's sliding, sliding down my throat. Right then I *do* gag and start spitting the bits of paper into my hand.

"What if Jett Dupuis could see you now?" Riley says with an especially defined eye roll.

The thought of Jett seeing me right now makes me suck in my breath so fast, I actually swallow some of the note. I hold my stomach and try not to cry. "Hey!" I call out, but Riley is already clomping down the narrow stairs. "How do *you* know about Jett Dupuis?"

The Secret Butterfly Garden is quiet after she leaves. Breathless, almost. I wander the room, trying not to look at the dead butterfly corpses, the beauty that's been snuffed out like a candle. The last thing I see as I close the door is the Giant Pink soaring through the couple inches of open window. I'm glad it's safe, that it's still alive.

I wonder if the Giant Pink is sad that all the other butterflies are dead. Then I laugh at myself for thinking that the butterflies have actual brains, with actual thoughts.

That night I lie in bed, my mind flitting about. I left my door cracked so I could hear Riley come home. She's been gone for hours and hours. I rack my brain trying to figure out what Key Number Six is supposed to open. *Just use your head*, Grammy Claire wrote. I'd torn apart her bedroom again, but the only thing ever hidden in there was the padded envelope taped under the bed.

Before dinner, Butler Reginald had paced the floor and finally called the police. Not to report his car stolen, but to try to find my sister. I told him she was with her boyfriend, praying Riley hadn't gone back to the airport to try to fly to California. If Daddy privately called her cell with a new airline ticket, leaving me alone, I'm not going to speak to him for a month.

My eyes sting when I realize that my daddy probably wouldn't even notice. I'd have to ignore him for at least *three* months. I miss Grammy Claire more than ever so I spend a while crying in my room, and then eat dinner alone.

Madame See served me quietly in a flowered Oriental dress that isn't really a muumuu, but kinda sort of. Bowing, bowing, bowing with the rice, then the seasoned battered fish, and then with a bowl of ice cream. I asked her if she knew the recipe for chocolate chip cookies and she shook her head. "No understand. More fish?"

Next, I'd wandered each floor, cruising through the empty guest rooms.

Then I sat in Grammy Claire's library and pulled out every single book. Flipped the pages. Checked for secret compartments. Hollow panels in the walls. I tipped over the armchairs, rolled up the rug, and patted down the drapes. Nothing.

Nothing!

Rolling over in my bed, I picture the words on the note again — and try not to think about half the note sitting in my gut. Paper can't hurt you, right? I'd flushed the other half, the soggy bits, down the toilet. Didn't need to burn it because the ink had washed away in my mouth. Can ink poison you? I wish there was a computer in this house so I could look it up. I wonder what the phone number for poison control is.

. . . you'll be undertaking a secret journey, which this key will reveal. Just use your head.

Not three seconds later I hear the soft shushing of feet on the staircase. Throwing off the sheet, I run to the crack in my door and peek out. It's Riley sneaking home. A few of the clocks downstairs chime out a single bong. One. One o'clock in the morning that is.

My sister hurries to her room so fast I don't even have time to intercept her. *Dern!*

Secret journey.
Use your head.

The words come together in my head with a clunk.

A secret journey means I'm going somewhere. Meaning I'm not staying here all summer with Riley sneaking in and out and nothing to do but eat notes and try not to get poisoned.

If I'm going on a journey, I need to pack. Which I'd done two days ago in order to come here. But this was Grammy Claire's house and Grammy Claire's clues and puzzles. She trusted me to *use my head* and figure it out. Because she wants *me* to find the clues.

I snatch Key Number Six and step into the dim hallway. The second floor is lit by a night-light shaped like a purple water hyacinth. In my bare feet, I race downstairs to the closet built under the staircase. Gently, I press the small half door open. It lets out a loud creak and I stop, breathing hard. Hoping nobody heard it.

Under the stairs it's pitch-black like a cave. Inside all that darkness lies a stash of Grammy Claire's suitcases and trunks, old and new, with wheels and without. And one of those suitcases has a lock that fits my key! I just know it.

First, I need a flashlight. Or matches.

The musty smell of the house creeps into my nose as I crawl back out of the space and head to the kitchen. Moonlight drifts through the window so I don't need to turn on a light.

The appliances look like they're sleeping. Shadows in the corners watching me, waiting to see what I'm gonna do. The clock on the stove looks like a face with buttons for eyes. Cracks in the porcelain are crooked smiles, eerie and creepy.

Slowly, slowly, slowly, I open the cupboards and drawers, smelling soy sauce and cumin mixed with the tang of mandarin oranges sitting in a bowl by the flour canister.

At last I find a small flashlight. Perfect. I switch it on and off to make sure it works. Not too bright, just enough.

Ten seconds later, I'm back at the small half door under the staircase and shining the flashlight into the recesses. It's a good thing I'm not *too* scared of the dark. Except there might be lots of dead bugs. But that's Riley's undoing, not mine.

There! I hurry over to the stash of suitcases and trunks and old-fashioned hatboxes. I can barely stand up and the top of my head skims the low ceiling as the roof slopes down and the space gets smaller with each step.

I brush off a dusty spot on the hardwood floor and kneel down, reaching for the first suitcase. There are four of them and two trunks. Key Number Six is too small for the trunks and too big for the suitcases. I'm skunked. My chin wobbles as I squeeze my eyes shut. I thought for sure I'd figured out what Grammy Claire meant about a journey and using my head.

When Riley and I were younger we used to play hide-and-seek, and under the stairs was one of my favorite places to hide. I'd peek out the crack of the little door to see where she was. For a long time, I could fit without scraping the top of my head. One year, I grew a couple of inches and didn't know it until I smashed my head into the low ceiling during one of our midnight games. I remember the cut and Grammy Claire washing the blood out of my hair, putting ointment on it, then rocking me to sleep in the chair in her library.

Riley was unsympathetic. "Try a new hiding place," she'd told me in her superior tone. "I always find you in here."

After that I hid under the desk in the library. One time I was so quiet listening to Riley calling my name up and down all the staircases that I fell asleep. The cubbyhole of the desk was small and perfectly sized. So cozy I curled up and dreamed about being a real princess in a real castle, not the old Doucet Mansion, until I heard Grammy Claire calling me for dinner. I can still remember the sizzling smell of fried catfish and hot balls of fried cornmeal, my favorite summertime dinner. The same meal she'd told Madame See to fix me last night when we arrived.

I remember Grammy Claire teaching me to fish on the bayou. Pulling up my first catfish from the muddy river bottom.

I'll never make any more memories with her. I have to live off the ones I already have, which means I gotta hang on to them tight. I wish I could stuff them into a memory jar. Too bad nobody has invented one yet. I'll bet they'd make a million dollars!

Crawling around the stack of suitcases, I shine my light into the far corners. I have nowhere left to look. A small, boxlike shape appears under a stack of two-by-fours tucked into the deepest part of the storage space.

Holding the flashlight in my lap, I pull the box toward me, bumping my head again. My hair falls over my face and I brush it back, the heat making me sweat. The air is thick and stifling back here.

The last piece of luggage is an outdated makeup case. Not a soft, zippered bag, but oblong-shaped with hard, molded edges — very old-fashioned. And boasting its very own lock!

My fingers shake as I insert Key Number Six and twist. The lock snaps and a silver metal tab flips up, pinching my skin. Sucking on my finger, I shine the flashlight inside. Flowered material, puckered with age and wrinkling along the edges where it's lost its glue, lines the inside of the case. The faded cardboard pieces are also curling. The case contains the most adorable little trays. Compartments for eye shadow and pencils and brushes and lipstick.

The top tray folds out by a set of metal levers. Below it is an envelope with my name on it!

I can't stop myself from letting out a cry. "Oh, Grammy Claire, I found it, I found it!" I laugh, wiping at my eyes and rubbing my nose across my arm. Something I've never done in my life.

The clocks across the hall chime the half hour, but I have no idea how much time has passed. My eyes burn I'm so tired, but I rip open the envelope and tear into the letter. It's the shortest one so far.

Dearest Tara,

You used your head, my darling girl — although I hope that pretty head isn't damaged this time. Congratulations! Even so, you will probably not feel that this is a victory at all as you move deeper and deeper into this dangerous journey. Be brave! All will be well. I promise. Just remember the nipwisipwis and how much they need you.

All my love forever,
Your Grammy Claire

P.S. Keep digging

What does that mean? My legs cramp and needles shoot up my feet. I want to crawl back to my pillow, but I have four more keys! And this letter says nothing about Key Number Seven.

Feeling depressed, I fold the compartments and tray back into the makeup case. All of a sudden, I stop. A second tray is hidden underneath the bottom cloth-covered cardboard. My breath catches. Grammy Claire had said to keep digging!

Sticking my fingernails into the tight edges, I finally manage to loosen the cardboard, which is papered in blue primroses. After I lift it out, I stare at a silver clasp purse in the glow of my flashlight. The purse is beautiful, shiny, and very chic. A fancy purse for wearing with an evening gown. Breathing harder, I twist the metal pieces of the curved clasp apart.

A stack of green money stares back at me. I can hardly believe my eyes. Hurriedly, I start putting the bills inside the lap of my nightgown. When I reach the last one, my whole body is humming in shock. There are twenty one-hundred-dollar bills! Two thousand dollars!

I count them over and over again, double-checking. What is this money for? Why has Grammy Claire given it to me? This is getting more and more mysterious.

Then, between two of the Benjamin Franklin bills, a note slips out. Holding up my flashlight, I read:

Hide this money! *Now repeat that seven times.*
You will need good old Ben on your journey. Key
Number Seven will show you where you're going
and have further instructions.

"And don't forget to destroy this note," I say out loud as I repeat the identical line of warning that has appeared at the bottom of all of Grammy Claire's clues.

Tucking the cash back into the silver purse, I snap it shut, stick it back into the makeup case — and decide to leave it right there inside the storage room. In the darkest recesses of the under-the-stairs closet. Where else in this house will this much money be safe? If I put it in my room, Riley might find it. What if Madame See decides to dust? What if Butler Reginald decides to take down the drapes and send them out for dry cleaning? I worry the money will not remain safe even here, but it's probably been hiding inside the makeup case since last summer, when Grammy Claire was last here.

As I crawl back over the junk, I snap off the flashlight and stand up, gripping Grammy Claire's note in my fist until I can burn it. I really don't want to eat it again.

Peering into the face of one of the hall clocks, I see that it's going on two a.m. Rubbing my tired eyes, I head to the kitchen to burn the note.

That's when I hear a stirring above me. A door closing. Soft, stealthy footsteps. My heart thuds and my ears tingle. Who is it? Where are they going? And do they know I'm standing smack-dab in the middle of the entry hall?

My pulse pounds as I wait and listen. And wait and listen.

I stand like a statue for so long, my legs start to ache.

The sounds fade into the night. Did I imagine it? Was it just Riley going to the bathroom? My sister usually makes a lot more noise than that.

Suddenly, the stairs creak. *Creak, creak, creak.* Right above me! Someone is coming down, not five feet away.

The creaking stops and I can't hardly breathe.

Goose bumps rise on my arms. Maybe someone is watching me right now from the blackness through the banister. The thought spooks me so badly I force my legs to return to the little closet under the stairs and hide behind the door.

Keeping the door cracked the tiniest sliver of an inch, I wait and listen. The creaking on the staircase starts up again and a moment later a figure glides past me. I think I'm going to have a heart attack. What if it's an intruder?

My mouth is dry as I strain to see who it is. After I count to three, I open the door another inch. Someone small with short dark hair reaches the end of the hallway and turns the corner into the dining room.

Leaving the safety of the closet, I flatten myself against the wall and tiptoe closer, hiding behind the grandfather clock.

Silently, Madame See creeps through the dining room, heading back toward her own bedroom on the other side of the kitchen. A second later, her door closes with a click.

Madame See? What's she doing up in the middle of the night? And upstairs! Where she has no business snooping around.

Finally, I let out a ragged breath. The new note is turning damp in my sweaty hand. Which reminds me — Grammy

Claire forgot to give me the clue for finding the lock for Key Number Seven. What if I can't figure it out? What if I let my grandmother down? And what about all that money I just found?

Prickles of worry nag at me. My head hurts thinking about it.

When I start to tiptoe back upstairs, I let out a gasp.

The purple butterfly that flew through my bedroom window the day after Grammy Claire's funeral comes tearing down the hall straight at me like it's gone crazy. Its wings are going a hundred miles an hour, zooming right for my face.

Chapter Fourteen

We are like butterflies who flutter for a day and think it is forever.

~ C A R L   S A G A N ~

I clap my hands over my mouth and try not to scream. My voice is hoarse as I whisper, "How did you get all the way down here from the Butterfly Garden?"

I'd closed and locked that laboratory door. I know it. Or had I? My stomach sinks. Now I can't remember. I'm afraid for the butterflies because of all those *other* butterfly corpses. I'm supposed to protect the *nipwisipwis*. But how can I protect a garden full of dead butterflies?

I don't know if Grammy Claire wanted me to find the garden full of alive, flying butterflies — or dead ones, because my job is to figure out how they died. I'm so confused!

The purple butterfly darts around my head. Back and forth and around and around until I feel dizzy. I hold up my hand but it won't even alight on my finger. "What do you want me to do?"

The butterfly races down the hallway, then comes back and zips around my head three more times. Finally, I get it. "Okay, okay, I'll follow you."

The purple wings get even more frantic when I make a detour to my bedroom and grab Key Number Five to the laboratory, shoving Key Number Six that opened the little makeup case with the others in the locked box.

The hallways are narrow and dark, the light from the moon painting the tall windows at the end a grayish color. I slow down when I reach the steps that lead up to Grammy Claire's laboratory.

There's no air-conditioning up here and the small staircase closes in on me. I'm perspiring, the hair on my neck heavy and hot.

Pipe organ music comes through the walls and I try not to shudder as the shadows watch me. It's spooky being up in the middle of the night, alone. I try not to pull the chain for the hallway light. Try not to creak the floorboards, like Madame See. Seeing her creeping around the house in the middle of the night still freaks me out. She has her own bathroom. There's no reason for her to be upstairs.

The purple *nipwisipwis* flutters wildly at my ear, and it comforts me. Like it's watching over me, and strangely, I don't feel so alone.

When I insert the key, I can hear my heart thudding inside my head. *Thwap, thwap, thwap! Thud.* My fingers tingle as I touch the doorknob and turn it, but the door isn't locked! I must have forgotten when Riley and I left. How could I be so stupid?

Did someone else have a key? Maybe someone had broken in, like they tried to do at Grammy Claire's bedroom door? Someone — like Madame See? I turn cold and clammy as the thumping in my throat grows stronger. I think I'm gonna choke. The Butterfly Garden was left unattended and it's my fault. My mind whirls with possibilities. The door doesn't feel like it was broken into. Nothing is jammed into the keyhole or bent. When I grabbed Key Number Five a few minutes earlier, it was still in its place, right where I'd put it.

Someone else has a copy of the key to this room!

The door creaks as it opens and the sound makes me jump. I wonder if everyone downstairs can hear it — if they know I'm up here.

I wonder if Madame See will hear me and return. I'm not sure I can look her in the face again. What if she's a thief? Or an escapee from a mental hospital? Did Butler Reginald get good references for her?

My sweaty fingers grip the edge of the door, staring into the shadows of the garden room until my eyesight blurs. When I finally step through, my feet are icy cold. Goose bumps run up and down my legs. Maybe I should just leave and run back to my bed.

But the purple butterfly won't let me go back. It keeps fluttering behind me, not letting me turn around. Keeping me on an invisible leash like I'm a human pet. It would be funny if I weren't so scared.

When I glance upward, my stomach soars straight into my throat.

The sky through the windows above is beautiful. Starry and glittery like someone sprinkled glue and then shook a bottle of sparkly confetti. The moon glows silver. The entire garden is bathed in the moon's light and I don't need to turn on any lights.

I start circling the room, wondering if the purple butterfly with its yellow-tipped wings will show me which direction it wants me to go.

I walk over to Grammy Claire's desk and the butterfly darts in the opposite direction. Then hovers waiting for me to catch up. Like we're playing Hot and Cold. I get Warmer when the butterfly leads me into the center of the garden. I try not to look at all the corpses, the dusty, broken wings, the pile of small blue butterflies. We stop at the round table underneath the rose arbor. The table where I found Grammy Claire's envelope earlier today.

I still have the flashlight so I click it on, and the table comes clearly into view. It's a table without dust, which is strange, but there is something else lying on its surface. Something horrifying. The air shudders; music vibrates. I'm vaguely aware that the music sounds different. It's closer. Right in my ear. And it's not the wheezy pipe organ music.

But I can't figure out where it's coming from because my throat closes up, even though I want to scream real bad. On the table lies the Giant Pink butterfly. The one that burst through the window in Grammy Claire's bedroom. I know the shades of pink and ribbons of green. The remarkable size of such a magnificent butterfly.

"Nipwisipwis," I whisper, and my voice chokes.

The Giant Pink is dead. Its wings torn apart, its body broken, its antennae —

I turn away, covering my face, and then I'm crying, bawling my eyes out. My chest hurts, my stomach clenches. I think I might throw up.

The purple butterfly zooms right into my face and my eyes are so blurry it looks like its attacking me. Then I realize, with a huge shock, that it's trying to comfort me. Or maybe it wants *me* to comfort *it*.

I hold out my hand and the butterfly finally alights, its frantic wings slowing, its little eyes staring at me.

"Nipwisipwis," I say again, and then I give a start when the

butterfly cocks its head at me, as though it's listening. "What happened here? How did she die?"

And then I start to cry even harder because I know deep in my heart that the Giant Pink butterfly didn't die of old age.

It didn't have an accident.

Its life span didn't just run out.

It was murdered.

Chapter Fifteen

I'll be floating like a butterfly and stinging like a bee.
~MUHAMMAD ALI~

How could such a horrible thing have happened? And it's my fault. I'm the one that killed it because I didn't lock the door properly. I didn't take care of the *nipwisipwis* like Grammy Claire asked me to. I let her down. I *failed*.

I glance up, wondering if my grandmother can see me from heaven, knowing how disappointed she is in me. "I'm so sorry!" I sob, sinking to my knees in front of the table where the giant butterfly lies smashed to pieces. "I'm sorry," I repeat, knowing that I'm not only telling my dead grandmother how terrible I feel. Now I'm talking to the Giant Pink, too. And the purple butterfly who led me here.

Madame See had been upstairs. I heard her come down the main staircase. I saw her with my own eyes, and there's a good chance she might have been up here in the laboratory snooping around. Our cook might be a butterfly killer! Grammy Claire said I could trust Butler Reginald, but she didn't breathe a word about her cook and housekeeper.

Through blurry eyes, I glance around the garden room. There isn't another butterfly like it. No other pink corpses. Because of my carelessness, I helped kill a species that was about to become extinct.

The thought of that just makes me cry even harder. My nose drips until I'm miserably soggy. Taking the edge of my nightgown, I wipe my face because there aren't any tissues. And I'm not a girl who wipes her nose on her own clothes!

Am I having a breakdown like Mamma? The idea terrifies me, but I can't think about her right now.

The purple butterfly moves to my arm, soft as a whisper, so light I can barely feel it. The wings stay closed, like it's bowed over and mourning its friend, the Giant Pink.

Tears keep dribbling out of my eyes as I glance up at the sky glittering with jeweled stars. "Grammy Claire, I need you. I need you so bad. Everything is a mess. Mamma, Riley, the butterflies. I don't know what to do! Tell me what I'm supposed to do!"

Riley.

The thought of my sister makes my face heat up.

Riley smashed that moth back home. On her dresser. Didn't even think twice about it. Didn't even care that it wasn't *really* a moth. That it was actually a butterfly.

Did she do this? Perhaps my own sister is the killer. She does have a past record.

Maybe the Giant Pink flapped in her hair, scared her. It *is* humongous.

'Course, it doesn't make any sense that Riley would follow it up to the top of the house and splatter it all over the table. And she certainly wouldn't smash it in Grammy Claire's bedroom and then bring it here. I glance at the smear of pink-and-brown wings against the wood and it makes me sick.

Riley and I had been getting along better the past two days, but suddenly I hate my sister. Hate her now more than I ever have in my whole life. Anger surges in my gut. My head pounds. I want Riley to go back home. Or go to California. I wouldn't give two hoots if she spent the rest of her life on the beach until she rotted away in the sand. I hate Daddy, too, who hardly ever calls, and wouldn't even come to Grammy Claire's funeral. My own mamma doesn't care enough about me to get her sorry self out of the South Wing and *live* like a normal person.

Suddenly, I hate everything and everybody.

"Stay here and stand guard," I tell the purple butterfly. "If someone comes, fly through that slit in the window and escape."

I wonder where the translucent butterfly got to. It's hard to see in the dim light. Shadows of laboratory equipment and shelves of old books and filing cabinets surround me like quiet statues.

It must be out flying or sitting somewhere sleeping. I just hope it's safe. Shivers run along my arms as I wonder if the invisible, mirrorlike butterfly is watching me right now.

The purple butterfly flies down to the table again where the pink lies. Folding its wings, the creature goes still. Like it's guarding the deathbed of its best friend.

Who would have thought? Is this what Grammy Claire was researching? Intelligent butterflies? The idea is mind-boggling crazy.

Maybe it's a sign that *I'm* crazy. Maybe I'm dreaming this whole thing!

But deep in my heart, I know I'm not.

When I leave the laboratory, I lock the door very deliberately, double-check it, and stomp downstairs to Riley's bedroom.

I slam the door open, cringing a little about waking up Butler Reginald and Madame See. But they're old and it's a long ways downstairs so they probably can't hear what's happening up here anyway.

Riley appears asleep. Only a sheet covers her, and one bare foot is hanging out.

She doesn't move when I walk in and close the door. I feel hiccups coming on from all the crying, but I suck it in and stride over to the bed, ripping off the covers.

Suddenly, Riley opens her eyes and stares at me. I jump just a little. It's creepy the way she opens her eyes like a zombie waking up from the dead. She pops the earbuds out of her ears. The sound of hard rock comes through the little black pieces.

"What are you doing listening to music at two in the morning?"

"What are *you* doing awake and wandering around? Didn't you ever hear of knocking first?"

"I didn't think you'd wake up if I knocked."

She rises on her elbows and peers into my face. "You sleep-walking, Tara?"

"Of course not. I'm not a girl who sleepwalks."

"Always a first time for everything."

"I came in here to tell you that I hate you. I hate you!" I repeat for emphasis, wanting to throw something.

She yawns, big and loud. "That's nothing new."

"How could you kill it?" I shriek. "You're a murderer!"

She sits up, her spiky hair sticking out in weird angles. "Have you lost your friggin' Pantene Princess mind?"

The smashed-up butterfly is imprinted on my brain, and everything feels bleak and miserable. "They would never hurt you! Those butterflies are special, can't you tell? They were Grammy Claire's butterflies! I'm supposed to protect them!"

Riley switches on her bedside lamp, and I blink in the bright light after wandering the dark house for an hour. "You don't make a lick of sense. Grammy Claire's butterflies?" She stares at me. "Oh, you mean that Butterfly Garden in her lab upstairs."

"I saw it, all smashed on the table. You're not only a serial killer, you're — you're sadistic!"

She cocks one of her plucked eyebrows. "Wow, what a big word; where'd you learn that?"

I'm getting better at rolling my eyes. "From your music albums, where else?"

She snorts and lies back down. "Oh, you mean that group called Sadistic Rain?"

"You're the only one who *knew* the butterflies lived there."

"Yeah, because I was with you, remember? They've probably been in there for a long time. Died while Grammy Claire was gone this past year."

"I'm talking about a Giant Pink that was alive. It flew into Grammy Claire's bedroom yesterday."

"Never saw it, don't know what you're talking about. Can I go to sleep now?"

Frustration makes me shake. "Why are you still awake?"

"I always listen to music while I fall asleep."

"It's the middle of the night."

She shrugs. "I was talking to Brad. We usually say a second good-bye on the phone after a date."

I never knew my sister was so romantic. The latest note in my hand is getting wrinkly with sweat from my palm. "You never saw a Giant Pink butterfly?"

Riley sighs. "No! You're running around in the middle of the night chasing butterflies?"

"I —" I stop, not willing to trust her. "I wasn't doing nothing."

She gives me a look. "Yeah, right. And I'm Dracula's daughter. Go to bed, Tara. You're starting to bug me. I'm tired."

I'm tired, too, but I don't say it. My mind is whirring away. "You promise, cross your heart and hope to die, that you didn't see that butterfly and kill it up in the Butterfly Garden?"

She flops back onto her pillow, reaching for her earphones again. "Promise, cross my heart, et cetera, et cetera."

"Soooo," I say slowly. "If you didn't kill the butterfly, who did?"

"I guess you're gonna have to figure that out all on your own," Riley says. "But I got an alibi."

I frown at her. "What do you mean?"

"An alibi. That's a police term for proving I wasn't anywhere near the scene of the crime. I was out with Brad, remember? So I couldn't have killed no butterfly. Get it?"

"You were out with Brad," I repeat, feeling my anger deflate. She's right. She does have an alibi.

"Uh-huh." She shuts her eyes and shuts me out at the same time.

I mutter a couple of curse words, and then punch the mattress. "So that means you left me here with a killer! Alone!"

"Give it up, Tara." Riley rolls over and starts to snore.

When I close her bedroom door, I stare straight up at the ceiling, pretending I can see through the two floors above me into the Secret Butterfly Garden, even though I actually can't. What if all those species are going extinct? The purple and pink and transparent as well as the dead blue ones? Maybe Grammy Claire was trying to save them. Maybe she was breeding them so the world wouldn't lose them forever.

The ends of my hair are wet by the time I finish sucking on them and crawl back into bed. I peel back my fingers and look at the crumpled note. The ink has stained the skin of my hand.

I read the words one last time. I should have already burned the note, but I'm too tired. Unless someone kidnaps me in my sleep, I'll hang on to it until I can flush the pieces down the toilet.

A second later, I jump up and make sure the windows are locked. Then I get up a third time and double-check the lock on my door. Finally, I crawl under the cool sheets for the last time, triple-checking the box of keys.

I stare at the smudged note before I turn out the light.

Hide this money! Now repeat that seven times.
You will need good old Ben on your journey. Key
Number Seven will show you where you're going
and have further instructions.

"Hide the money, hide the money, hide the money." I murmur it seven times, burying my head into the downy pillow. The money in the suitcase should be safe right where it is. I already burned the clue to the makeup case, and nobody saw me go into the closet after midnight. I just hope Butler Reginald doesn't get it into his head to do some spring cleaning under the stairs. Or pack up Grammy Claire's possessions for a yard sale.

Benjamin Franklin's face printed on all those hundred-dollar bills floats before my closed eyes. "Good old Ben on my journey," I repeat. "Ah!" I sit up so fast I whack my skull on the headboard.

I know what Key Number Seven unlocks.

The clue is in the note after all.

There's a reason Grammy Claire stuffed hundred-dollar bills and not a pile of twenties into that secret compartment. Now it all makes perfect sense.

Chapter Sixteen

How does one become a butterfly? You must want to fly so much that you are willing to give up being a caterpillar.

~ANONYMOUS~

Naturally, I oversleep the next morning, and when I wake, the sun is hot on my face. I pull on shorts and a T-shirt as fast as I can, then socks and sneakers instead of sandals. I'm going somewhere real dirty.

In the bathroom, I burn the little scrap of smeared paper I held on to all night long. The black, burned pieces flutter into the toilet and I flush. Twice, for good measure. *Then* I wash the ink off my hand, scrub the sleep out of my eyes, and brush my teeth.

When I pound down the curving staircase, I don't smell breakfast cooking. Butler Reginald is vacuuming the great room and has a tray of cleaning supplies to wax the furniture, dust the clocks, and mop the fading ceramic-tiled floor.

"Good morning, Miss Tara," he says, waving a gloved hand.

"Um, are there any eggs or toast?" I ask.

"Madame See left a note informing me that she was off to the grocery store. We hadn't laid up too many days of supplies," he adds in his soothing accent. "But she left fruit and some homemade bread and honey on the table. Help yourself."

I'm relieved our cook isn't here and I don't have to face her. "Madame See can drive a car?"

"Of course, Miss Tara. Why not?"

"I just — well, I just didn't think she knew much English."

"It's difficult to live in America and not drive, isn't it?" Reginald says musingly. "She doesn't say too much, but I believe she can read English well enough. Many people aren't comfortable in a second language."

"Well, I'm going down to the bayou for a while," I tell him, fibbing right to his face. "Wanna see if the baby frogs are out yet."

"Right-o," Reginald says. "I did that myself as a boy on holiday, but didn't realize girls liked to frog hunt as well."

"Just depends on the girl, I guess," I tell him, crossing my fingers behind my back, since I'm *not* a girl who *ever* goes frog hunting. I might run up and down a pier to scare some new kid at school, but frogging is best left for boys. And girls like Livie Mouton whose family eats them for Sunday supper.

"Would your Grammy Claire want you so close to where the alligators nest? I'm not sure I'm comfortable with this excursion."

I wave my hand as I slink toward the door. "Oh, don't you know? Alligators are more scared of us than we are of them."

Butler Reginald puzzles over this as I pound out of the great room, setting off the pipe organ. The eerie music floats down the hall while I grab a bunch of grapes from the antique sideboard, a slab of bread and honey, and head for the back door — the same vine-draped door that Key Number One opened on our first day.

I pat the pocket of my shorts where Key Number Seven lies securely.

Popping grapes into my mouth, I head down to the banks, sitting on a stump under the shade of a cypress. Spanish moss floats over my head in grayish swags of drapery.

Chocolate-colored water laps the shoreline. The current swirls around a cluster of cypress knees that stick out of the mud like gnarly witch fingers.

I see the shape of a V moving out in the middle of the bayou and watch a nutria poke its head up, carrying a stick between his teeth. A heron calls from somewhere across the water and the cypress forest on the opposite shore is thick and silent as a swamp.

I gulp down the last bite of bread and lick my fingers. Under cover of the trees, I sneak back through the tall weeds and overgrown flower beds and head for the barn. Red paint peels in long strips, and a fence encloses part of the acreage where Grammy Claire used to ride her horse.

Last summer I got to practice riding the gelding. Grammy Claire borrowed a neighbor's horse and we went riding along the bayou together in the morning before it got too hot.

I smile to myself. My grandmother's horse was named Ben.

Short for Benjamin Franklin.

"Very tricky, Grammy Claire," I murmur, dashing for the door of the barn where a padlock hangs hooked through a metal latch. "Yes, yes, yes!" I cry, pulling out the key. My hands are shaking so bad it takes me thirty seconds to get the key in right and yank the round, solid bolt out of its slot in the lock.

I pull open the door, scoot inside, and lean against the rough wooden door. Dust streams through a bank of windows, reminding me of the day the first butterfly came.

That seems so long ago now, but it's only been three days. "Okay, Grammy Claire," I say out loud. My voice is muted by bales of hay and a dusting of straw on the cypress plank floor. "Where'd you hide the next clue?"

Old Ben's gear still hangs on the walls. Saddles and frayed rope. An old steel trough has been shoved into the corner; otherwise the barn is empty. Ben must have been sold. A big room with an extra-tall roof. Hotter than heck. Airless. Sweat dribbles down my face and the nasty smell of manure lingers.

My eyes scan the walls and I wonder where the next letter is. Hope someone else hasn't found it. I picture Grammy Claire hiding the letters, boxing up the keys before she died. Did she do it last summer or longer ago than that, thinking I'd be lots older? Probably, but I'll never know.

The barn is so empty . . . no hiding places.

Was I wrong that the clue about *Ben* should lead me here?

Sucking on my hair, I start circling the building. The tools and riding equipment are rusting. There aren't any taped letters anywhere. 'Course, if Grammy Claire put them in the barn, it would be obvious to anybody who walked in the door!

Ben's watering trough! That has to be it! Just like that envelope taped under Grammy Claire's bed.

I sweep my hands through dirt and bugs in the bottom of the steel tub, gulping hard so I don't throw up. After stirring up the straw, I know there ain't a thing under that layer of filth.

Next I try to look underneath the trough, but after pushing and pulling, it's so heavy I can't budge it. Grammy Claire knew I wouldn't be able to move it by myself. Or am I supposed to get Riley to help me push it over so I can look at the bottom of it? Should I trust her now?

I blow out a big breath of air and rub a hand across my hot face.

I want to hold Grammy Claire's last words and secrets and notes close to my heart. Just for myself. Maybe it's selfish — but the letters, the clues, the keys — are all I have left of her.

I stare at the walls, the roof's peaked beams, the high windows. Scuff my feet along the floor. Nothing is under all that straw. There is *nothing* else here!

I want to cry.

I want a shower.

I want some chocolate chip cookies. And ice-cold milk.

I want to jump into the bayou and get the sweat off, but there's probably gators and I'm not stupid enough to get eaten.

"Think, think, think," I say, walking back outside. I was so sure I'd been right! Benjamin Franklin hundred-dollar bills. Ben, the old horse, who liked to nibble on my fingers when I ran out of apples. And I'm not a girl who lets animals snack on her fingers.

My nose starts running as I blink back all that stupid water filling up my eyes again.

Pressing my back against the barn door, I think back on the last two letters. Grammy Claire kept talking about a journey. Money for a journey. *Secret journeys. Going on a journey that the next key would reveal.*

So far Ben and the barn hadn't revealed a goll dern thing.

Okay. Horses took you on a journey. Suitcases were vital on a journey. Money helped you buy plane tickets and souvenirs and meals. What else is out here on the property that has anything to do with a journey?

I bite my lips as I lock the padlock and stick Key Number Seven back into my pocket. Walking around the barn, I keep to the shade, but even the shade is hotter than heck. Not a breeze ripples the surface of the bayou. The whole world has come to a sluggish standstill.

I keep walking, wondering how Mamma's doing. Even though I like Butler Reginald's proper London accent, I'm not sure I want to stay here all summer. I wonder if it's very dangerous to take Grammy Claire's skiff out on the water by myself. I wonder if Riley will go with me. Probably not. Maybe Butler Reginald will go with me. When he's not cleaning or shopping, he's talking on his cell phone a lot. He told me that he has relatives and friends both here and in England, and now that he's back in the States it's easier to telephone than on the island where phone service is spotty and unreliable.

I find myself staring across the property at Grammy Claire's old boat.

Journeys! Boats!

Jumping over a tangled bush, I race to the water's edge. The cypress pirogue is tied up on a rack. Stained, and splintery, and upside down.

I'll bet dollars to doughnuts that Key Number Seven unlocking the barn was a decoy to put somebody off the trail. Without the clues I burned, nobody would know where exactly to look.

I place my hands on my hips. There's nothing taped to the pirogue. Or tied to it, or glued to it. Finally, I get on my hands and knees and crawl under, scratching my legs on sharp, prickly grass. Lying on my back, I look up inside the shadowy, hollowed-out boat.

I don't see anything. Anything! I cover my eyes with my hands, feeling a sob jump into my throat. I've run out of clues. My brain is fried. Maybe I have heatstroke.

Grammy Claire is gone and I'm never gonna see her again. The knowledge of that crashes over me all over again. So painful I think somebody punched me in the chest. I cry for a while, feeling sorry for myself.

When a beetle starts crawling up my shirt, I let out a yell and sit up, whacking my head on the wooden seat of the boat.

"Ouch! Goll dern it!" I'm suddenly so mad I want to spit, and I am *not* a girl who spits. But there are some days I *do* want to be a girl who spits.

Rubbing my forehead, I realize that when I'm sitting up most of my body is inside the boat. The world is blocked out, light chinking where the grass meets the edge of the cypress. Reminds me of the tight, suffocating space under Grammy Claire's bed.

I get on my knees, flick at a few more beetles, then brush my hands against the wooden slats of the bottom of the boat, hoping I won't find a spider's nest. Something crackles.

I start laughing as I rip off a wad of tape and then an envelope.

"Miss Tara," a voice says from the other side of the cypress.

"Um, yeah," I say, still on my knees, my head inside the pirogue.

Butler Reginald's voice comes again. "Are you quite all right, dear girl? Shall I help you out from under there?"

"Um, sure." I realize that I could conk my head again if I try to unfold my legs and arms from around the two bench seats sticking upside down from the bottom of the canoe.

"Easy does it," Reginald says, helping me slide my arms down. "A bit lower now; turn your head to the right. There you go. You've got it."

Leaving the envelope where it is for the moment, sunshine stings my eyes as I crawl out and slowly get to my feet.

Butler Reginald squints at me, gardening gloves on his hands. A wheelbarrow filled with dead branches sits near a hedge of azaleas. He even does yard work. "I'm sorry if I've interrupted your time alone, Miss Tara."

I blink at him. "That's okay."

He gazes out at the bayou with its slow-moving water. "I miss her, your Grammy Claire. After so many years working

158

together and traveling and facing dangers — it's just difficult to believe that she's gone."

I nod at Butler Reginald, realizing again that he's mourning her, too. That he's sad and in shock like the rest of us.

"Sometimes there are no words to express such a great loss, are there?" he adds softly, and then sniffs. "Well! Back to work. At least we can put her old home back to rights."

"Thank you," I whisper, not moving a muscle as he hefts the wheelbarrow and walks it around the side of the house. "See you later!" I call out. He lifts a hand to me and then disappears.

Quickly, I crawl back under the boat, grab the large manila envelope, and clutch it to my chest. My name is on the front and the seal is mashed together with an enormous puddle of unbroken purple sealing wax.

I'm thrilled to pieces I found the next clues — and there are only three more keys left! I run straight for the water's edge so I can be alone, my heart pounding so hard I think it's gonna burst. I find a tree stump where it's not too muddy. Water bugs skim the surface and a few mosquitoes try to check out my ears but I swat them away and break the purple wax seal.

Several items spill out all at once. "Oh, no!" I cry out, grabbing at them before they can float away under the elephant ears.

There's a map! Undoing all the folds and creases, I see lots of blue. And a string of islands. The heading reads *Micronesia* and *Islands of Chuuk*. I start giggling at the islands' names I can't read because they're in the language of — what? Chuuk? Chuukese? I'm not even sure how to pronounce that.

I run my finger over lagoons and grottos and a bay and more tiny islands spreading out across the blue of the South Pacific. There are a few towns on the islands, but not many. Small mountains, but not very high. I wonder if there are waterfalls. I've always wanted to swim in a waterfall.

Black Xs are marked on the map. One X is a mile from some village. Another X is on a part of the island where there are lots of pools and lagoons and inlets and a ridge of cliffs. The third X lies close to the beach.

With Grammy Claire gone, I'll never know what those Xs mean.

Chewing on my hair, I stare across the bayou, reminding myself that I still have Grammy Claire's house. And her letters. And the memory of her love to hold deep inside my heart.

Tucking my knees tight under my chin, I also know that it's not enough.

Riley's not enough.

Mamma's nowhere close to enough.

And Butler Reginald ain't even in the ballpark of knowing how to comfort me.

After folding up the map again, I retrieve the white envelope tucked inside the big manila one. Actually, there are two white envelopes, one more bulky than the other. I open it first, curious. And out drop four airline tickets.

Four airline tickets!

The tickets look like coupon books, and as I peel back the layers, I see that the tickets were booked with the Chuuk Travel Agency. Booked without dates, open-ended tickets for coming and going. I'm so astonished I think I have a whole kaleidoscope of *nipwisipwis* flying around in my stomach!

There's a ticket with my name on it, Riley's name, Mamma's name, and Reginald Godwin's.

I'm going to the islands of Chuuk! I really am going! "Oh, Grammy Claire," I whisper. "You knew I would still want to go, you knew it. Thank you, thank you!"

Finally, I open the second envelope.

Dearest Tara,

You probably think it's silly and overly cautious, but I arranged all of this just in case. Lately, my work on Chuuk has become dangerous. For two years I've been watched. Someone is stealing from me. I don't know who, but I'm absolutely certain of why. That's why I'm taking precautions — and why I insist that you burn the clues. And why I've put you through so many keys and letters and cryptic notes. I pray the envelopes' seals remain unbroken, and that you find them all.

Someone wants to hurt the <u>nipwisipwis</u>. To steal them, and destroy them. I cannot allow that to *happen. They are precious. They hold a secret the world is not ready for, but which someone is willing to kill for. I often make myself crazy thinking about each person I know on the island and wondering who wants the butterflies. And who might want me dead.*

A horrible thought crashes across my brain, and I nearly fall off the stump. My sneakers squish in the mud as I try to stay seated. Grammy Claire's work was dangerous? Could this be why she died? Because of her secret *nipwisipwis*? Someone was watching her, stealing from her?

Cold drenches my entire body as a horrible thought knocks me over. Was my grandmother killed? Murdered? The car accident . . . maybe it was not an accident at all?

Tears splash onto the slick cover of the map, and I'm hardly breathing as I read the rest of the letter.

My list of suspects is fairly small, but frightening. Because I know them all personally. And yet, I'm in the dark about potential motives.

1. Alvios
2. Tafko
3. Mr. Masako

4. Family members of Alvios?
5. Mr. Masako's brother, Klate Masako, who used to be in prison for theft?
6. Members of the island government, the mayor?
7. Scientists at the Institute of Research for Lepidoptera? But they're all in Guam!
8. Reluctantly, I add the name Eloni, and he's just a child!

The most important reason you and your mamma and sister are going to the island is for the reading of my will. Reginald Godwin being my butler is a bit of a joke between him and me. He is not a butler in the traditional sense. Mostly, he's a trusted friend, personal bodyguard on my travels, and my attorney. My will is kept in a security box at the village bank. You will find it — with the right key — the date and time are in a future letter.

The other reason, Tara, and just as important, is that I want you to see the island where I've been living and working the past five years. I want you to experience how special it is and the wonderful people there. And I want you to see my spectacular _nipwisipwis_. I can't wait to look down *from heaven and watch you. In Chuukese, they call heaven <u>naangenu</u>, the place we came from and the place we return after death. Wherever I am, I will be with you in spirit. Always.*

All my love forever,

Your Grammy Claire

"You forgot a name," I whisper after I finish reading the letter. "Madame See. Maybe she's the one you feel watching you, hovering in the background. Spying on you. Because she's tricky. She fooled Butler Reginald enough so that he would let her come here to the bayou. So she can snoop right in your very own house. Which makes her even more dangerous."

My stomach does several queasy flips as I run my hands over the creamy stationery paper. "But I know she's watching. And now I'm watching her."

Chapter Seventeen

We delight in the beauty of the butterfly, but rarely admit the changes it has gone through to achieve that beauty.

~MAYA ANGELOU~

I picture Grammy Claire sitting at the desk in her laboratory writing the letters, assembling the keys, humming, and smiling. She thought she was leaving the keys and clues for me in case she died of an illness or had an accident. But she did it because she was going to be murdered. My Grammy Claire was killed. The car accident was *on purpose.*

I'm so sick to my stomach, I think I'm going to puke any second.

My mind goes back over the past two weeks. Our telephone ringing off the hook with calls from the police and the Bayou

Bridge attorney's office. A police report arriving special delivery. Miz Landry taking everything up to Mamma in the South Wing while I cried in my room and beat my pillow.

That's probably why Mamma went into hiding. She can't face that Grammy Claire might have been murdered. Murdered because of the *nipwisipwis*.

Gripping the brochure and the letter, I close my eyes. It's like a nightmare.

With Grammy Claire dead, the killer is now free to steal her research. And steal the butterflies. The *nipwisipwis* are completely unprotected without her.

Goose bumps break out along my arms and legs. The killer must have come to Grammy Claire's house first. Killed the butterflies in the laboratory. Or taken any that were still alive.

Which meant the killer had been here at this house before Riley and I arrived. And they were most likely already back at the island, taking everything out of Grammy Claire's laboratory.

Now I understood the secrecy of Grammy Claire's letters, the urgency, the precautions she'd taken, the clues that only I could figure out.

After stuffing the letters and airline tickets back into the envelope, I roll off the stump onto my knees, shudders crawling up my back. Breakfast rises into my throat as I stare into the cypress and tupelo. Shade dances across my face as I try to hold still. I will not throw up. *I will not.*

But I can't stop the sob that bursts out of my mouth. Tears burn like liquid fire, and I cover up my face with my hands. The sun is hot and sticky, but I'm lying in the mud and grass like a wild, crazy person.

I know for certain now that I have to protect the *nipwisipwis*. That's why Grammy Claire wrote the letters to me. And I will need Riley's help, even if she kicks and screams the entire way across the Pacific.

"We have to leave now," I mutter. I need to talk to Riley. And Butler Reginald. And pack. And catch a plane.

And yet, I'm still wondering, what *is* the secret of the butterflies? Why hasn't my grandmother told me already? Blowing out a deep breath, I try to grab at my crazy thoughts when the sound of crunching leaves makes me jerk my chin up.

From the house, Riley walks toward me, determined, her eyes looking down at the ground like she's watching out for snakes.

I break out into another uninvited sweat.

When she reaches me, Riley clears her throat. "Miz Landry sent a letter yesterday, and it just arrived certified delivery."

I shake my head. I don't want to hear more bad news. "Mamma —"

"Just read it." Riley thrusts the envelope and paper at me.

Darlin' Riley and Tara,
  I'm sorry to write and spoil your holiday, but I must tell you that your mamma ended up getting those nasty bank

*papers yesterday and they're gonna take the house right out
from under us and we both been so upset and crying and
I'm so sorry to give you such terrible news on your vacation,
'specially with your grammy so recently passed (God bless
her generous soul!), but your mamma ain't doing too good so
the doctors been here and recommending she might need a
few days in a hospital to get her to feeling better so you
don't worry about a thing, she's in good hands and I won't
never let anything bad happen to her, you can count on that
for sure, so you both just <u>Take Care</u> of yourselves, call me if
you need to, and I will see you in a few weeks.*

   Lots of hugs and sugar,
   Miz Emmaline Landry

Riley kicks her boot into the mud and sprays bits of grass.

"It's really true we're gonna lose the house?" I ask her.
"Think we should sell Grammy Claire's house to keep the
Doucet Mansion?"

Riley chews on her lips, not looking at me. Suddenly, she
screams and throws a rock against the bark of the tupelo, split-
ting off a few pieces, which go flying into the muddy water.

I think she's more upset about everything than she lets on.

"Who's gonna buy this dump out in the middle of nowhere?
The Doucet Mansion is just a dumb old house, but it's *ours*. And
why do people keep dying or going away or getting checked
into hospitals? I hate them all!"

She's talking about Grammy Claire and Daddy and Mamma.

"I'm outta here so bad," Riley mutters, stomping off.

"Wait!" I screech. Chasing after her, I jerk at her arm and she whirls around. "You can't leave!"

"Who's gonna stop me?"

"Me, that's who! Grammy Claire got it all arranged before she died. *You* have to come with *me*." I thrust the manila envelope at her. She pulls out the airline tickets and reads the fine print, her lips moving.

"Are you out of your freaking mind? I'm not flying clear across the ocean to some pathetic, dinky island with a boring laboratory and another bunch of dead butterflies!"

"But you have to! Grammy Claire told you to! With me! And Mamma."

Riley lets out a couple of curse words, stomps in the grass, and yells again. "I hate my life."

"Listen to this," I say, reading her part of Grammy Claire's letter.

The most important reason you and your mamma and sister are going to the island is for the reading of my will.

Riley frowns. "Her will, huh? Only way we can save our house is if Grammy Claire's got a million bucks stashed under a sand castle. And it probably already got washed away!"

"Ha, ha. That is *not* funny."

"About as funny as a million bucks that doesn't exist."

I resort to whining. "You *have* to come. It's the rules."

"I don't follow rules."

Before she can leave again, I show her the rest of the letter. Then I whisper, "Don't you see? Grammy Claire was killed for her butterflies. We have to go. It's a matter of life and death!"

"I don't want to hear it, Tara! Don't you get it? I. Don't. Want. To. Hear. It."

And then my big sister actually breaks down. Before I know it, she's sobbing her guts out, and within ten seconds, she's running away from me and out of sight.

I pick up the airline tickets she dropped in the prickly grass. I know that I have to go. Not only for Grammy Claire and to save our home, but for Mamma. And me. And Riley, too.

Because my family is breaking into a million pieces.

That night, tucked between the cool sheets of Grammy Claire's bed, I write a letter of my own.

To Shelby Jayne Allemond,

I need you to pass the letter inside to your mamma, Miz Mirage, as soon as possible. I know she's a <u>traiteur</u>, a healer, and that sometimes I've called her a swamp witch with the

other kids at school, but since we're going to be in Bayou
Bridge Middle School next year, I figure it's time to let
bygones be bygones —

I stop writing as the buzz of cicadas outside roars louder.
The words aren't coming out right like I want them to.

The Giant Pink floats through the open window and circles
my head, tickling my ear, lighting on the long strands of my
hair where I've chewed the ends off all day long.

I start the letter over again. Wish I could text or e-mail, but
there's no cell service out here and no computer. Grammy
Claire has a computer in her laboratory, but the Internet was
switched off long ago.

"Okay, okay, I'll be nicer to Shelby Jayne in my letter," I mutter to the Giant Pink.

When the butterfly flits her wings, she's so beautiful I feel
like crying. A tear slips down my face when I think about how
this butterfly was one of Grammy Claire's special ones.

Wait a minute.

I blink.

I'm seeing things.

There is NO Giant Pink any longer. I saw her with my own
eyes, dead on the fourth floor.

Rubbing my hand across my nose, I swipe away tears, dis-
gusted with myself.

The memory of the Giant Pink is so powerful. Almost like the creature's spirit is still here in this house. Something about that butterfly is making me want to be a better person.

I swallow my pride and my past and begin again.

Dear Shelby Jayne,

Could you please pass along the letter inside to your mamma, Miz Mirage? I know she's a <u>traiteur</u>, one of those folks who heal people with herbs and prayers. And I know that I used to call her a swamp witch with the other kids at school — and, well, I really <u>am</u> sorry about that. It wasn't nice and I know it's not true. At least, I know it now.

Turns out <u>my</u> grandmother knew <u>your</u> grandmother. Isn't that strange? Turns out your grandmother and your mamma have helped my family before, and since we're going to be in Bayou Bridge Middle School next year, I figure that maybe we could start all over again. So I hope you can forgive me for everything that happened last year when I tried to make you jump off the bridge. I want to start over. I really do.

Truth is, I'm desperate. My mamma is real sick and I'm not sure the sickness she has can be helped by any doctor or hospital. I also need my mamma to get the airline ticket I've stuck inside with this letter. The ticket is a matter of life and death and she needs to get it before someone takes her away and locks her up. It may be too late already!

My mamma needs a healing real bad. Some medicine, some herbs, some prayers, whatever a <u>traiteur</u> does to help folks.

Please help me! Please.

Your friend, I hope!

Tara Doucet

After I finish the letter to Shelby Jayne, I write a second letter to her mamma, Miz Mirage, explaining Mamma's depressed condition. Then I tuck the two letters and the airline ticket inside a manila envelope and address it. If I get Butler Reginald to drive me to the post office first thing in the morning, Shelby Jayne and her mamma should get the letters day after tomorrow. It'll take that much time to get packed, close up the house here, and get seats on a flight. That'll give Miz Landry time to get Mamma to the airport in New Orleans so we can all get to the island together.

When I finally snap off the lamp, the room plunges into darkness. The house settles around me. Creaky. Whispering. Wind moaning around the eaves.

I can't shut my mind off. I'll bet Grammy Claire's killer wants my keys, and whatever is on the island. They've already been here in this house, looking — and someone smashed the Giant Pink last night.

Springing out of bed, I race to the door and triple-check the lock. Then I grab the straight-backed chair sitting in the corner and jam it under the doorknob. Then I stack it high with all sorts of books and junk from my suitcase. If someone does try to get in, I'll hear them right away.

Wish I had a hammer or some kind of big stick. Or one of Daddy's twenty-twos locked up in the gun case back home. I wonder if Riley's asleep. I wonder if I should jump into bed with her, but she'd probably just kick me out.

Crawling back under the covers, I lie there stiff as a board. Organ music floats overhead. The wind rises and the oak leaves rattle. Soon the sound of raindrops plinks against the window. That's the last thing I remember, but my right hand is tightly closed around Key Number Eight and Key Number Nine. Key Number Ten digs into my left hand.

The last three keys will open the locks I need to find on Chuuk. I wonder what they are . . . a second laboratory? A secret journal with scientific calculations that will save the world?

With every hour I'm getting closer to the reason Grammy Claire died — and the reason the butterflies are so priceless.

Chapter Eighteen

We are closer to the ants than to the butterflies.

~GERALD BRENAN~

The next day I stick my letter to Shelby Jayne and Miz Mirage through the slot at the post office.

Two days later we're packed, snacks purchased from the Piggly Wiggly, and our airline departure confirmed. Beef jerky, chips, and a large bag of M&M's for Riley. We also have lunch at the Yellow Bowl in Jeanerette.

Butler Reginald eats cleanly and precisely, his napkin tucked into his shirt collar, his knife scooping food onto his upside down fork.

The Yellow Bowl is crowded and my fried catfish is divine, even though tears bite at the corners of my eyes. Grammy

Claire used to bring me here when I'd visit. She always said that the Yellow Bowl had been sitting in the same spot since she was a teenager.

"Life has certainly turned upside down these last few weeks." Butler Reginald's voice trails off and he dabs at his eyes with a napkin. "Truly extraordinary, you finding those airline tickets!" I like to listen to the genteel sound of his accent. Makes me think of books set in a charming English countryside — or high tea, scones, and clotted cream. Then Butler Reginald adds, "Your grandmother thought of you with her last breath."

I really don't want to see a grown man cry, so I go use the restroom while he gets control of his emotions. In reality, I let out a few of my own tears and then wash my face with cold water.

The next day I'm saying good-bye to Grammy Claire's house. My stomach feels like a swarm of butterflies is having a party.

The staircases from top to bottom are littered with Riley's clothes, combat boots, makeup bags, and backpacks. The air reeks like a chemical factory. My sister must have used ten bottles of hair dye just that morning. Her hair is now a very deep shade of magenta.

My throat gags and my eyes burn. Swirling my own hair over my shoulder, I'm grateful that Grammy Claire passed on her long and silky hair genes to me.

I refold all my clothes again, excited to leave, but wanting to give Mamma enough time for a visit from Miz Mirage to work her healing magic so Mamma will be at the airport waiting for us. I even telephoned Miz Landry the day before to pack Mamma a suitcase.

Anticipation thumps against my ribs, but there's a good dose of fear and dread, too. What if the Doucet Mansion is locked up with chains when we return from the island? Does Daddy know we might be on the streets after summer is over? What about the killer on the island — and how am I supposed to save the *nipwisipwis*?

Stuffing the plane tickets under my stash of sandals and flip-flops, I rush out the door.

Riley is standing by the hall window overlooking the bayou. She doesn't move when I skid to a stop. Never seen her so still and quiet. It's unnerving.

She presses her forehead against the glass, staring at something while she rubs her right foot against her left leg in the Doucet fashion. I wonder what she's thinking about.

When the floorboards creak, she whirls around. "What are you doing sneaking up on me?"

"I'm not sneaking up on you!"

"You better be packed and not make us late to the airport — or I won't go at all."

"Don't threaten me!" I shoot back. "Besides," I add, softening my voice like Miz Landry, "I'm not the one with junk all over the house." Then I run upstairs to make sure Grammy Claire's laboratory is securely locked.

First, I sit at her desk and wander the room until dinner. I keep waiting for the purple butterfly to return, but it never does. I fear that it's dead now, too. Maybe I'll never know the secrets about Grammy Claire's butterflies. I keep thinking the secret is here and I can't see it. Or somebody already stole it, and I'm too late.

On day four after writing my letters, a hot breakfast appears on the dining room table. Waffles, maple syrup, grits, and bacon, but I can't hardly eat, even though it's delicious.

"Did you know that there isn't a ticket for Madame See?" I tell Butler Reginald, wondering what he'll say. Does he suspect our cook, too? I can't ask. My lips must remain sealed.

"She's decided to go to San Francisco where her family lives," he informs me with a small smile. "Eventually, I will need to employ another cook, although I suppose I'll wait until our return to the States. Meanwhile, we will have to fend for ourselves."

I try to return the smile, but I'm afraid it comes out crooked due to a bad case of nerves. It's all I can do not to start straightening rug fringe and alphabetizing the spices!

After saying good-bye to Grammy Claire's bedroom, I fasten the windows, stare at the Bayou Teche's rippling muddy waters, then double-check my packing.

Clothes, sandals, bathing suits, sunscreen: Check
Matches for burning important notes: Check
The carved box of ten keys: Check
Grammy Claire's personal notes to me: Check
Airline tickets and map of the island: Check
$2,000 from Grammy Claire:

My heart drops with a thud. I forgot to get all that cash still sitting underneath the stairs!

I run to the opposite window overlooking the drive. Butler Reginald is helping Riley pack the car with all her junk. A taxi has arrived to collect Madame See. She's standing off to one side in a long dress and those old-lady black shoes that housekeepers usually wear for comfort. She's got a hat and sunglasses on her head, two small cases at her feet.

The coast is clear! As soon as Riley pulls out her cell phone and Butler Reginald helps the taxi driver with Madame See's belongings, I *race* downstairs.

The clocks begin chiming, the pipe organ breathes a few wispy notes, and I'm ducking under the stairs, stumbling over to the little case in the corner. Fast as I can I open the lid, lift up the secret bottom flap, and reach in.

My fingertips brush against — nothing.

Swiftly, I sweep my hands over the faded old material again and again, but there are only little pockets of dust and crumbs in the corners.

The money is gone.

I start hyperventilating.

Daylight comes through the small staircase door and I hurriedly bring the makeup case into the light. I pull out the false cardboard bottom again, staring until my eyes burn, but the case is truly empty.

Prickles of terror run down my neck, zap my knees, and then my toes.

Someone came in here and stole the money. *My money.* Grammy Claire's money!

That's when it finally dawns on me that I didn't use Key Number Six to open the latch on the makeup case. Somebody picked the lock during the last few days — and it's still unlocked.

The thief has to be Madame See! She's the only one with a bedroom downstairs. She's small and sneaky and always kept herself hidden away in the kitchen. It was Madame See I saw on the stairs after midnight. Madame See must have seen me that night! Seen me watching her behind the crack in the door. She'd glided right by me back to her bedroom, cool as you please. She's a regular burglar! Grammy Claire must have been suspicious of her. That's why Madame See isn't returning to the island with us. She's probably the one that killed the Giant Pink, too!

And now she's escaping in the taxi!

Clutching the little case under my arm, I duck out from under the stairs, fly through the front door, and race down the porch steps.

"Butler Reginald!" I scream.

He turns toward me, then runs to my side. "Miss Tara, what is it?"

"Madame See! Madame See! Where is she?"

Butler Reginald points to the road where dust creates a tail of brown behind the yellow taxi. "She just left. Why? Whatever is the matter? You look quite flushed."

"It's too late," I moan. Madame See took the money I need for Chuuk. I'm trembling so hard, I sink to the ground. And I'm a girl that never sits in the dirt on purpose.

The sun burns my head. Tears blur my vision so bad I can't see straight.

"Oh, my dear girl," Butler Reginald says. "Here, let me help you." He sets me on my feet and pats my shoulder with a large, comforting hand. "What can I do to help, Miss Tara?"

"Nothing," I choke out. "Unless you have a forwarding address for Madame See."

"Well, now, I'm not sure," he says, looking flustered for the first time ever. "We said our good-byes; I gave her the last pay-check, and bid her a long and happy life."

"I guess I just gave her a two-thousand-dollar bonus," I mutter bitterly. I've failed Grammy Claire. I should have kept the money safe. But most of all, I hate Madame Erial See with a passion. Even if she did make the best gumbo I'd eaten in the last year.

Chapter Nineteen

This magnificent butterfly finds a little heap of dirt and sits still on it;
but man will never on his heap of mud keep still.

~JOSEPH CONRAD~

I stand at the gate and wait for a full hour, but Mamma never shows up.

I'm the last one to board, but Mamma never shows up.

I stare at the airplane door until the flight attendant shuts it. When she locks it, my stomach twists. Nobody pounds on the other side to let them in, and the captain's voice comes over the loudspeakers.

I keep waiting to see if I will get a message from Miz Landry or Miz Mirage Allemond, but I don't, and Mamma's ticket goes unused.

Riley sticks her earbuds into her head, closes her eyes, and eats M&M's one at a time, in the same order for hours. Green, red, yellow, brown, green, red, yellow, brown. I feel nau-se-ous.

Across the aisle, Butler Reginald reads newspaper after newspaper until I think I'm gonna be sick to my stomach from staring at the headlines. Finally, I watch a movie on the little screen with my own set of headphones that come in a cute plastic bag that snaps at the top.

After that, I stare at the blues and greens of the ocean zooming in all directions for thousands of miles until I fall asleep with my head against the small airplane window. When I wake up, I find that I've been drooling, and quickly wipe my mouth.

I am a girl that *never* drools!

We fly all night. The hum of the airplane rumbles underneath us. Through slitted eyes, I see the soft shadows of the flight attendants, and all I can think about is revenge against Madame See for stealing my two thousand dollars and smashing the Giant Pink.

I have to trust that Grammy Claire hid some extra cash in her house on the island, but even if she did, I still hate Madame See.

And I try not to hate Mamma. Mostly I try not to think about her locked away in the South Wing. If I do, I'll either start screaming or crying — and I can't do either. One thing a Southern lady with countless Paris generations in her blood does well is to hide her emotions and problems and tears.

We land in Guam in the middle of the night and transfer planes. By this time, I'm so groggy, I fall asleep in the narrow seat right away. When the sun comes over the horizon and the attendants bring us breakfast on little trays, I spot a string of islands in the distance. A bubble rises up in my stomach. I'm finally going to see Chuuk! The island of the *nipwisipwis*!

As soon as the breakfast trays are collected, the seat-belt sign flashes and the captain prepares us for descent. The ocean grows closer. Frothy whitecaps sparkle dizzily under the sun. I try not to think about crash-landing and swimming to the island. We pass over two small islands and head for the biggest one, but it's a ring of white cliffs, rocky inlets and bays, capped by a jungle of green.

"Does anybody live down there?" I can't see a single sign of habitation. What if we have to camp on the beach while crabs pinch our toes and fleas bite under our arms?

"Oh, yes," Butler Reginald says with a laugh. "The trees are such a dense canopy you can't actually see the village from so high, but it is there."

"*The* village?" Riley says, coming back to life. "As in one village. One. Period?"

"The village is very modern. Even comes equipped with electricity and running water." He says this with a straight face but I finally realize he's teasing.

My face feels itchy and my eyes crusty from sleeping in an

airplane all night, but I can't stop staring. Chuuk is beautiful and lush, straight out of a movie.

There's only one landing strip at the tiny airport. We even have to use a set of rickety metal stairs to get to the tarmac. A blast of hot, humid air slaps me in the face like a wet rag.

Butler Reginald removes his coat and mops his face. "You'd think I'd be used to it by now," he says, stepping to the soft, melting asphalt. "But it always takes me by surprise."

Riley tries to suck in air. "I can't breathe, I can't breathe!"

The other passengers stare at her as she lurches down the metal stairs like she's drunk.

I wonder if she knows how ridiculous she looks.

The steamy atmosphere seeps into my skin like a sauna, and I swear I'm walking through hot liquid air. Time for living in my swimsuit.

Inside the terminal, we drag our suitcases off the baggage carousel, and then we're back outside, sweating on the curb.

Butler Reginald marches down the curb lined with cars and buses. "I'll round up a taxi, girls. Stay here with the luggage."

"I have to go to the bathroom," I tell Riley.

She's chewing on a piece of gum and popping bubbles between her teeth. "Well, hurry!" She rolls her eyes. "Why didn't you go already?"

I race back inside the airport, my sundress sticking to my skin, hair plastered to my neck, and look for a restroom sign.

Another flight has landed within the last thirty minutes and now there are crowds of people collecting baggage, reuniting with family, the sounds of a language I don't recognize surrounding me.

Spotting a restroom at last, I head for it, when a woman wearing a long, colorful dress and those old-lady black shoes with thick soles slips out the restroom door. She starts walking in my direction, then cocks her head, and spins around on her heels to head for the other end of the terminal.

It's Madame Erial See! I'd swear on a stack of bibles it's her. The hunched shoulders, the short dark hair, the funny clothes.

"Madame See — !" I call out, but the words die in my throat. She's too far away to hear me, and moving fast. Catching my breath, I race toward her, but in an instant, the woman disappears into a throng of people all converging toward a set of glass doors at the far end of the terminal.

I *know* it's her. The abrupt change in direction makes me think she saw me. She's trying to hide from me. Because she's the one who stole my money!

But why is Madame See here in Chuuk? That makes absolutely no sense! Isn't she supposed to be going to San Francisco? Then I realize that she was most likely traveling on our very same flight! We had seats in the front of the plane and I'll bet she had a seat in the back — hiding her face behind a newspaper.

Seeing her here on the island is very, very peculiar. She must have followed us. Deep in my gut, I know she's here to hurt the butterflies. And I'm supposed to stop her.

Someone jerks my arm and I'm staring into Riley's smudged eyes. "Will you come on already? We already got the stuff loaded in the taxi. You are so slow, Tara."

"But I haven't been to the bathroom yet!"

"What have you been doing?"

"Riley, I saw Madame See! Down there at the end, walking out to the sidewalk!"

"You mean our cook? Yeah, I saw her, too — like I just saw a flying saucer."

"You don't have to be sarcastic."

"Would you just *go* already?"

"Go where?"

"To the bathroom! If you don't go now, you'll be using a palm tree. Reginald Dude says it's a two-hour car drive around the island to Grammy Claire's house."

Running as fast as I can, I use the facilities, wash my sticky hands, and then race to the curb where the only person smiling is the taxi driver. He introduces himself as Alvios and shakes each of our hands like we're all new friends and going to a party. He has a head of thick black hair, a flowered shirt, sandals, and speaks broken English.

Alvios! He was on Grammy Claire's list of suspects. In the

number-one position, too. I stare at him from the backseat. He *seems* nice. Not sinister at all. But appearances can be deceiving. Take Madam See for instance!

Leaning out the car window, I gaze back at the Chuuk International Airport as Alvios starts the engine. *Madame See, what are you doing here? Are you here to steal Grammy Claire's* nipwisipwis*?*

We drive down a main street that looks like it was last painted when Grammy Claire was born. A couple of restaurants, hotels, the Chuuk island post office, and various little boat and bait and scuba-diving shops.

Alvios points out shops and restaurants like we're tourists and have never been here before. Well, which we haven't. I like the musical lilt in his voice, but Butler Reginald waves his hands at the dashboard like he's shooing at a cat. "Keep going, my man. We're out on the west beach side, in Professor Claire's house."

Alvios bobs his head and repeats, "Miz Claire! Miz Claire! Yes! Yes!"

It's strange to hear Grammy Claire called Professor Claire. Rolling down the window, I smell the salt air, letting it wash over me.

Once out of town, we wind through palm tree–lined roads, my head banging against the roof of the taxi until it aches and my eyes smart. The roads are horribly rutted, muddy, and much of the ground is covered in deep puddles. Cars slowly pass each other.

"I'll bet we're not going over ten miles an hour," Riley mutters to the window.

"I plan on enjoying every single minute," I tell her, looking up at the blue, blue sky. Even if I don't stop sweating for the next week.

I'm pretty sure three hours have gone by when Alvios finally stops the taxi. "Here! We here, girls! Here!"

"But there's nothing here," Riley says, sagging against the cramped backseat. "You made a wrong turn."

The driver laughs, his big white teeth sparkling. "I have no wrong turn! Nope!"

I feel sorry for my sister in her black shirt and big old, hot boots. Sweat trickles freely down her face, but she pretends it doesn't bother her. "So where the heck is the house? I need a shower."

"There!" our taxi driver tells us. "See? There!"

Rays of sunlight glint through mangrove forests, clusters of palms, and hibiscus shrubbery. A beach covered with perfect white sand lies just below the rise we're standing on and beyond the trees. We have our very own private beach — how supremely wonderful is that? The water is so blue, so clear, it doesn't seem real. The air smells like flowers and salt and summer and sunlight. But when I stare back into the jungle, I don't see a house, either.

"Hey, what about that shower?" Riley says again, looking miserable. Her magenta hair is sticking straight up on half her head and plastered flat to her skull on the other half.

"Do we *have* running water and electricity?" I ask.

Butler Reginald laughs and gestures up ahead. "The house is right there, girls. Through the trees. Cast your eyes heavenward."

Then I realize what I didn't before. It's like I'm looking at a mirage, and my heart crashes like a perfect blue wave.

Grammy Claire's island house is actually a tree house.

The next moment, a boy comes swinging down a rope from one of the ledges of the house and races toward us. He whoops and hollers, a blur of long dark hair, tanned legs, and bare feet, kicking up sand and bark and hibiscus petals along the path.

"Who is *that*?" Riley drawls, rolling her eyes.

Butler Reginald says, "He's your grandmother's hired assistant. His name is Eloni. He's thirteen, nearly fourteen, I believe."

Eloni! The last name on the list! The one person Grammy Claire did not want to write down. I never expected him to be close to my age. Or so happy and friendly. Imps of jealousy surge through me. And Grammy Claire hired him to be her assistant? To do what? Why couldn't I have lived here and been my grandmother's personal assistant?

My chin quivers. Why didn't she move *all* of us here five years ago? Or even just *me* if Mamma didn't want to come?

The boy stops in front of us and gives a solemn bow. I blink at him and he grins. He's wearing a pair of blue shorts with ragged edges and a thin T-shirt. I have a feeling he put on the shirt just for us. On the drive here, we'd seen lots of houses and huts situated under clusters of palm trees. People walking along the roads. Many of the boys and young men not wearing shirts at all. A smooth-shaped stick lies in a deep side pocket of his shorts. I can see carvings decorating it as several inches poke out, and I want to look closer.

"I'm Eloni," he says, bowing to us. Then he shakes my hand and Riley's hand. "Professor Claire's personal research assistant. Very happy to meet you, misses." I notice that his English is much better than Alvios's. Like a hundred times better. I wonder if Grammy Claire taught him.

Riley sighs and starts dragging her baggage toward the trees. I'm dying to explore the tree house myself, and I don't want my sister to see it first. Grammy Claire called me here. Riley is only here because she has to be.

"Don't exaggerate, Eloni," Butler Reginald tells him mildly.

Eloni's eyes go wide and dark. "I do not exaggerate, Mr. Butler Reginald. I am her assistant, and she will tell you so."

Eloni speaks formally, and yet there is an excited, eager lilt to his voice that I can't help liking. Am I supposed to like him? Or should I ignore him? Or watch him and see if *he's* the bad guy? I'm so confused! Eloni is also taller than me, but not too tall. Not many boys are taller than me, so I can't help liking him. But not more than Jett Dupuis back home, of course!

My grandmother's research assistant hurries to help unload the trunks and suitcases. I watch him and Alvios embrace and chatter. Then I marvel that this island is so friendly, strangers would actually hug each other.

The taxi driver slams the trunk shut and then his and Eloni's sandals crunch on the path as they haul the luggage to the tree house staircase. When they embrace good-bye, Eloni speaks a string of words in another language, Chuukese probably. Something with long, convoluted words and run-on sentences. The taxi driver waves good-bye to us all, his smile as wide as the horizon.

Nervously, I rub the back of my right foot against my left leg. "Does everyone around here hug everybody else? Even if you don't know each other?"

Firmly, Riley says, "I refuse to hug anybody. I don't care who they are."

Eloni starts to laugh, and Riley gives him one of her best glares. "The taxi driver is not a stranger. He's my grandfather."

"Your grandfather?" I ask faintly. "But he looks so young. Like your dad. Or an uncle."

Eloni's eyes flick across my face and then he shrugs. "We are lucky on the islands of Chuuk. We have so much fun, we stay young and healthy. We eat a lot of tuna, too."

I can't help laughing, his comment is so unexpected.

Riley makes a face. "Tuna? Does Grammy Claire have any steaks in her freezer?"

"Where *is* Miss Professor Claire?" Eloni asks. "Is she in town for shopping? I can do errands so you can enjoy time together." His eyes dart beyond us, toward the taxi, which is empty but for his grandfather, who revs the engine.

I swear it's the bright sun sparkling on the water, or maybe the coconuts high in the palm trees overhead, but my eyes start watering. I blink again, super hard, and will myself with every ounce of resolve I possess not to cry. Not until I get inside the house. Not until I find a private spot.

Butler Reginald's voice lowers, and I glance away, unable to watch his face. "I have very sad news, Master Eloni. Professor Claire is not with us any longer. She was buried over a week ago. But these are her granddaughters, Miss Riley and Miss Tara Doucet."

Eloni's face clouds over as he glances between us. He shakes his head, as if he can't quite believe what he's hearing. "Not possible," he finally whispers. "No. No."

"I'm afraid it's true," Butler Reginald continues, and I'm so grateful I don't have to say anything. "It has been a very sad month, and that was the reason I left the island so quickly ten days ago when I received the news. But Miss Claire planned this trip for her granddaughters a long time ago. While they enjoy the beach and a little vacation, I will be shutting down the house, tying up loose ends, and then we all return back to the States."

"You m-mean —" he stutters. "You mean I will never see Professor Claire again?"

Butler Reginald puts one of his big hands on Eloni's shoulder to comfort him, and my eyes just keep watering and watering, so I duck my head and sprint after Riley. After taking a couple of deep breaths, I gaze into the jungle of palm trees and mangroves, thinking about Grammy Claire living and working here. She was right *here* just a few weeks ago. And the house really *is* a tree house.

The tree house has regular walls reinforced against the huge limbs, and floors bolted into the tree trunks. Thatched roofs perch atop each room, and bamboo walkways join each room from tree to tree. It's absolutely fantastic.

A bubble of excitement rises in my stomach. "Can we go inside?"

"Is there a hotel back in town?" Riley says.

"Running water," Eloni tells us. "Electricity. Bathrooms. The works!" He sounds proud, even if his face looks red and splotched like he's trying not to weep. "*Nesor annim. Etiwa.* Welcome to Chuuk."

"Um, yeah, okay," Riley says, so rudely I want to punch her. "Do we get to pick our bedrooms?"

Eloni frowns. "Not many bedrooms," he says, but Riley immediately thumps her way up the staircase into what looks like the main part of the house, crashing her duffel and back-pack into the banister.

I cringe and glance at Eloni, knowing he's in shock over Grammy Claire's death. "I'm sorry. She's a big pain in the you-know-what. And thank you for the welcome," I add, trying to be a good Southern girl. "I'm really, *really* glad to be here."

"That makes me happy, Miss Tara."

"Um, just call me Tara, okay?"

Eloni gives a formal bow again. "I'm very sorry for the loss of Miss Professor Claire. This news makes me so very sad."

I brush away the water in my eyes. "Are you really my grand-mother's errand boy?"

Eloni pulls himself up even taller. "I am no errand boy. I am Professor Claire's laboratory research assistant."

"I believe you," I assure him, but *now* I know the reason why my grandmother had to add his name to her list of suspects if he had access to her research. "Is there really a laboratory out here?"

"I will show you, Miss Tara! I mean — just Tara." Eloni shrugs, pink creeping into his face.

"I'm only twelve. Not some lady of the house."

"Me, I'm thirteen."

We grin at each other and I glance away, a flush creeping up my neck. Then I chant Jett Dupuis's name inside my mind so I won't forget it.

"I saw my grandmother's laboratory back home. It was filled with" — I pause, wondering if a thirteen-year-old boy could be a spy — "lots of dust." Grammy Claire's words flit through my mind: *Trust no one.*

Eloni pauses on the first step of the staircase and leans close, his black eyes on my face. "Professor Claire told me that if you were ever to come, I should tell you about the research."

Tingles run up and down my whole body. "She did?"

"Can I ask?" Eloni lowers his voice to a mere whisper. "I mean — at her laboratory . . . in her house far away . . . did you see the bu — the *nipwisipwis*?"

Chapter Twenty

What the caterpillar calls the end of the world, the Master calls the butterfly.

~RICHARD BACH~

Eloni *knows* about the butterflies! This boy really knew my Grammy Claire. I whisper back, "Yes, I saw them! But they're" — I start stuttering — "th-they're gone."

"You mean dead?"

I stare at him. "How do you know that?"

Eloni ducks his head, like he's hiding his own emotions. "I know the *nipwisipwis*," he says quietly. "And you will, too."

His words give me shivers, but someone starts to yell and I jerk my chin up. Riley is running back and forth on the bridge walkways that attach the various rooms of the tree house. "The place is locked! How are we supposed to get in?"

I pound up the stairs behind Eloni as he takes me and Riley to the front door. Butler Reginald retrieves the suitcases from under the giant palm in the front yard, and climbs the stairs, bumping the luggage against his knees.

The wood of the front door is etched with a picture of a gigantic lagoon with more than a dozen islands and the bumps of the coral reefs. "Looks like a regular door," I say, smoothing my fingers over the carvings. "Not the door of a tree house."

"This tree house *is* a regular house. With regular doors," Eloni adds. "Very sturdy, very safe and secure. This picture is the Lagoon of Chuuk. Professor Claire paid our best island carver."

Riley jiggles the doorknob. "I'm desperate for a shower and a bed, people!"

My older sister is not good when she's tired. Come to think of it, she's just barely tolerable when she's rested.

"Do you have a key?" I ask Eloni.

He shakes his head. "Professor Claire doesn't give me a key to her home."

His English is pretty excellent, actually, even with the Pacific Island lilt. I like the warmth and friendliness of it. The way his tone goes up at the end. Butler Reginald had said that the older people mostly spoke only Chuukese, but the children learned English at school.

"So how do we get in?" I ask.

Riley paces the bridge connecting another room of the tree house, and it looks like she's standing at a back door. "This door is locked, too!" she calls out. "Where's our butler dude?"

"I'm right here," Butler Reginald says behind me, perching the luggage on the top step. "I wonder if the house key was in her personal belongings after, the, uh, accident." His voice drops and I bite my lips trying not to think about that. "The police would have given her personal effects to your mother after the investigation."

"The key is back home?" Riley spits out, and I brace for another screaming fit. Then she gives us an evil grin. "Guess we'll just have to break in."

"You're not gonna break down Grammy Claire's tree house!" I yell. The image of Key Number Eight pops into my brain. Quietly, I add, "Um, I think I have the key."

Riley gives me her iciest stare. "If you don't unlock that door in the next three seconds, I'm gonna strangle you."

Eloni glances between us, his eyebrows shooting clear into the dark hair falling over his eyes. Butler Reginald heaves a small sigh. I think he's becoming resigned to Riley's temper.

"She's only joking," I tell Eloni, digging into my backpack until my hands close around the right key. The others are packed in the box in my main suitcase. "It's called sisterly love."

Ten seconds later, the key fits the lock and the door swings wide.

"First dibs on bedrooms," Riley calls out.

In a split second, my sister is gone, poking her head into each room, clomping her feet while I stand in the tiled entryway where little piles of sand have blown into the corners like welcome visitors.

Grammy Claire built a tree *house*. Emphasis on the house. Because it is. A home with rooms of bamboo and beautiful swirly wood inside the walls and along the doors. Wide windows show off the blues and greens of the lagoon below, trimmed by pristine white sand.

In the back of the house, the kitchen and bedrooms overlook a forest of giant palms. It's a jungle of massive shrubs, thickets of tall bamboo, and mangrove trees whose roots and branches spill along the forest trails.

The hall bath has running water and a real shower. And I adore the cozy dining room with its plush cushions on the chairs and a window seat stacked with Grammy Claire's books.

In the kitchen, a faint smell of citrus and chocolate hovers. A pineapple is rotting on the counter after so many weeks. The refrigerator stands mostly empty, except for half-used bottles of dressing and sauces.

Eloni and Butler Reginald divide the suitcases among the three bedrooms, and then our butler flings open the windows, letting in a warm, salty breeze from the ocean.

I wander the house, tiptoeing, testing the flooring, wondering if I'll fall through and hit a tree trunk — or the ground and crack my skull. Soon, I forget about walking in the tops of the trees, and admire the shade falling through the windows, making me feel warm and cozy.

Grammy Claire's possessions are everywhere. Her books. Her dishes. Her clothes in the closet. Mud-caked sandals still sit by the back door. Pictures of me and Riley on the shelves. Mamma and Grammy Claire when my mamma was a girl. Sitting in a pirogue on the Bayou Teche. An old framed photo of my grandfather in his uniform during the war.

Like she'd left to go on vacation.

Which she did.

And will never come back again.

But now I'm here. My throat is tightly wedged with emotion, and it hurts.

I find a glass in the cupboard, recognizing it as the same style as our Doucet crystal back home, and run the water, peering through the curtains at a red-and-yellow bird perched on a branch across from the window. The bird watches me but doesn't fly off.

I explore the front of the house again, passing through a narrow hall that leads to an outdoor walkway — which leads to another room of the house separate from the main house.

Hesitantly, I cross the bridge walkway and try the door. It's locked.

Inserting Key Number Eight again, I turn the doorknob and step inside. Overflowing bookcases greet my eyes. Walls covered in graphs and charts. A messy desk, unlit lamps, two filing cabinets side by side in the corner. Grammy Claire's Chuuk office.

And there are pictures. Dozens of photographs of *nipwisipwis* hanging on all four walls. *Nipwisipwis* in every variety and species and color. Brilliant, dazzling purples and oranges and yellows. And Giant Pinks. Small blues. Species of white and green with feathery wings.

I gaze at the Giant Pink photo and shivers slither along my arms like a snake. "Oh, Grammy Claire, what happened to you?" I whisper. "Why did you have to die? Who killed you?"

The door bangs open and Eloni stands there. "Miss Tara, I will show your bedroom now. Suitcases inside already."

"Thanks."

The boy stares at me and his eyes are dark and soulful.

I shiver again, trying to shake off the melancholy feeling. "What?" I finally ask. I have to admit, it's sort of nice when boys stare at me, but this is different, peculiar.

Eloni shakes his head, as if to clear his thoughts. "You look like Professor Claire when you watch the photos of *nipwisipwis*."

I'm startled, but then I realize that he's complimenting me. I'm glad I look like Grammy Claire, and I know I look like her when she was young. Must be the Pantene Princess hair. "Thank you. I — it's hard —" Abruptly, I stop. I'm not going to tell a perfect stranger how much I miss my grandmother, but I find myself wanting to confide in Eloni. He seems innocent, gentle. I'm drawn to him. I want to be friends, but I'm not sure if I'm supposed to. Grammy Claire should have given more details in her letters!

An explanation shoots into my mind. Maybe she wrote those letters before Eloni started working for her. Because there are no dates on them. A month ago? A year ago? Two years? "Hey, how long have you worked for my grandmother?"

Eloni turns his head. "Almost a year. When I become twelve. Professor Claire is very generous to my family. She let me help her with the *nipwisipwis*."

I point to the pictures of the butterflies. "A Giant Pink came through her bedroom window. It was absolutely beautiful. I've never seen a butterfly like it."

"Yes, the Giant Pink is very special butterfly." He walks along the rows of butterflies, pointing to various species. "The purple butterfly, they are — you hear — I mean that they are soothing. And the small blue . . . so fragile and delicate."

I noticed how he hesitates, choosing his words carefully. "There were dozens of the blue *nipwisipwis* in her labora-tory," I tell him. "And they were all dead," I add, trying to shock him.

Eloni holds still for a moment. "The blues don't live long. Very short life."

I spot a series of maps on the opposite wall. One map is the entire world cut into pieces, like a globe opened up and displayed. There are individual maps of all the continents. And a map of the South Pacific with endless blue water and clusters of islands spread across like dots on the ocean.

"Is this the island we're on right here?" I ask, pointing.

Eloni nods. "That is Weno, or Chuuk. The islands of Chuuk are many, but we are on the main island. The capital." He circles a big area of the Pacific Ocean with his finger. "All these islands are Micronesia. Hundreds of them."

"I can't believe I'm so far from home."

"This will be your home away from home," Eloni tells me with a smile, and I think he means it. "Or maybe you will come here to live all the time."

"But — but my mamma is back in Louisiana. And my daddy. Well, he's in California."

"Why?" Eloni asks me, and his voice is innocent, curious.

"Actually, I don't really know," I answer. I'm suddenly desperate to chew on my hair. But I can't in front of him so I pretend to straighten the maps.

Eloni's eyes flicker over my face, and I think he senses my anger at Daddy and my hopelessness about Mamma. I need to hide my feelings better. Eloni and I stand there, not speaking.

As if testing each other. Waiting for the other to bring up the subject I *know* we're both thinking about.

Finally, I can't stand it. "*Where* are the *nipwisipwis*? And where's the laboratory — Grammy Claire must have one here!" Eloni watches my waving arms as my voice rises louder and louder. I feel a little silly getting all crazy so I immediately drop my arms as well as my voice, trying to be patient.

Eloni opens the two side windows and I can hear the pounding of the surf below. Grammy Claire's office is perched in a tree, the last one of the thicket, and when I glance down there is nothing below us, only sand and surf and waves. I feel like I'm floating over the earth, anchored to nothing.

My grandmother's assistant leans out the window closest to the sea — and his head is so far out, I start wondering if he's going to jump through the opening and started climbing the palm trees! "Um, Eloni?"

He smiles mischievously. "I will show you a laboratory. Will that be good?"

I prop a hand on my hip, wondering how many laboratories there are around here.

Eloni reaches out and grabs my hand. "Then come with me!"

We go flying out the door to the walkway, but Eloni doesn't head back to the main house. Instead, there's a little gate he opens, and a small flight of stairs going downward. My feet stumble on the narrow steps.

Eloni holds my hand super tight so I don't fall and as soon as my sandals hit the next walkway I'm down a third set of stairs and running straight for the forest. It's cool and dark and smells sweet with the scent of ripe fruit and dead leaves. I run with him through clusters of palm trees, and then there's another flight of stairs going up again.

Straight in front of us, another little house — or room — is set off by itself in the shadowy cluster of palmettos. "Do you have the key?"

"Yeah, I think so," I say, fumbling in the pocket of my sundress with my free hand. Because he's still clutching my left hand in his own.

I *used to be* jet-lagged, and I *had* been thinking about a bath and a nap, but not anymore. I'm nervous holding the hand of a boy I barely met, but his palm is cool and firm and steady — and — and I like it. But maybe this is just island friendliness, and actually means nothing.

"If your key opens the door, it is meant for you." He gives me a big grin. "Which will mean you are meant to be here, Miss Tara."

My stomach flies into my throat and my heart pounds louder than the crashing waves on the distant shore. The key twists in the lock and there's a clicking noise. "It fits!" I breathe out.

Eloni turns on a lamp against the shadows. The little building is cooler under the trees, more private, darker — and right away I see that it's Grammy Claire's island laboratory. Tables, cupboards, vials, and microscopes and a mountain of paperwork on a far table.

"Look at the miniature trees and shrubbery!" Green is sprouting up through cracks in the floorboards, creating bushes and shrubs and vines right inside the room.

"Professor Claire wanted a special place to study them."

"Nipwisipwis," I whisper, feeling dizzy. "That's your language, right?"

He smiles, and a warm glow spreads through me. "It's the old language of my tribe and we all still speak it. My grandfather was teaching Professor Claire. She wanted to talk to the *nipwisipwis.*"

I stare at him and my throat swells up with emotion. "They're friends, then? Your grandfather and my Grammy Claire? I mean *were* friends."

"Still friends," Eloni assures me. "Dying doesn't stop friendship and love and family."

Tears sting at my eyes. His words are true. Death doesn't stop love. Memories keep on going, forever, and so does love. "I like that," I finally choke out. Because I'm a girl who *never* cries in front of boys.

"I will show you a wonderful thing, Miss Tara. Professor Claire — her experiment is good."

A strange thrumming begins in my chest. Eloni opens

another door, which leads to a second room — a room very much like the butterfly garden in Grammy Claire's house back home. There are a couple of tables, but the tables have been swallowed up by masses of vines growing straight to the roof. Tendrils of cool green leaves brush against my face as I follow him through the maze of vines.

When we reach the end of the room, Eloni releases my hand and points up into the emerald foliage. "Do you see it, Miss Tara?"

I shake my head. I don't know what I'm looking at. But suddenly I do see it. A light green shape, about the size of a fat finger, smooth and perfectly formed, clings to the slender trunk of a small vine.

"Did that used to be a caterpillar?"

"Professor Claire was trying to grow more *nipwisipwis* in the laboratory."

"Are *nipwisipwis* different from any other butterfly?"

Eloni laughs. "*Nipwisipwis* is the word for all of my island's special butterflies. They come from caterpillars, just like other butterflies. Then it is a larvae. After the larvae eats and eats, it makes a cocoon, or pupa."

"I'm trying to remember my science lessons."

Eloni doesn't make me feel stupid like some boys do, laughing when the girls don't know all the answers right away. "While the pupa sits on the leaf inside the cocoon, the caterpillar is changing. They call that metamorphosis." He says the word slowly, and I can tell Grammy Claire taught it to him.

"I remember now. It's called a chrysalis."

"That chrysalis up there has been changing. Not so green. More clear."

I raise my eyes to where he's pointing and let out a little gasp. "It *is* getting clear! And this is the same kind of chrysalis as that dark green one over there?"

"Soon two butterflies will fly here in the laboratory. Watch — the chrysalis is getting ready."

Neither of us moves as the chrysalis slowly, achingly, begins to crack apart.

Several minutes later violet wings are fluttering outside of the chrysalis. Then the head, legs, and antennae break free. All at once, the butterfly is sitting quietly on the edge of its chrysalis.

"That was fast," I whisper. "How long has it been changing and waiting to be born?"

"Two to three weeks. Some longer, some not so much."

"Did Grammy Claire know this was going to hatch right now?"

"Everything is on the charts. I will add today's birth for this *nipwisipwis*." Eloni glances up at a clock on the wall, then retrieves a thick file folder and a clipboard with an attached pen.

"But why would my grandmother leave if she knew she would miss this today?"

Eloni raises his eyes to mine. "Professor Claire made plans to come back with you. In time for the hatching."

I swallow hard, pressing my lips together so I don't cry again.

"And see?" Eloni adds softly. "You made it right on time."

When he squeezes my arm, I turn my head away. Grammy Claire had everything planned — everything! "It's not fair!" I finally burst out, pulling my arm away.

"Miss Tara, don't be afraid. I want to cry for Professor Claire, too." Eloni presses a fist against his chest. "But she is right now watching. From *naangenu*."

"What does that mean?"

Eloni grins at my attempt to pronounce the word. "It means 'heaven.' Where the gods live. And one day, we live there, too."

His words calm me as I watch the butterfly sitting on the branch. I'm afraid it will fly away and disappear, just like all the other butterflies. "What's the butterfly going to do next?"

"The wings are wet. Now they dry. Soon they will open and fly."

Palm leaves sway in the breeze outside the window. I hear birds calling in the distance, the buzz of insects close by. I stare at the butterfly until my eyes glaze over, and then suddenly the wings begin to flutter and unfold. With the movement of the wings, I hear a faint humming. Like music. Angel music.

"Is someone playing a flute or something below the laboratory?" I whisper.

Eloni shakes his head, not speaking as the violet butterfly spreads its wings wider and music dances along the warm, salty air. But the wings are not a violet color anymore! As they dry, the hue darkens, turning deeper purple every second. The purple is dazzling and rich, outlined in lemon yellow, just like Grammy Claire's pound cake. It's the very same species of butterfly that flew through the window of my room the afternoon of Grammy Claire's funeral!

I feel shaky as I realize something else, too. The day the first butterfly came, I'd heard music, faint and otherworldly. "Eloni! Do you hear that music?"

He smiles a wry smile. "I do, Miss Tara. It's beautiful, isn't it!"

"Is the butterfly creating that music?"

Eloni's smile grows wider, his teeth glinting in the shadows, but he doesn't answer my question.

I stride across the room toward the map on the wall. There is only one map here, unlike the numerous maps in the study back at the tree house. It's very detailed.

"Is this the island we're on right now?" Eloni nods as questions and answers are firing in my brain. "What is this over here?"

"It's called the Beautiful Empty."

"Why is it empty? Nobody lives there?"

"Very rocky, no farming, no fresh water. Lots of coves and caves."

"Caves?" A tingle runs down my neck.

"Underground caves. Many sunken ships from the big war in the lagoon. When my grandfather was a little boy. They are Japanese ships when Japan invades Chuuk. The Americans came and bombed and all the ships sink."

"I remember Grammy Claire telling me about ships rotting underwater in the lagoon," I say. "Have you dived down there?"

"You can see Japanese guns and machines still on the ships. Bottles and tea sets. Cups, books, coral growing." Eloni's eyes dart to the purple butterfly stretching out its wings. It's getting ready to fly.

I grab his arm and shake it. "The Beautiful Empty is where the butterflies live! The *nipwisipwis*! I'm right, aren't I?"

"Professor Claire said you would figure all things out."

My throat feels thick as I glance into his black eyes. "How do you say thank you?"

"Kinissow."

"Kinissow," I repeat, and Eloni nods in approval.

I'm struck silent as the purple butterfly flaps its dazzling wings and rises into the air, floating around the room. My ears are tinkling with the sound of a heavenly harp. I'm trembling all over as I stretch out my hand and the butterfly lands on my finger.

"This butterfly seems to know you, Miss Tara," Eloni says quietly.

We stand close together as the butterfly opens and closes its wings. The same species that kissed my heart the day of Grammy Claire's funeral. The purple butterfly that seemed to know what I was thinking and feeling. Like it had a *brain,* and a heart and soul of its own.

I stare into Eloni's eyes and dare him to tell me the truth. "This island has more secrets, doesn't it?"

Chapter Twenty-one

Caterpillars? Pupas? Cocoons or chrysalis?
Only God knows the mysteries and secrets of a true nipwisipwis.
~PROFESSOR CLAIRE THERIOT CHAISSON~

The sixth butterfly wakes me the next morning, touching its wings to the tip of my nose.

I shoot up in bed and try to remember where I am, then realize that I'm lying under the cool sheets of Grammy Claire's big bed. I'd decided to use this room because it made me feel closer to her.

The butterfly hovering overhead is velvet black with a striking dab of bright blue paint on its wings. I've never seen anything like it. Why do I feel so much better whenever the butterflies are nearby?

As the new butterfly dances around the room, I pull out the last two keys — and wonder where Grammy Claire's next letter is hidden.

I'm certain there are more secrets on this island. Secrets Grammy Claire has kept hidden — and Eloni refused to tell me yesterday.

Do the *nipwisipwis* contain special DNA that gives them a bigger brain? Do they have intelligence, the talent to create music, or the ability to change a person's mood? My mind is a jumble of confusion with a thousand questions.

And I think I'm hungry.

As I watch the ceiling fan twirl, I picture the purple butterfly breaking free of the chrysalis and then humming and whirling around my head yesterday. Like magic.

I can't help thinking about Eloni and his grandfather, too. There is something very peculiar about them that I can't figure out, either.

Grammy Claire's tree house bedroom is similar to her room in Louisiana, but instead of a window overlooking the Bayou Teche, the view is a private beach. Instead of polished wooden floors and crown molding, the ceiling is a crisscross of bamboo. An ivory-colored gauze tent encloses the bed, making me feel safe and cozy.

Her clothes are still hanging in the white wicker wardrobe, her shampoo toppled over in the shower, scientific magazines strewn on tables out on the balcony.

I'm in a tower room at the top of a tree-house castle. Gnarled limbs greet me through every window and leaves flutter against the glass. Finally, I roll out from under the sheets. The rugs are soft under my toes. Below the balcony, the sea is calm, soft, slow waves rushing into shore with a mesmerizing rhythm.

The butterfly floats about the room, dancing on each piece of furniture, fluttering into the bathroom and out again. I can't help laughing. "What are you doing?" The butterfly is like a curious toddler, wanting to touch everything in sight.

Bouncing along Grammy Claire's shelf, the butterfly alights on the edge and sits there, opening and closing its wings while it waits for me to catch up.

I'm not sure I want to look at the pictures. Photographs of my family. Mamma and Daddy on their wedding day. Riley and me as babies. Toddlers with toys and birthday cakes and school portraits with missing teeth.

There are also photos of us with Grammy Claire on vacations, boating on the Bayou Teche and fishing. Snapshots of alligators sleeping on the banks.

Kneeling down, I study the pictures of my grandmother over the years. Mamma always made us go to a professional studio and have a family portrait done whenever Grammy Claire visited.

The photos are arranged in order, starting back when I was about in kindergarten and ending last summer when we took our last family portrait in Lafayette. I peer closer at the photograph and let out a gasp.

Maybe it's the makeup.

Maybe it's the lighting.

Maybe it's not either of those things.

Grabbing the last several family portraits, I study them back to back. I'm positive Grammy Claire looks a little bit younger in each photograph. There are fewer wrinkles, less folds along her neck, and not as many smile lines around her eyes and mouth.

A peculiar prickling runs up and down my neck as I think about Eloni's very young-looking grandfather. Grammy Claire shed five years off her age — maybe ten years — in those pictures. Maybe island paradises make everyone happier and more carefree.

Maybe not.

And maybe now I know why Grammy Claire taped the photo album underneath her bed with one of the letters. It wasn't just for past memories, it was a clue, and I didn't even know it.

I scramble to get dressed. "I have to find the next letter!"

After yanking on my yellow swimsuit, I throw a skirt and white blouse over it. While combing my hair, I think about how Key Number Eight fit the front door of the tree house as well as Grammy Claire's laboratory. But neither the tree house nor the laboratory had any letters with my name on them. "How do I figure out what's next?" The velvety butterfly cocks its head at me, as if it's actually listening, then flutters through the window. I run across the room and crane my neck to see where it goes.

The *nipwisipwis* dives down through the trees toward the laboratory. Maybe that's where it came from. But the laboratory, even though there are a few chrysalises ready to burst open soon, is cleaned out. I'd searched it last night. The desk and drawers were empty of anything personal, the filing cabinets bare.

Grammy Claire had taken her files and put them somewhere else. Even Eloni had seemed surprised to discover that the room was virtually empty. Why would my grandmother do that before she flew to Louisiana? She knew she was coming back, right?

Before I head to the main house for breakfast, I hurriedly finish unpacking. The sight of Grammy Claire's personal clothes and soap jabs me in the heart. Like she's just gone out for the day. Or away on a holiday. Not dead.

I grab the last two keys from the secret lining in my suitcase, stuff the box inside the luggage and the suitcase deep into the closet. I open Grammy Claire's most recent letter from the makeup case and scan the last part — and that's when I finally realize where I will find the lock for Key Number Nine.

"Riley!" I call as I head out the door. Key Number Eight also locks Grammy Claire's bedroom door. Locking it makes me feel a teensy bit better, although if someone really wanted to, they could probably break down the door.

When I get to the main house, I stop short. There's a strange sound of moaning, followed by a little sob. Faint and far away. The windows are wide open, letting in cool morning air. Letting the moaning sound creep inside, too.

I run in circles through the main room, the kitchen, the dining room, and the foyer, but I'm alone. "Who is that?" I shout. "Where are you?"

"It's me — out here!" Riley's voice comes from beyond the front door. Flinging it open, I see her sprawled at the bottom of the tree-house stairs, the ones we'd climbed just last night. And she's lying in a really weird position, her legs splayed out in an unnatural position.

The sight of her makes me cringe, and I start running down the steps toward her. "Are you okay?"

"Stop!" Riley screams. "Don't run! You'll fall like I did. The stairs are slick and wet."

"Did it rain last night?"

She rolls her eyes. Even when she's hurt my sister can be sarcastic. "Look around, Tara. Do you see any wet ground? Any puddles?"

"No, but you don't have to be like that."

"Sorry, but my foot really hurts. I think I sprained my ankle."

I glance back at the steep flight of stairs and then at my sister lying backward on the ground at the bottom. "You're lucky you don't have two broken legs and a concussion."

Riley looks me in the eye. "I'm lucky I'm not dead."

"Are you serious?"

"Look at the stairs again. There's water pooling on each step and it's mixed with some sort of oil, making it really slick. I slipped and landed all the way down here. My back is killing me. I think it's all scraped up, too."

I shiver in the warm sun. "Guess those combat boots saved your neck."

"These stairs were just fine last night."

I lower my voice as I slowly walk down, gripping the railing. "What are you saying?"

"I'm *saying* that I think somebody tried to hurt me. Or you." By now we're whispering. It suddenly feels like the coconut trees have ears. Anybody could be hiding inside the thick mangroves, listening. "I got a phone call this morning saying there would be a car to take us into town. I came running out and — down I went, skidding over all the steps." Riley wipes a hand across her eyes, and I'm pretty sure she was crying before I got here.

"Who was it?"

Riley shrugs. "Thought Butler Dude arranged for a taxi. He

knew I wanted to get cell service. There's not a blasted thing to do out here."

Oh, how wrong she is! Grammy Claire's keys jangle in my pocket as I help her into a sitting position. "Grammy Claire actually wants us to go to the bank."

My sister grimaces as she peels her sock down. The skin is swelling fast around her ankle and turning green. "You're dreaming, Tara."

"It's in the last letter — with the two —" I stop. I almost said *two thousand dollars.* "I figured it out this morning after I woke up."

Riley's eyes search the trees. "Something creepy is going on. Maybe we should catch the next plane home."

"No! We have to stay. Grammy Claire's will . . . it might have enough inheritance that we can save our house. And help Mamma. Make her go to a doctor. Someone killed the Giant Pink, and I have to find out why. I have to find the killer. Grammy Claire's killer."

Riley swallows hard, shaking her head as she stares at me. "You're talkin' crazy. This whole thing is crazy."

"Where's Butler Reginald?"

"I saw him hike down that road earlier. Said there was a local woman who sells breadfruit and mango for breakfast. And then he said he'd go back to town and buy groceries. Should have done that yesterday before we came out here. The cupboards are pretty bare."

The sound of an engine comes through the trees. "Come on, let's get back into the house. We should put your foot in some ice water."

Before I can help Riley up, a car arrives. A small, dark blue compact with tinted windows, crumpled doors, a missing fender, and no tire rims. A faded *CHUUK ISLAND TAXI* sign has been screwed into the sides of the rear doors.

My stomach tightens. I suddenly feel very small and vulnerable sitting out here. I want to lock us inside, shut the windows, and pretend nobody is home.

Eloni jumps out of the passenger side. Then a man opens the driver door and climbs out. No, he's not a man. Well, he is, but he's younger. Sort of a much older teenager. He's tall and big and there's a solemn expression on his face like he's not very happy. His hair is short except for the topknot braid running all the way down his back.

"Miss Tara!" Eloni cries out, running over. "You're awake!"

"What do you mean, I'm awake?"

"We came a little while ago. All doors were closed and quiet. We went down to the beach to check out the tides for fishing."

They had been here earlier. I don't like what that could mean.

Riley bursts out, "Why don't you check out the staircase? You guys do that? Spraying water and oil on the steps?"

"Shh!" I hiss at Riley. She is so in-your-face sometimes!

222

Eloni looks shocked. "I never — why would I hurt the home of Professor Claire?"

"I don't know. You tell us."

"Riley!" I hiss again.

She rolls her eyes in the biggest eye roll of the year. "I coulda been killed, gone over the edge. Landed facedown with a split skull!"

She's going over the edge, but she's right. She could have been badly injured, maybe even killed. I have a very sick feeling in my stomach. And I don't think it's from missing breakfast.

Eloni's face is pale. "Let us help you into the house. Find medicine bag or first aid. Oh, and, Miss Tara, Miss Riley. Please to meet my brother, Tafko."

"*Tafko* is your brother?" Tafko is another name on the list in Grammy Claire's letter. I start feeling dizzy and a little bit scared. Suspects are everywhere! Maybe Riley and I should hire a bodyguard!

Eloni looks up at Tafko with a look of pride. "He begins college soon."

"Knock it off, Eloni," Tafko says in a quiet voice. He's the opposite of his younger brother. Reserved. Quiet. Or maybe he's sullen and mean. I narrow my eyes, wondering about him. About the coincidence of their arrival, and Riley's accident. "Don't go bragging. I may end up fishing again for the winter."

Eloni's face brightens again. "Tafko got our grandfather's old taxi for today. We go down the road to —" He cups his hands around his mouth to whisper. "To show you the *nipwisipwis*."

"Grammy Claire's *nipwisipwis*?"

Eloni nods, obviously excited.

Still sitting on the bottom step, Riley mutters, "I wouldn't go anywhere with these guys, even if you paid me."

"You wouldn't?" Disappointment sears me. I want to see the butterflies. I *have* to see the butterflies.

"Can you take me into town to the bank, too?"

Tafko shrugs and then nods.

"I need to wrap my ankle and put it up so the swelling doesn't get worse," Riley says.

I look from my sister to Eloni and then to Tafko and back again. I know we need to stay safe, but why would Grammy Claire hire Eloni if she didn't trust him? Why would she live here if she didn't trust the citizens of Chuuk? If she thought her life was in danger?

Before anybody can say anything else, Butler Reginald drives up in a rented car, and jumps out when he sees us all gathered around Riley sitting on the ground. "Riley! Tara! What happened?"

"Hey, Butler Dude," Riley drawls. "Got some stairs for you to clean up."

Butler Reginald frowns as he examines the steps and then Riley's ankle. "A day or two off your feet and you'll be up and around again, as long as you're careful. Now if you'd been wearing sandals or flip-flops, you would probably have a broken leg, or worse."

"Just put me on the beach with my bikini and suntan lotion and I'll be okay. I'm not gonna waste my vacation sitting in a house with no food, no television, and no computer."

The next half hour is spent doctoring Riley. When Butler Reginald learns of my plans to take a drive around the island, he assures Riley that I'll be okay. "I've known these boys since they were very young. Tara will be safe, you have my word. If not, they will answer to me. Besides, nobody can get off the island. At least not very far."

"See?" I tell her, stepping out of reach as Riley tries to smack me.

"Just get me some junk food," she calls from the couch.

Butler Reginald says, "You're sure you'll be fine while I go into town for groceries, then, Miss Riley?"

"Hey, I'm almost eighteen. I'll be a good girl so I can go out tomorrow."

As soon as I climb into the blue taxi, Eloni says, "First, we should go to town. The bank closes at three. If we go to the butterfly coves, you might miss the bank."

I agree, but I can't decide which is more urgent, seeing the *nipwisipwis* or unlocking Grammy Claire's security box. I'm also hoping there might be some cash. I have nothing for food, taxis, or tours — or an escape, if I need one. Rage bubbles up every time I think about Madame See with my money.

Eloni is a regular tour guide, pointing out where the wild birds live, which beaches are the best for shell collecting or swimming, and the locations of some of the sunken ships. "See? Tourist boat on the water there. Diving down to the ships."

I picture all those sunken ships lying just offshore. Lying for decades in their watery grave. Are skeletons still buried in the drifting sands?

By the time we arrive at the Bank of the Federated States of Micronesia, my hair is wind-blown and my heart is pounding with anticipation.

Tafko stays in the car and pulls out a well-used banjo. He plucks at the strings, pulling a melody out of it that makes me think of waves and sun and sadness. He kept giving me sideways glances as we drove into town, and I tried to ignore him. As he strums his banjo, he pulls a few brown nuts out of a plastic bag and starts chewing on them. His mouth begins to turn red from the juice of the strange nut. It looks like blood, and I turn away.

"Those are betel nuts," Eloni tells me, and all I can do is smile in silence.

"Wait here," I tell him as we enter the bank and see a row of plastic-covered chairs in the waiting room. After we sit down, I get up again to head for the bank manager offices, and then turn back, perching on the edge of my seat. "Can I ask you a question, Eloni?"

"Yes, Miss Tara."

"Well, first, you can cut the Miss Tara business. I just want to be Tara, okay? Remember?"

Eloni grins. "Okay!"

"Um." I bite at my lips, and then decide to just blurt it out. "How old is your grandfather? The taxi driver from yesterday? Alvios?"

"Oh, he's old." Eloni ducks his head just a little.

"Do you know his age?"

Eloni ponders the bank's high ceiling. "Not sure, Miss Tara. I mean, just Tara."

I stare him straight in the eye. "I think you know and don't want to tell me."

His eyebrows fly straight up his forehead. "Why would I do that?"

"Because" — I lower my voice — "I think it's part of the secret. The secret of Chuuk."

He returns my gaze, and I can tell he's trying not to blink.

I lean closer, not letting him off the hook. My long hair falls over my shoulder, brushing our arms. I want to grab a chunk and start chewing bad. But I summon my best self-control and dig my fingers into the seat cushion.

Finally, Eloni lets out a sigh. "You win. My grandfather is young. Only fifty."

"Liar."

His eyebrows jump again. "Sixty?"

I fold my arms across my chest and shake my head.

"Well, maybe seventy. . . ."

"You said he was a little boy during World War II. Which means he's gotta be more than seventy. Yet he looks like he could be your father."

"Here on Chuuk, we grow old slowly."

Eloni says this so solemnly, I burst into laughter. "Eloni, you're a bad liar."

When I glance up, the bank manager is bearing down on us. When he learns that I'm Claire Chaisson's granddaughter, he immediately escorts me into his office. The one with gold lettering on the door spelling out his name, Mr. Masako. The bank manager is also on my grandmother's list of suspects — and has a brother who was in jail! My palms start to sweat.

Mr. Masako's thick hair is pure white and his eyes are chocolate brown. He's wearing a rumpled suit and looks like he'd rather be sitting in a hammock with a lemonade. After expressing his condolences on the news of Grammy Claire's accident, he says, "I can see the resemblance. I would wager Professor

Claire looked just like you when she was younger. Now how can I help you?"

"I need to open her security box," I tell him, my voice jiggling nervously. "I have the key," I add, holding it up. Key Number Nine is not very big. *Bank of FSM* is stamped across the side. Words I hadn't noticed until recently.

After he has me fill out some forms and show my passport, Mr. Masako finally leads me into a back room where there is a private booth for patrons to open their security boxes. He brings me an oblong gray box and shuts the door — and I wish that Riley were here because I can hardly breathe.

The box of keys has led me to this moment. Grammy Claire's will is going to save me and Riley, our home, and Mamma. I can't wait to read her next letter, too. It's been days since a new letter.

My hands are shaking when I insert Key Number Nine and the lock makes a tiny clicking sound.

Chapter Twenty-two

Not quite birds, as they were not quite flowers, mysterious and
fascinating as are all indeterminate creatures.

~ELIZABETH GOUDGE~

The metal lid squeaks, and I let out the breath I'd been holding when I see a thick manila packet tied with string. I
unwind the string, open the flap, and there's a large official-
looking envelope with the name of a Chuuk Island attorney's
office. A second, smaller envelope is inside with *Tara Doucet*
written on the front.

I open the stamped and official envelope first.

The Last Will and Testament of Claire Theriot Chaisson. It's dated
from last year.

I don't understand all the legal words, but I scan the lines and get most of it.

Grammy Claire gives everything she has to my mamma, Riley, and me. I'm not sure what everything is exactly, but a huge wave of relief fills up my chest. I picture good doctors for Mamma. Fixing our house. Dance lessons and college — and, well, everything again. Everything the Doucet Family Trust Fund has swallowed up over the last hundred and fifty years.

I wonder about the tree house, and I think about bringing Mamma here. Maybe she just needs to get away from our stuffy old house and lie on the beach. Get some sunshine, drink guava juice, and read a stack of books.

I'm so excited about the next letter from Grammy Claire that I rip the envelope a little.

My darling Tara,

Etiwa! Welcome to the islands of Chuuk. My home away from home — in a tree house, to boot! How do you like it? And isn't the island stunningly beautiful? A taste of heaven, for sure. Or naangenu, as the people say.

I hope Eloni showed you the laboratory and the current metamorphosing chrysalis. Quite astonishing, isn't it? Humbling to see God's creatures in their dramatic finery. Almost a

*spiritual experience. You will notice that there are
no Giant Pinks in the laboratory or in my home.
There is a reason for this, which will be revealed
later.*

My eyes widen, thinking about the smashed Giant Pink. Was it dangerous? Poisonous? Was someone trying to save my life and Riley's by getting rid of it?

Why doesn't Grammy Claire just *say*? My mind is constantly churning with possibilities. I'm tired and my eyes burn. I know my grandmother was afraid, and she should have been if someone killed her. Even with all the secrecy, she wasn't careful enough. But there's no time for a good cry. I have to figure out what she wants me to do — and how to save the *nipwisipwis*.

*You should still have one more key, and it
unlocks the most dangerous location of all.
I cannot even give you any clues because I'm
afraid of who is watching you. I'm afraid of what
they might already know, or that they might steal
this letter from you, so I can't take that chance.
You will have to rely on your wits, your brains, your
courage, and most of all, your good heart to find
the final lock. You must do your best to save the
nipwisipwis from those who will inflict experiments*

and certain death on them. My beautiful
creatures are facing extinction. And if my
research is stolen and there is free access to the
<u>nipwisipwis</u>, no longer will the island's butterflies
fly free and help the native people as they have
for centuries. They will be gone forever. They
cannot be manufactured in laboratories and
sold to the highest bidder — that will eventually
kill them, too. They need the freedom of the island
to truly live and grow and be what they were
meant to be.

I read the words over and over again, looking for clues, and there is nothing. Nothing! My heart thumps hard and painful. My palms are sweaty even though it's air-conditioned in the bank.

Don't forget to enjoy the beauty of the island.
I hope you brought lots of swimsuits and
sunscreen!
And most of all, remember, my lovely
Tara, I will be with you in the darkest hour.
Always. I have not left you alone. Trust Riley. Show
her this letter. Trust your mamma to do the right
thing. I know she loves both you girls very much.

*So . . . until we meet on the other side, know
that you have all my love,
    Your Grammy Claire*

"Oh, Grammy Claire!" Her letters make me feel like I'm gonna break into pieces all over again. "I want you to watch me *here* — not *there* — wherever there is!"

"Miss Tara, may I help you?" It's Mr. Masako, the bank manager. He probably heard me crying. "Are you all right in there? Can I call someone for you?"

I had wondered if there was a telephone at the tree house, and of course, there is. Grammy Claire and I used to call each other, but Mamma always had the number written down at home. I feel *so* stupid! I'm completely unprepared. Hurriedly, I fold the letter, tuck it back into its white envelope, and clutch the thick packet to my chest.

After I draw back the curtains, I show the bank manager the Last Will and Testament and try not to let my voice waver. "Can you tell me what all of it means? What property or houses my grandmother owned? How much money is in her bank accounts? And do you think I can get some so Riley and I can get around the island for the next week?"

I listen to my own desperate questions and cringe, knowing he won't really give me access to Grammy Claire's bank accounts — even if I am her heir. I'm sure there are piles of paperwork and attorney stuff to go through. And it's all gotta be done by Mamma, not some twelve-year-old girl.

But I hate being dependent on Butler Reginald. Besides, he's no longer technically employed by Grammy Claire and earning paychecks. I should have asked Mamma for some cash before I left, but I was in such a rush, I didn't even think about it, although Mamma's own bank account is probably empty, too.

Mr. Masako studies the will for several minutes, and then takes off his reading spectacles. "Please come with me, Miss Tara."

"Is everything okay?"

"Is there an adult you can call? Your mother?"

I shake my head. "My mamma is back home. Riley's here, but she's at Grammy Claire's house with a sprained ankle."

He frowns. "I see. Please come into my office."

As I pass Eloni, he says, "You okay, Tara?"

I nod, fiddling with my hair, trying not to stick a whole lump in my mouth. Trying not to straighten the crooked pictures and toppled magazines in the waiting room. "Be right back."

I sit down in a green chair and Mr. Masako brings me a cup of water from one of those water dispenser machines. Tension rises in my throat. Bad news is coming.

"Miss Tara, I need to tell you that your grandmother actually drafted a new will. About a month before her trip to visit you."

"Why would she do that?"

"I don't know, and I must admit that I was dismayed. Claire Chaisson always arranged her banking and legal business with our lawyers. And yet this time she went to a different firm."

"Is that legal?"

Mr. Masako gives me a small smile. "Of course. A person can do whatever they like with their personal affairs. We were surprised, but these things happen."

My ears are buzzing as I wonder if she changed banks because *he* truly is a suspect. "Do you know what's in the new will?"

"I'm afraid I don't have a clue. Or why she would want to change it, since the will you have right here is obviously the correct path — that her next of kin inherit everything."

A terrible pain settles in my stomach.

"Of course, that doesn't mean your grandmother took you and your mother and sister out of the will. It could be that she merely added a few details, or wanted to make sure that anything new that had come up over the last year was included."

I nod, trying to breathe. That had to explain it. Because of the *nipwisipwis*. There was a new will because of the secrets. The keys. My brain hurts just thinking about it.

"So who is the lawyer with the new will?" I ask. "Where can I get a copy?"

"It was drawn up at Kanador Attorneys-at-Law, which is only a few blocks from here. They'll have a copy of it, but will probably request that you make an appointment. There *is* someone else you could ask. Which would be infinitely easier and faster."

I sit up in my chair. "Who?"

"Mr. Reginald Godwin."

That's when I feel very stupid. Grammy Claire had told me he was her lawyer. He probably had worked for the Kanador law firm. He'd have the latest, *real* will! "What about her bank accounts?" I ask. "Is there any way to get twenty bucks or something?" If something happened — like Riley falling over one of the walkways — we couldn't even hire a taxi to get us to the hospital or the airport if we needed to escape! I make a mental note to ask Riley if she's got cash on her.

Mr. Masako looks down at the file of papers again. "I'm afraid that your grandmother cleaned out her accounts right before she left for the States."

"But why didn't she tell me in the last letter —" I stop, horrified that I mentioned the letters to someone besides Riley. I'm also in shock. Someone is lying to me. But who — and why? "So, um, what did Grammy Claire do with all her money?"

Mr. Masako gives me a sad smile. "I'm afraid I have no idea. Your grandmother didn't confide in me. Our bank patrons usually don't divulge their private business."

A minute later, I stalk out of the bank. "I don't understand any of this!" I burst out.

Reaching out a hand, Eloni stops me from running straight into the street. When he touches me, that peculiar tingle surges again in the pit of my stomach. "Professor Claire was in an unexpected car accident," he says gently. "No time for warning you."

I let out a shaky breath. "She set up everything — and then it all ends up being for nothing." I'm suddenly homesick and afraid and I want my mamma to hold me and make everything better.

Tafko zooms up in the blue, crumpled taxi and leans over to roll the window down. He doesn't even look at us as we climb in.

"What's wrong with him?" I whisper to Eloni in the backseat.

Eloni whispers back, "He doesn't like to come to the bank."

"Why not?"

"He used to work here, but Mr. Masako fired him."

I'm startled. "Why?"

"He never told me. Mr. Masako is a new manager. The old one moved to Pohnpei."

Everyone I meet seems to have some sort of secret. Perhaps that's why Grammy Claire told me to trust no one. I want to trust Eloni. I really do, but maybe I'm not being smart. Or I'm being taken in by his open charm and attention. And the nice feeling when he takes my hand.

Does Tafko's firing from the bank have anything to do with Grammy Claire's will? And what *were* he and Eloni doing right before Riley fell down the stairs?

My gut tightens as we head out of town on a completely different road. "Where are we going?"

Tafko doesn't answer. He's drumming his hands on the steering wheel and listening to music, earplugs in his ears, just like Riley.

Eloni rolls down his window as we bump along and swerve to avoid potholes. "Remember? We're going to the *nipwisipwis*."

Yes. And I want to see them so badly. "But I thought they were near Grammy Claire's house."

"This is a shortcut. We follow the beach roads."

I sit back and try not to worry about, well, about *everything*. I feel the wind on my face, but the roads are terrible, bumpy, jolting. My teeth bang together whenever we hit a hole.

Tafko whistles to his music, but otherwise stays silent.

Suddenly, the little car spins on the slippery sand as we leap off the road onto the beach. "Hang on!" yells Eloni.

We bounce over flat, hard sand, tire marks zooming away behind us. Waves crash along the shore and I can taste salt on my tongue. Shades of blue and turquoise and white shimmer as far as I can see. It's perfect.

Behind us, the island rises up like a volcano. Mountains, mounds of jungle and dark green forests, so dense anybody could be hiding just inside and I'd never know they were there.

The open beach becomes smaller and narrower as the shoreline dips and turns. Sunshine trips across the water, sending up bright sparkles of light, and towering palms heavy with coconuts hug the sand.

I'm breathless with the beauty.

Tafko slows as he maneuvers the car around a final curve. I feel a tug in my throat. We're inside our very own little lagoon. It's small and private and there's not a soul in sight.

My stomach jumps with nerves as I glance at Tafko. *Not a soul in sight* means that if I were to disappear Riley would never know where to find me. Tafko is just quiet, I tell myself. He's reserved, not Grammy Claire's murderer. Madame See stole my money and is lurking somewhere on this island right now. I need to find out which hotel she's staying at. She's the only real clue I have. Somebody else could have sneaked into our house and killed the Giant Pink.

Which could mean Tafko. But he was here on the island.

My thoughts are making me crazy!

"We get out here," Eloni says, reaching over to press the button on my seatbelt. "Too difficult to drive now."

The sand sinks under my sandals. A boat is bobbing out on the whitecaps. Maybe I'm not so alone, even though this beach feels completely isolated. "Who's out there?"

Eloni shades his eyes. "Another tour boat."

I suppose I could create an SOS if I needed to. If I had matches. My white top might work if I ripped it into pieces. Hmm. White blouse against white sand. Maybe not.

Tafko stays with the car, strumming on his banjo as he sits on the sand. He gets up to grab a pad of paper from a backpack in the trunk and starts scribbling.

"He writes music, too," Eloni says proudly. "For his girlfriend."

"He's romantic?" Maybe a guy with a girlfriend isn't so bad. Tafko talks so little, I wonder what they ever discuss.

"Hey, Tafko," Eloni calls. "We'll walk back to Professor Claire's house. Not that far from here."

Tafko lifts a hand in salute, then scoops up his banjo and paper and jumps back into the taxi. The sound of the engine fades quickly across the sand and within moments all I can hear is the soft, rippling waves whispering as they break the shoreline.

I follow Eloni over a patch of black lava rock, stepping in and out of shallow tide pools, and then up over more rocks. The giant palms and mangroves bend over us like giants.

As we walk, Eloni says, "Tafko reminded me to tell you about our party for you."

"A party for me?" I'm surprised and don't know what to say. I didn't think Tafko liked me. He seemed to be in a bad mood and would rather be somewhere else.

"We are having a feast for you and your sister. And Mr. Godwin. Tafko and my cousins are hunting tomorrow. They will catch a wild pig. My mother and aunts are going to cook much food."

I bite my lips, thinking about Grammy Claire living here, being here on this very beach, talking Chuukese with Eloni's grandfather. Teaching Eloni English. Working together. Eating dinner with them.

"Will you come?" Eloni asks. "Professor Claire was a part of my family. I was only eight when she came to live here."

I realize that I never responded. I can't help smiling at him. "Yes, I'll come. Never ate wild pig before."

"It's the best meat on the island. Well, sea turtle is my favorite."

I let out a laugh as we climb above the boulders and reach another flat, open space. The sand is still warm from the sun as I kneel and look down over the beach. The sounds of the waves seem as if the ocean is murmuring a secret.

Late afternoon comes on, and the sun begins to sink just a little.

"When the sun is at the horizon they will come."

Terror grips me. "Who comes!?"

Eloni laughs and bumps his shoulder into mine. "The *nipwisipwis*."

"Oh. You mean right here?"

He nods and gestures at the dark forest behind us. "They live in trees. And in the caves."

"What caves?"

"The caves underneath us."

I stare at him, surprised. "There are caves underneath us? Will the sand fall in?"

"Made of lava rock. Thousands of years old." Eloni gives a laugh. "We have caves and sand and palm trees and boats. It's an island. Like all the islands out there in the lagoon."

A lone seagull circles overhead in the blue silence. "I think you're teasing me."

Eloni wiggles his eyebrows and just smiles.

I finally let out my breath and some of the tension inside eases. "I'm hot," I admit. "Can we go swimming?"

Eloni nods as he squints at the sun. "We have an hour until we see the show."

"What do you mean by a show?"

"Soon you will see," he says mysteriously. In an instant, he's scrambling back over the rocks, jumping through the tide pools, and running straight for the beach. I watch him pull off his shorts and T-shirt and throw them to the sand.

Copying him, I throw my skirt and blouse to the sand, too. It's strange not to have blankets and water bottles and a picnic basket and books for a beach excursion. Strange not to see another single soul anywhere. Very strange to run into the blue, sparkling surf next to a boy I met only yesterday.

We splash each other and head farther into the sea until we're up to our waists and the waves are coming faster. As we jump the waves, we start talking about our families and school and movies. The sand is pebbly and rough under my feet, but the water is deliciously warm, like a bath.

"Just need a bottle of bubbles," I say, turning around to float on my back and stare at the clouds. I scoop at the water, trying to stay on top. Eloni swims effortlessly.

"You're a good swimmer," I tell him.

"The village elders throw babies in when they're born. We learn to swim right away."

"Are you serious? What keeps a baby from drowning?"

He grins at me, his dark eyes shining, and I know I've been had. "You are easy to fool, Miss Tara Doucet."

My cheeks burn and I splash water at him. Eloni ducks under and comes back up again, shaking his head and flinging water like a dog.

I'm not usually the one teased. I'm the one everybody looks to for answers. I'm the one who tells everyone else how to do things and when to do them. I'm the Doucet Princess. But out here, I'm not anybody. I'm a stranger, just some no-name tourist. But really, deep in my heart, I just want to be Tara. I want people to like me. I want Eloni for my friend. I want my sister to like me. And my mamma to love me.

Tears fill my eyes and I pretend it's the salt water. Or the sun.

"Hey," Eloni says. "Let's go dry off. They're coming."

He creates a final humongous splash, hitting the edge of his hand against the surface of the water, which sends a plume of spray into the air.

They're coming. The words fill me with an intense thrill.

I run out of the sea, water dripping, clumps of sand crawling down my wet legs. We flop straight down on the hot sand to dry off, and I'm not even shy about Eloni seeing me in my swimsuit, all covered in a layer of sand.

"You will be an island girl," he tells me. "The sand makes you sparkle."

I try not to turn red as he keeps looking at me. "Maybe Grammy Claire gave me the tree house in her new will and I can come here whenever I want to."

"You must be independently wealthy."

I shake my head, a jolt of reality stabbing my chest. "Nope. Not anymore. My great-great-great-grandmothers were, but not me. Although I — I —" I stumble and stutter, and I'm a girl who never stutters. "I always pretended I was, back in Bayou Bridge." I take a gulp. I've never admitted that to anybody before, not even my best friend, Alyson.

"Here it's no matter," Eloni says, digging his toes into the sand. "We all live the same. Fishing, boating, singing, dancing — and waiting for tourists. Here on Chuuk you can be one of us."

Emotion tugs at me and I'm not sure what to say. "Thank you," I finally whisper. "I mean, *kinissow.*"

Eloni claps his hands and I can tell he's happy I remembered how to say that in Chuukese.

The sun feels good on my face and I comb my fingers through my hair as it dries. I notice that Eloni still has that same stick in his shorts pocket when we arrived our first day. He carries it with him constantly, in fact. At times, I see him whittling on it with a small knife.

I get up my nerve to ask. "What is that stick you have? Did you make it?"

He pulls it out of his pocket, holding it flat across his palms. It's about six to eight inches long. A slender, dagger-shaped piece with carvings on each side. Eloni digs out a pocket knife and shows me how he carves the soft wood. "We carve our favorite things into it." He points out the details of a fish with beautiful fins arched over a wave. Along the other side is an array of stars and constellations and a sliver of moon that is stunning.

"Do all Chuuk boys make these?"

"Yes. Every boy carves his stick different. We know which stick belongs to which boy. This is my first one to make so it's smaller than the older boys like my brother, Tafko."

"Do the sticks have a certain name?"

Eloni's face turns a little red, and he keeps his eyes on his hands. "It's called a love stick."

A love stick. It sounds romantic.

"It's a tradition."

"Yours is beautiful," I tell him, and I mean it. The crafts-manship is gorgeous. "What do you do with it after you've finished carving?"

Eloni brushes his finger across a new notch in the fin of his flying fish. "When a boy in the village wants a girl to know that he likes her or wants to court her, he pushes the stick into the bamboo wall of the girl's hut at night when everyone is asleep."

"Does the girl recognize whose stick it is when she sees it?"

"If she's been watching. She feels the stick's design and if she does not like the boy, she pushes the stick back out of the wall. But if she wants the boy, she pulls it through the wall toward her and keeps it."

"That seems easy. Better than a phone call."

Eloni grins at me. "Our carved sticks are our cell phones."

I laugh and our eyes meet for a split second, then I look away, studying the waves, tasting salt on my lips, thinking of Grammy Claire right here on this very beach.

Not two seconds later, Eloni leaps up. "Miss Tara! They're here, they're here! The *nipwisipwis*!"

I jump to my feet and brush the sand off the back of my legs.

"There!" Eloni says as he points to the ledges of rock where the caves are hidden.

Seconds later, butterflies emerge from the tops of the trees. Hundreds of them, flapping crazily in the slanting sun. So many colors, so many wings! Lemon-yellow butterflies as bright as daisies! Soft, dusky orange ones. Pale blues; deep, dazzling purple; velvety black; chocolate brown.

I stand still as swarms of *nipwisipwis* fly straight toward us. I can't move. I can hardly breathe. Within moments, thousands of them are over our heads, floating, shimmering, flitting, flapping, darting, skimming, dancing. They're lighter than air, more beautiful than anything I've ever seen in my whole life.

"Look," I say, tugging Eloni's arm. "There are *green* butterflies!"

I can tell he's pleased that I'm so excited. "The green ones can hide in the forest," he tells me. "No one knows they're there!"

"These are the butterflies Grammy Claire has been studying all these years," I say softly, stunned at the secrets she's been keeping the last five years.

Eloni's face is skyward as I sneak a peek at him. He stands as still as I do, as though seeing them for the first time, too. And yet, I know he's been here dozens of times. Watching him, I can feel that he loves the butterflies as much as my Grammy Claire did.

Something tightens in my throat and I point, shaking. "Over there! Look — they're coming up from under the ground!"

Giant Pink *nipwisipwis* are swarming up from the underground caves, spilling into the sunlight, streaming toward the sky.

"Run!" Eloni shouts, and I race after him over the sand, bounding up the rocks until I can see into the shadowy overhang that hides the grottos and caves.

Standing there on the ledge as the Giant Pinks fly up from their hidden, underground world, tears begin running down my face. A peculiar joy throbs inside my heart.

"There are no words to describe this," I whisper, my eyes watering.

Eloni comes closer. "That's the home of the Giant Pinks. Hundreds of them."

"They're gorgeous, Eloni. I don't even know why I'm crying."

He nods, watching me. "Everyone who sees them the first time weeps with the beauty."

Then Eloni holds out his hand to me and I stare at it, excited and afraid all at the same time. Finally, I clasp my palm to his, and he grips my fingers tight as we run back toward the ocean, leaping over the rocks and hitting the sand with our bare feet at the same time.

We run like maniacs. Back and forth across the beach. Splashing our toes in the warm, foamy surf as the Giant Pink *nipwisipwis* join the rest of the butterflies in a flickering swarm above our heads.

A tornado of colors and butterfly wings spins wildly around us. When I close my eyes, I feel the brush of their velvet softness, the vibration of magic as they circle and enfold me in their world.

And I hear music, too. Beautiful angel music filling my ears and mind and heart.

The underground *nipwisipwis* grotto is the first of Grammy Claire's secret mysteries on the island of Chuuk. I know there's more to come, and I'm both thrilled and terrified.

Chapter Twenty-three

In nature, a repulsive caterpillar turns into a lovely butterfly.
But with humans it is the other way around:
a lovely butterfly turns into a repulsive caterpillar.

~ANTON CHEKHOV~

Two mornings later when I cross the bridge to the main house, Riley is sitting on a chair, her foot wrapped and resting across a second chair. "How's your ankle?" I ask, pouring juice.

Riley yawns. "I think I just twisted it real bad. The swelling is down and I can walk on it, if I'm careful."

As I sip my juice, I feel restless and worried. Key Number Ten is like a weight in my pocket. I carry it with me everywhere because I know it's the most important key of all. I sleep with it under my pillow, too, but I'm no closer to figuring out what it unlocks. What if I never do? What if I totally fail to save the butterflies? My gut hurts just thinking about it.

Butler Reginald brings me a bowl of delicious baked breadfruit. He's also sliced up a fruit salad of kiwis, papaya, strawberries, and mango, which drips on my plate.

I lean over, examining the scratches on my sister's face. There are a couple of dark purple bruises on her arms, too. "Does it hurt?"

"Butler Dude washed me in antiseptic and told me not to pick at the scabs."

Butler Reginald lays down napkins and forks. "Picking at the scratches will leave scars. Something a young lady does not relish on her face. At least in England they don't."

Riley rolls her eyes at him. No one is spared the eye roll, not even Butler Reginald. "I haven't done that since I was six years old. Give me some credit." She eyes our butler as he flicks the switch for the overhead fan. "You know, Butler Dude, you're more like a nanny than a butler. A big ole softie."

He gives a mocking bow, teasing her back. "I'm glad to know where my talents lie, Miss Riley, but this morning I will be in full attorney mode. We will do the reading of your grandmother's will. No reason to put it off, and I'm sure you girls are anxious."

My stomach jumps. I knew this was coming, and I tried not to think about it when I went to bed the previous night. Instead, I just wanted to relive that unexplainable feeling as I stood on the beach with thousands of butterflies swarming, ready to carry me off to a magical land. The whole world had felt like it was expanding and exploding, and my soul was huge and bursting and full of love.

I don't tell Butler Reginald or Riley about the key to the security box at the bank — and that I've already been there. That there was only an outdated will. And an empty bank account.

I bite into a strawberry, thinking. Grammy Claire's last letter hadn't given me *any* clue for Key Number Ten. I'm completely in the dark.

As Butler Reginald runs soapy water in the sink, I think about the butterflies retreating back to the mangroves and underground cave as the sun set. The world had been stained a fiery orange and red. Streaks of clouds drifting across the sky.

Afterward, Eloni and I walked back to the tree house. It was about three miles straight through the trees and across some sand dunes. The unpaved roads were rough and winding. Walking had been faster than driving. I wonder if I could find that beach on my own.

After dinner, Riley and I had sat on the balcony under the soft lantern glow and listened to the whispering of the sea. For once, my sister didn't spend the evening with heavy metal plugged into her head.

"Tomorrow I *am* going to the beach," she'd said. "I can't go back home with white legs."

"You mean you're actually going to take off those horrid boots?"

"Sarcasm doesn't become you, little sister."

"Yeah. You own the patent on sarcasm."

"Very funny. Those boots saved me a trip to the hospital. Surgery. A cast for six months."

I'd been grateful that the accident hadn't been worse, too. But what kind of threat were Riley and me? Who would want us dead? We didn't know anything. Except I did have Key Number Ten. The most precious one of all. It wasn't doing me a bit of good, though.

I push my breakfast bowl away, thinking about the new will, sick to my stomach.

Butler Reginald dries his hands on a towel. "Ready, girls?"

He's wearing his official black suit and white shirt, looking sharp and pressed. "Why don't we convene in the living room in five minutes?"

My heart is thudding by the time Riley plops herself onto one of the couches.

A knock comes at the door and Butler Reginald answers it, ushering in Eloni; Tafko; Mr. Masako, the bank manager; and Alvios, Eloni's grandfather.

I rise in my seat, completely surprised, not expecting any of them. My heart begins to thud.

After everyone says *Nesor annim* for "Good morning," they begin taking seats. Butler Reginald serves juice and cookies, like we're at a Garden Club party. I just want him to hurry up and read the will!

Finally, our butler/nanny finishes passing napkins and clasps his hands. "I'm sure you girls are wondering why I've invited Mr. Masako and Alvios here this morning."

"You could say that," Riley tells him.

"Mr. Masako and Tafko signed your grandmother's new will as official notarized witnesses, so I thought it best to have them present this morning."

Learning that bothers me. Maybe it's because I don't quite trust Tafko. The idea of a new will drawn up right before Grammy Claire died greatly bothers me, too.

Butler Reginald unseals an official-looking envelope, pulls out a sheaf of papers, and then shows the final page to Tafko and Mr. Masako. "You can verify that these are your signatures?"

The men look at the inked handwriting and nod in agreement.

"Let us dive right in so as not to take up your day — and so the girls can resume their vacation."

I take a deep breath and grip the edges of my chair.

Butler Reginald clears his throat. "The Last Will and

Testament of Claire Theriot Chaisson, resident of Bayou Bridge, Louisiana, and concurrent resident of the islands of Chuuk.

"I, Claire Theriot Chaisson, testify that I am of sound mind and body and do hereby bequeath my estate in the following manner:

"Number One: My home in Louisiana will go to Rebecca Chaisson Doucet and her daughters, Riley and Tara Doucet.

"Number Two: The residence and laboratory on Chuuk were rented to me for my research purposes as commissioned by the Chuuk government and will be returned to the State of Chuuk within thirty days of my death."

There's a tug at my chest when I hear this. The tree house never truly belonged to my grandmother — and would never belong to me and Riley, either. Not even for a vacation in the future.

"Number Three: My scientific research I am giving to the Institute of Research for Lepidoptera located in the Federated States of Micronesia. In conjunction with this decision, I declare that the rest of my estate, my savings and stock holdings, as well as the remains of my late husband's estate will be used to run the Institute of Research for Lepidoptera for the next decade until further funding can be obtained."

Riley sits up in her chair and frowns. "Say that again in English?"

Butler Reginald turns a shade of apologetic pink. "A year ago your grandmother commissioned me to set up a legal foundation for the continuing research and protection of the butterflies here in the Micronesian Islands. As her estate executor, I will be overseeing the Institute. I have also been commissioned to hire a new scientific staff to continue the research and harvest of the Chuukese lepidoptera species."

I watch Riley chewing on her lips, and I know she's annoyed. "What does that mean?" I say under my breath.

"It means that Grammy Claire willed her research work to Butler Dude — and whoever he wants to hire."

"But you're not a scientist, are you?" I ask Butler Reginald.

He shakes his head. "I'm not a PhD, but my undergraduate work was in biology before I received my law degree. I also have a master's degree in lepidoptera research from Yale." Butler Reginald clears his throat. "I know this is difficult, girls. You were hoping to receive the bulk of your grandmother's estate — not only hers, but your grandfather's that she frugally saved since his death. But her lepidoptera work here on Chuuk was more important than anything else."

"More important than us?" My voice is wobbly and tears sting my eyes, but I quickly look at the floor, my hair swinging down so nobody can see my splotchy face. Especially Eloni.

Riley shoves back her chair, sputtering, "Grammy Claire knew we were about to lose the Doucet Mansion! That Mamma can't work — she's got no other skills besides flower arranging and giving parties! I don't know much about houses, but I do know that Grammy Claire's house on Bayou Teche is a wreck

257

and will need thousands in repairs and updating to sell. So me and Tara owning it doesn't help us at all! And Daddy —"

I cry out, willing her to stop before she says anything horrifyingly embarrassing. Eloni tries to catch my eye, but I can't look at him.

Riley does stop, in the nick of time. She glances at me. "It's our secret, right, Tara?"

"Thank you," I whisper. We both have been pretending for months that Daddy is living as a rich movie director in Hollywood. And that it's only a matter of time before we go live with him when he returns from filming "on location." But in reality, Daddy's a used car salesman and his new wife is a waitress trying to break into the movies. And they're middle-aged! It's embarrassing. It's pathetic. I never want to live with them.

And now I'm sitting in a tree house on an island paradise watching my whole life crumble. Losing those two thousand dollars to Madame See hurts worse than ever. Riley and I have nothing but two old, falling-apart houses with mortgages. And a mamma who can't even get out of bed and onto an airplane.

A sob chokes my throat as I rise to my feet. I'm not sure I can walk straight.

"I'm terribly sorry, Miss Riley and Miss Tara," Butler Reginald says. His voice is so kind and gentle it only makes it harder to hold the tears back. It's not his fault he can study butterflies and be a lawyer both. He just does the paperwork that his clients tell him to do. "Are these your certified signatures?" he asks Tafko and Mr. Masako once more, as if to assure me it's all legal.

They both nod, giving me sympathetic looks, and I can't take it anymore. Running across the room, I fling open the door and race down the open-air walkway to Grammy Claire's bedroom.

I throw myself on the bed and cry into the mound of pillows. I cry so hard I think I'm gonna throw up. Not only are my parents useless, but my life is pathetic and miserable.

I cry so hard the pillowcase gets soaked. I can still smell Grammy Claire's scent. Her hair spray and lemon-pound-cake smell. The memories, so sharp and real, only make me cry harder.

The next instant, Riley smacks the door open and slams it closed again.

I roll over, staring at her, my Pantene Princess hair sticking to my wet face. "What do you want?"

She limps to the bed and drapes herself across the un-rumpled side. "I want to get out of here and go see Brad back home. I want to tell Daddy to get lost. I want to yell at Mamma to get herself into a hospital. Grown-ups have messed up our lives, little sister. Even Grammy Claire."

I cover my ears. I don't want to hear what she's saying! "It's not true!" I shout at her. "She loved us. She loved me. It says so right here in her letters!" I pull them out from under the mattress and spread them across the bed. "See, see?"

Riley glances at the pages and shrugs. "It's just a bunch of words. Actions speak louder than words." I hate what she's saying about Grammy Claire, and I'm about to tell her how much I hate her, too, when she suddenly reaches out and touches my hand. "I'm sorry the real world has crashed down on you today, Tara, but I always thought you put her on a pedestal."

"She's *not* a liar! I know it." I say the words, but do I *really* know it? Grammy Claire never breathed a word about any of this. And we talked on the phone every Sunday! She was fine. Normal. Her letters were normal, wonderful, filled with love and concern. I'm so confused I don't know what to think. Maybe she was getting dementia. Maybe she was just selfish and all she cared about were her *nipwisipwis*. After all, her letters were full of those butterflies! Maybe she loved them more than me. The thought is so devastating, tears start streaming all over again. I think I'm going to choke and die right here.

"Okay, Tara, get a grip," Riley says gruffly. "It's not the end of the world."

I glance at Grammy Claire's pictures strewn along the shelves. The ones where she looks younger and younger each year. "But it is the end of the world. *You* get to leave because you already graduated high school, but Mamma's useless. Daddy's *more* than useless, and Grammy Claire is dead. I'll end up in some foster family!"

The thought is a true nightmare and I flop backward, putting the pillow over my face. I start sobbing so hard I swear my heart is going to actually burst. There will soon be blood spilling everywhere and the closest ambulance is almost two hours away.

Riley kicks off her combat boots and lies down next to me, not speaking, just waiting for me to finish bawling and hiccupping. I take a good, long while, and I wonder if she'll really stay until I'm done. A couple of times I peek out from under the pillow, but she's peacefully gazing at the ceiling.

Finally, the tears and the hiccupping slow down. I lie there for another five minutes, listening through the window to the ocean roll in and out. Then I sit up. "Well. Someone is lying."

Riley lifts her eyebrows. "You think so?" Sarcasm *drips* from her words. I love it.

"But who? Grammy Claire? Tafko and Mr. Masako? Eloni? The bank? Butler Reginald?"

Riley lets out a big sigh, and I think she actually doesn't have any answers, either. "Oh, Tara, I want somebody to be lying, but probably nobody's lying. Grammy Claire got so caught up in her research, living way out here, that she didn't realize how bad things were at home. She probably thought giving us her house *would* help us. Grammy Claire was pretty great, but she wasn't perfect. She left us for this island thousands of miles from civilization, for cryin' out loud. Whose grandmother does that?"

"You're not helping, Riley!" I feel like we're back where we started. But if I'm honest with myself, I did think Grammy Claire was perfect. I wanted her to be perfect. I don't want to think about her putting more importance on the *nipwisipwis* than me. But she did.

I glance at the row of framed photographs again. I think about Eloni's grandfather. What's the connection? Did Eloni's grandfather and my grandmother have something going on together? Both of them were aging backward. Getting younger. What sort of experiments was my grandmother doing?

"Guess I can't fault Grammy Claire for getting caught up," I tell Riley. "I've never seen anything so beautiful, so spectacular in all my life."

"What? You mean the butterflies? When did you see them?"

"The day before yesterday. With Eloni."

"Where do they live?"

"Maybe three miles from here. It took an hour to walk back, but if you didn't know they were there, you'd never realize that thousands of butterflies are hatching in the mangroves."

Riley grunts, but I can tell I've impressed her.

I shoot up, blinking. "But Eloni knows the secret! I know he does — and there *are* secrets out here nobody wants to talk about. I'm pretty sure somebody besides Grammy Claire has been lying."

"But we don't know who, Tara. You can't walk around calling people liars."

"Well, maybe not lying, but they're hiding something. Something big!" I clap my hand over my mouth. "And Madame See! Remember? She's here, too. Sneaking around the island!"

Riley shoots up next to me. "That's right, I forgot about that! Okay, I'm getting confused."

I stare at the letters strewn across the bed, and remember that Grammy Claire told me to trust Riley, so I spend the next hour telling my sister everything, from the beginning. She gets a fresh ice pack for her ankle, sits in one of the wicker chairs on the balcony overlooking the beach, and reads every single letter from start to finish, even though she'd glanced through the first ones when we were back home.

I chew on my hair, watching her. When she finally finishes, she lays the last letter in her lap and says, "I'm impressed."

"With what?"

"That you figured out all the clues and keys. And it's *really* too bad the money is gone."

I can only chew more hair and nod.

"Will you stop that, Tara? It's disgusting."

I drop my wet hair and sit, sulking. Below us the waves roll in gently, leaving big swaths of foam.

"So what do you think the last key unlocks?"

I shake my head. "Already tried it in every single door here."

"And what was Key Number Nine again?"

"The safety deposit box at the bank. With the first will."

"Which is obsolete now," Riley mutters, leaning on the balcony ledge. "So what do you think Key Number Ten would open? What would it need to be?"

"I have no idea and the last letter doesn't have a single hint! Every other letter had a clue tucked inside, which Grammy Claire told me to burn." I lower my voice even though we're far from the bedroom door. Peering through the slats of the balcony railing, I look down to see if anyone is hiding in the trees. "Seems like I just heard a rustling noise."

"You're going paranoid on me now."

All of a sudden, Eloni appears from around the mangroves, coming from the direction of the laboratory. What's he doing there? I narrow my eyes, studying him. He must sense someone is watching because he suddenly glances upward and sees me and Riley bending over the railing.

"Hi!" He waves, grinning as big as ever. "Come down. The party is today! My grandfather started roasting the pig last night and it's ready to eat. You're coming, right?"

Riley shakes her head. "Don't think Butler Dude is going to want to drive us around."

"My family has a village. Down the beach. It's not too far. We can ride."

"Guess that explains why Grammy Claire hired him if he's close." Riley calls down again. "Hey, what did you mean by riding on the beach? Does your family have horses or something?"

"No, I mean dune buggy! In Professor Claire's shed."

I stare at Riley. "Grammy Claire drove a dune buggy?"

Riley stares back at me. "Guess she couldn't walk back and forth to the butterfly cove several times a day. Never thought about her having wheels. But it makes sense."

My hand flies to my mouth. "Key Number Ten! Do you think — ?"

"Shh! Don't say that out loud!"

My head hums with a thousand sudden thoughts. I race back inside the bedroom.

"You're coming, right?" I hear Eloni call up again. It makes me laugh. That boy is very impatient.

"Okay, we'll come!" Riley calls down from the balcony.

"Go behind the laboratory. Follow the path," Eloni tells her. "Mr. Butler Reginald says he will drive the car over later after he changes his clothes."

I hear Riley give a laugh. "A beach party with a roasted pig isn't exactly the place for a butler suit, I guess."

I'm too busy snatching up Grammy Claire's last letter. I scan the lines, searching for clues, searching for more. There has to be more! There wasn't an extra note with a clue this time, which means she had to hide it carefully within the letter. I didn't have to burn or swallow anything — *because Key Number Ten is the most important key of all.*

Slowing down, I read the entire thing again, not stopping so my brain won't keep interrupting. Certain lines jump out at me in a whole new way.

You will notice that there are no Giant Pinks in the laboratory or in my home. There is a reason for this, which will be revealed later.

You should still have one more key, and it unlocks the most dangerous location of all. I cannot even give you any clues because I'm afraid of who is watching you. I'm afraid of what they already know, and that they might steal this letter from you. . . .

You will have to rely on your wits, your brains, your courage, and most of all your good heart to find the final lock. You must do your best to save the nipwisipwis from those who will inflict experiments and certain death on them. My beautiful creatures are facing extinction. And if my research is stolen and there is free access to the nipwisipwis, no longer will the island's butterflies fly free and help the native people as they have for centuries. They will be gone forever. . . .

Don't forget to enjoy the beauty of the island.
I hope you brought lots of swimsuits and
sunscreen!
    And most of all, remember, my lovely Tara, I
will be with you in the darkest hour. Always. I have
not left you alone. Trust Riley. Show her this letter.

I had shown Riley the letter, and she couldn't figure it out. I'd done everything Grammy Claire had told me to do.

Other laboratories were trying to get the *nipwisipwis*. Why would they inflict terrible experiments? Why kill them? How did the butterflies help the native people? So many questions still to unravel.

But an idea begins to form in my mind, nagging at me. Key Number Ten unlocks a dangerous place — which means that Grammy Claire is *not* referring to the dune buggy. "Aah!" I yelp softly. *What* is she talking about?

And then I see it. The clue. Plain as can be, right in front of my nose.

My heart thumps as I try to catch my breath.

Grammy Claire's letter is set up like every other letter, where the clue always follows her information and warnings. Except this time the clue is so small and innocent, it seems completely insignificant. *I hope you brought lots of swimsuits. . . .*

Such a casual reference thrown into the letter in between the warnings. I think my grandmother is trying to tell me that I need a swimsuit to find the *dangerous location*. A swimsuit to find the lock for Key Number Ten.

"Riley!" I scream. "We're going to the party!"

Chapter Twenty-four

The air is like a butterfly with frail blue wings.
The happy earth looks at the sky and sings. . . .

~JOYCE KILMER~

Riley limps back inside and I signal to her to be quiet by putting a finger to my lips. We stand so close together that even if the room was bugged, nobody could hear us.

"Why are we going to the barbecue?" Riley asks, mouthing the words. "What about the dune buggy and the key?"

I shake my head, mouthing back in the faintest whisper. "There's nothing important *in* the dune buggy. The dune buggy is going to take us where we need to *go*."

"Maybe something is under the floorboards."

I shake my head again. "Wear your swimsuit."

"You're not making any sense."

I smile and pretend I have everything under control. "I know," I answer as calmly as I can even though my stomach is quivering and I'm suddenly tingling with nerves.

Quickly, we change into our suits, throw on shorts and tank tops, then grab towels. I stick my hand into my pocket, double-checking that I've got Key Number Ten with me.

As we cross the walkway to the outside staircase, I call out, "First one to the dune buggy gets to drive!"

"I'm the one with a driver's license!" Riley yells back, limping as fast as she can. For once in my life I have an advantage over her.

Jumping down the last three steps, I go flying past the laboratory and into the mangrove forest. Soon I see a little wooden shed that's been turned into a garage. I pull at the wooden doors, swollen by years of rain. With Riley's help, we finally get them open.

Inside the shed, there's a dusty dune buggy, filled with a layer of sand at the bottom.

"Looks homemade," Riley laughs, running a hand over the soldered metal frame. "Think it runs?"

I hold up Key Number Ten. "Only one way to find out."

"I'll bet Grammy Claire made this herself," my sister grumbles. She climbs into the driver's seat and we have a standoff.

"I'm driving. Grammy Claire gave *me* the keys."

"She told me to help you. And I have a license."

"You don't need a license to drive a dune buggy to the beach; anybody can do that."

"Not a twelve-year-old."

I narrow my eyes. "Just watch."

Riley runs a hand through her magenta hair, which is now fading to a weird purple shade. "Listen, Tara, don't be ridiculous. I'll drive so we don't end up flipping over or in a hole. You need to be the navigator. I don't know the way."

She quickly snaps the seat belt, and I know there's no way I'll be able to haul her out of the driver's seat. Finally, I climb into the passenger side. "You have to do exactly as I say."

"Fine. Give me the key." She's rubbing her hands, gleeful.

I practically stick my face into hers. "I've been safeguarding the keys all this time, and if Grammy Claire wanted you to have Key Number Ten, she would have given it to you. So *I* will do the honors."

"Fine! Just do it already!"

I pull the silver key from my pocket and feel a shiver run down my neck. It's the very last one. I'm finally here, almost to the end of my journey. Am I ready for what I'm going to find?

Inserting the key into the ignition, I find it fits perfectly. My sister pumps the gas pedal as I turn the key over. The engine growls to life.

"Woo-hoo!" Riley yells. "Let's make tracks!"

She backs out of the little garage and nearly runs over Eloni, who's standing there, out of breath, like he's been chasing after us.

"Hey, Eloni!" I shout. "Look! The dune buggy works."

"You are still coming to the barbecue?" he says. "Food is ready. We will eat soon."

My stomach growls. I *am* hungry. "Are you hungry?" I ask Riley.

"Starving. I think you talked me to death today. We didn't get lunch."

I think about the key and the clue and the caves. I'm so eager to go back I can't hardly stand it. And I'm dying to find what else Key Number Ten unlocks.

"The party is for you," Eloni reminds me. "And Riley."

"You mean, we're, like, the guests of honor?"

His eyebrows wiggle. "Best food in the whole islands. Best music, too. Where do you have to go?"

"Somewhere really, *really* important."

"Are you showing your sister the *nipwisipwis*?"

"Um, yeah. Grammy Claire told me to." I don't tell Eloni about the key, though.

He nods, but he looks suddenly apprehensive. "Riley needs to see the butterflies. But you need to meet my family. That's important, too." He says this in a solemn tone, and I wonder if there's more to the party than making new friends or being welcomed to the island.

Riley spins the steering wheel and the tires swivel. She's chomping at the bit to drive.

Eloni puts his hand on the edge of the dune buggy, staring straight at me. "You *are* coming. Right?"

I find myself blinking into his big brown eyes, and my breath catches. "I promise. Right now. Get in and show us the way."

It's only a couple hours past noon so we have hours and hours until sunset. And now we have wheels so we don't have to walk home in the dark.

"Good. Good." He jumps in behind me, his bare knees under his shorts sticking out in the cramped back space.

The tires spin as Riley steps on the gas. We shoot straight through the trees. Mangrove leaves whip past my cheeks. The path is not an actual road, but the dune buggy gets through perfectly.

Eloni's voice comes in my ear as he directs us, pointing with his hands right or left around the jungle of trees. The dune buggy lurches over mounds, and shoots through corridors of palms. A slithery voice in my head makes me wonder if the party is a trap. Another slithery voice tells me Riley and I should have protection if we return to the Butterfly Lagoon alone. A third voice reminds me of the secrecy Grammy Claire urged. The life-or-death situation of the *nipwisipwis*. When I return to the cove with the key and Riley, we have to go alone. Nobody else can know that we're searching for another lock for Key Number Ten — the most dangerous lock of all.

There's time, I try to tell myself. According to the Last Will and Testament, we don't have to give up the tree house for thirty days after Grammy Claire's death. Quickly thinking backward, I count the days in my head and feel a rush of panic. "Oh, no!"

"What's wrong?" Riley says as she makes a turn in the path.

"We only have three days until the house is turned back over to the Chuukese people. *Three days!*" I tell her. "We may *not* have enough time! What if I can't find the lock — ?"

Abruptly I stop, aware of Eloni sitting right behind me, his breath on my neck.

What if I've got the last clue completely wrong? What if I fail?

Riley glances over at me, squeezes my hand briefly, and then grips the steering wheel again.

The afternoon is bright and hot as we shoot out of the mangrove forest and hit the soft sand of the beach again. The dazzling blue of the water is always close, I've come to realize. It's never very far away.

Two more curves and we enter the clearing of a little village; houses of wood and concrete with metal or thatched roofs sit under trees along the beach.

As we drive, Eloni tells us names and relationships and I am completely confused. At least we're dressed okay. Little kids run around in shorts, barefoot, no shirts, playing with a ball. Girls younger than me wear a type of wraparound skirt in bright blues and pinks. I find myself wanting one so I don't look so out of place in my shorts and sandals. Even though Riley's got shorts on over her bathing suit, she's wearing socks and her combat boots. A sheen of sweat glistens on her face, and she looks really uncomfortable, holding herself apart after we park the dune buggy under a palm tree.

Bare-chested men wear a type of shorts/loincloth created out of swaths of red and yellow material around their waists. I recognize Alvios as he and two other older men tend to a roasting pig over a spit. The pig is sizzling and brown, the spit created under a barbecue hut with a thatched roof.

Women and teenage girls chat in their multicolored skirts, blouses every color of the rainbow. Dark hair spills over their shoulders. They all have beautiful brown or black eyes. They're also talking a mile a minute in Chuukese as they prepare food under a second thatched-roof cookhouse, kneeling in the dirt or on palm leaves.

I recognize roasting chicken, baking breadfruit, taro roots, pots of steaming rice.

A couple of other young men are arranging fruits in a wooden bowl. I hear Eloni call it a *unoong*. Another man appears out of the trees carrying a long paddle over his shoulder, a woven basket at each end of the paddle-like stick filled with green, melon-shaped breadfruit.

That's when I notice a few of the teenage boys and young men with sticks in their pockets or tucked in the back of their shorts as they set up an eating area. Carved love sticks like Eloni has. I can't help smiling, watching the boys and the teenage girls and young women talk and work together, trying to match them up and see which girl will get one of the beautiful sticks from a particular young man.

The smell in the air is heavenly. All that food. The smell of barbecue, fresh fruit, dripping pineapple, the sweet tang of ripe bananas and papaya.

My stomach growls just as Eloni grasps my arm to go introduce me to his family. "I heard that, Miss Tara."

"Just Tara."

"Just Tara," he repeats.

That's when I know that he calls me "Miss Tara" not because he forgets, but because he likes to tease me. I blush like crazy and glance away.

"Here is my mother," he tells me, pulling me over to a pretty woman with her hair tied in a heavy rope down her back. She finishes stirring a pot of steaming rice, and rises.

"Looks done, Maama," he tells her. "Now we can eat!"

She laughs, pinches his cheeks, and then kisses him.

"Maama, this is Miss Tara, Professor Claire's granddaughter." Eloni repeats it in Chuukese, the melody of the words rising at the end of the sentence. I wonder if I'll ever be able to speak it. But then I realize that won't happen. In three days I leave and will never return. And I'm suddenly so sad, I have to swallow hard before I can speak.

"Hello," I say. "How you do? That's what they say back home on the bayou."

Eloni's mother grins and I see his smile in hers.

"I'm very glad to meet you," I add.

She bows to me, then takes my hand in her warm palm and presses it with her other hand. "Welcome," she finally says, in stilted English.

"Thank you for inviting me and my sister."

She nods and motions for us to go play. "Cook. Eat. Soon!"

Next, Eloni introduces me to his older sister, Tana, who is wearing flowers in her hair and a beautiful swishy dress that brushes her bare feet. She's hanging out with several other girls who are just as pretty as she is with their luscious Pantene Island Princess hair and flowers and gorgeous eyes.

I suddenly feel very plain, with my white, skinny legs, stupid shorts, and a tank top, the straps of my swimsuit hanging out ungracefully.

Alvios greets me with a bow and a big smile, patting my hands in his, and I feel a teensy bit better. The older man is very easy to like, even if he worries me, too. There is no way this man is more than seventy years old. And why is he on Grammy Claire's list of suspects?

Hanging out under a tree, Tafko ignores me so I sniff and ignore him back. A few minutes later, Butler Reginald shows up with wet hair and a shiny face, in casual slacks and a patterned island shirt. He gives me a quick hug around the shoulders and I know he's still feeling bad about the reading of the will.

I'm glad I'm not at the tree house still crying. The party is a good distraction from the bewildering and melancholy news of Grammy Claire's will. I don't want to think about Mamma and losing our home. I don't want to look into the future without Grammy Claire.

I run my finger along Key Number Ten in my pocket and try to feel hope — not just hysterical urgency.

Minutes later, Tafko pulls out his banjo and starts playing a song. Then another older teen starts pounding on drums and someone else begins picking at a guitar.

The music floats through the open windows of the bamboo houses. Circles around the cooking fires, drifts across the palm trees, and loops around my heart, tugging hard.

Eloni moves me closer to the musicians sitting deep in the shade of the mangroves, and I'm glad to get out from under the burning sun. We sit on soft woven cloths spread across the spongy ground.

All of a sudden, the women are bringing over massive mounds of food in wooden bowls or trays perched on gigantic banana leaves. Hot chunks of pork meat, fish, bowls of rice, steaming taro.

"What is that?" I whisper to Eloni, pointing to something wrapped in a banana leaf.

"That's breadfruit that's been mashed with coconut milk and baked in the leaves in the coals."

Everything smells fantastic.

A boy near the band blows a conch shell several times and the sound vibrates in my heart. It's a signal for everyone to be quiet as Alvios stands and give a welcome in Chuukese. He smiles at me and Riley and Butler Reginald. "*Etiwa,* and welcome to our friends of Professor Claire," he says in his limited English. I can hear the happiness in his voice, but I also see sadness in his eyes. It strikes me suddenly that hearing about Grammy Claire's car accident has been a blow to Alvios and Eloni. They were friends of my grandmother, and Eloni and Alvios depended on the salary she gave them, which is now gone.

After that, Alvios sweeps everyone to their feet, shooing us to the center of the circle. Everyone digs into the spread, loading up banana leaf plates with food. We eat with our fingers, and I can practically hear all seven generations of French Doucet grandmothers tsking their tongues in my ear for eating dinner on the ground with my hands.

I feel happy and melancholy all at the same time. Sometimes I feel Eloni's eyes on my face. Riley stays quiet, eating piles of food as she leans against the bark of a palm tree. Filling her banana leaf over and over again.

As the food disappears and my stomach gets fuller and fuller, Eloni's sister, Tana, and her cousins walk out from behind the cluster of houses under the trees, wearing long dresses and grass skirts. Hibiscus blossoms and orchids adorn their hair. The musicians play and the girls dance and I'm mesmerized and envious all at the same time.

Eloni bumps my shoulder and smiles at me, gesturing to his sister and cousins. "How do you like it?"

I whisper back, "I love it."

"I thought you would."

The girls' hands and hips sway together, smooth and fluid, like water. Eloni explains, "Their fingers tell a story. That hand motion is for the waves of the sea. Those are raindrops. Our boats out on the water. Family. And love."

"I can see it," I tell him, feeling a thrill in my gut at how beautiful it is.

I never want the music and the dancing to end, but the sun is beginning to drop lower. We're probably only thirty minutes away from the Butterfly Lagoon by dune buggy, and there's still hours of daylight, but I'm restless to go. Terrified I'll run out of time and never find the last lock.

After the girls' final dance, the young men take over, showing off on their drums and guitars, playing fast and slow. I can feel the drumbeats inside my chest, and it's a peculiar sensation. Then it's only three drummers. Fast patterns pounding, competing with each other.

Riley stands and I watch her slip through the trees toward the beach. She motions to me. "Come on!"

I give a tight shake of my head, not wanting to be rude.

A few of the older men have lit a bonfire in the center of the sprawling group of people. The flames jump and swirl, crackling into the air.

Suddenly, Riley comes up behind me and hisses in my ear. "Look!"

"What?" She points through the trees and I see the figures of two people. They're not together, though. One is off to my right and the other, a smaller person, stands in the distance behind the drummers. Just a shadow in the dense mangroves. The first person does look familiar, the way he's walking.

"It's Mr. Masako from the bank," Riley says, just as I recognize him, too.

"What's he doing here?"

Eloni nudges me. "What's wrong?"

"Um, nothing."

Mr. Masako is furtively edging his way through the trees. I hadn't seen him at the party earlier as a guest of Alvios. I think he's recently arrived, but it's odd to see him hanging back, not entering the party like a normal person would do.

"He spying on us?" I say in Riley's ear.

"Dunno. Almost looks like it, though."

"Who's that other person?" I say a bit louder. "Behind the drummers." It's getting harder to talk as the drumming rises in volume and pace.

"Who do you mean?" Riley says, and I don't think she's seen the other person.

"Over there," I tell her, trying to point without being obvious.

A creepy feeling runs down my back as the shadowy figure moves deeper into the jungle. But as the person creeps forward, I catch a glimpse of shoulder-length black hair brushing the collar of a dress. Worn by a small, stocky woman.

My heart leaps inside my chest. It's Madame Erial See! Watching us! I felt her eyes on me — right before she slunk behind the trees.

Reaching out to grip Riley's arm, I lean over to tell her, but never get the chance.

A second later, there's two ear-splitting pops that rupture the air. Instantly, the bark of the palm tree I've been sitting next to spurts a shower of splinters. My cheeks sting from flying, razor-like slivers, and then shredded bark sprays over my hair, my lap, and my clothes.

I'm screaming as I fall to the ground. Riley screams next, and then Eloni starts yelling.

The next moment, I'm looking up into the swaying palm branches high above me, blue sky revolving, spinning, making me queasy.

"Miss Tara! Miss Tara!" Eloni cries. "Are you okay?"

"Am I bleeding?" I hear my own words coming out in a peculiar slow-motion way.

"You're not bleeding," Riley tells me. "But a bullet hit that tree. Only a foot away from your head." Her voice goes hard and steely. "You could have been killed, Tara."

I think about seeing Mr. Masako and Madame See not more than a minute ago. Uninvited guests. Hiding in the trees.

I try to sit up, but the world keeps rotating too fast and all that beautiful island food is threatening to come up my throat. My fingers are shaking as I pull out a few splinters from my legs and arms. The drummers have stopped. I hear women crying out. Were there more shots? Is anybody hurt? The press of people begins to throng toward me. I stare through the trees, trying to see Madame See or Mr. Masako again, but my eyes keep whirling as I glance across the musicians.

Tafko is not there any longer.

I don't see him anywhere.

Was he the one with the gun? Did he shoot? Or was it Madame See? Or Mr. Masako, who wasn't even invited to the party? Then I wonder if all three of them are in cahoots together.

"I think I'm going to be sick," I tell Eloni. I turn away, mortified, my stomach heaving.

"Tara!" snaps Riley. "You are not going to be sick!"

"I'm not?"

My sister hauls me to my feet as Alvios and some of the other village elders run up to us. The men examine the tree, Chuukese words going a mile a minute all around me.

The whole world tilts as I realize that somebody tried to kill me. Or were they aiming for Riley — or Eloni? No, Eloni had gone to fill his banana-leaf plate moments earlier. Did he know someone was going to shoot me and moved out of the way purposely?

I look at Eloni and his eyes shift to meet mine. I don't know what to think. I've never been more terrified in my whole life. I grip Key Number Ten in my fist until the ragged edges feel like they're cutting open the skin of my hand. The pain finally makes me move.

I don't know who to trust or believe any longer. All I know is that the clues and the keys aren't a game. It's life and death. Just like Grammy Claire warned me all along.

I think Eloni sees my thoughts cross my face because he darts forward, his brow creasing.

I don't wait. I can't wait.

Riley sees my thoughts, too, and the urgency to leave before Eloni can stop us. Before I know it, she's pulling me away from the crowd and dragging me back to the dune buggy. "Come on, Tara!" she yells, seizing my hand.

My feet start working, finally, and we're running for our lives.

Riley shoves me into the passenger side, and I hand her the key. Sand and gravel spitting, engine roaring, she turns the dune buggy around and heads straight for the beach.

Chapter Twenty-five

May the wings of the butterfly kiss the sun
And find your shoulder to light on,
To bring you luck, happiness, and riches
Today, tomorrow, and beyond.
~IRISH BLESSING~

We drive and drive — or fly and fly — sand spraying, lurching over dips and holes and ruts. Darting around piles of fallen coconuts from the trees above. Colorful birds soar from tree to tree; insects swarm the banana trees.

When we make the last curve and enter Butterfly Lagoon I'm relieved to see that it's deserted. The waves are more ferocious than they were two days before. Wind is frothing the sea.

"Come on," I tell Riley as she parks the dune buggy inside a mangrove thicket. "It's almost time for the butterflies to come out."

"Are we going to wait for them on the beach?"

"No, we're going to find the Giant Pinks. I think they live in the underwater grottos."

"Have you lost your mind?" Riley says, stopping as I begin climbing over the rocks and tide pools.

"Come on!" I demand, and she finally follows. Soon I'm scrambling up the face of the rocks, crawling on my hands and knees until I reach the overhanging ledge of rock. Ducking my head, I scoot under, afraid it's going to be black as night inside.

"Hey, wait for me," Riley says, panting as she slides under the ledge.

Once we're both under, we clamber down the other side of the sloping rock, a wonder world directly in front of us.

The Giant Pink grotto is spectacular. Not dark and scary at all. Rock formations create a domed low ceiling and slants of sunlight pierce the cracks and fissures, reflecting off a gigantic pool of water. A pool bigger than ten swimming pools combined. The seawater is so crystal clear, I can see all the way to the bottom, the blue color growing an even richer, darker hue where the water level is deepest. It's like a narrow canyon filled with the sea.

I kneel on the stone ledge, which runs along the perimeter of the grotto. "Look, way down near the bottom. Can you see those big turtles?"

Riley lets out a low whistle. "Wouldn't it be fun to swim with them?"

I stare so hard it feels like my eyes are bugging out of my skull. Crusted along the sides of the plunging rock walls are sprays of coral in every color of the rainbow. The living coral shivers and sways with the water's movement. Almost doesn't look real. More like a painting in a slow-moving underworld.

Getting on my stomach, I lay my palm flat on the water's surface, skimming my hand back and forth. The water is thick and warm. Riley lies down next to me and we stare down into the depths of the pool, pointing out fluorescent orange coral or the striped fish chasing each other far below. It's like looking into the world's biggest aquarium.

"So where are the Giant Pink butterflies you keep talking about?" Riley asks, rolling onto her back to stare up at the ceiling. We talk in hushed tones like we're in church. Every move we make echoes in the chamber and trembles across the water.

"Back in those dark recesses? Maybe they fly around during the day and only return to sleep at night."

Inside the cave, I finally feel safe. Part of me feels bad that I just left Eloni without saying a word, but I'm scared. The sound of that gunshot whizzing by my ear and shattering the tree keeps playing over and over again in my mind. "I can't believe I almost died a little while ago."

Riley scoots closer. "You need to find this last lock and we need to get off this island. Get the next flight back home. I'm serious."

I know she's right, and I hate to leave the butterflies unprotected, but I don't think there's anything I can do. I don't even know *why* I'm supposed to save them or help them. "I don't have any more clues. No more letters, no more keys. I'm stuck, Riley."

"I haven't told you this yet, but I heard a car motor and tires on the gravel in the middle of the night," Riley says next.

"Maybe someone just passing by?"

"Not much traffic out here — if you haven't noticed already."

"Eloni's grandfather has that taxi. And Tafko has a car, too. Maybe other villagers do, too. We're a long way from the main city. "

"Could be them, I guess." Riley shrugs again, closing her eyes. "But it seemed so close. Right under my bedroom window. Hey, wanna go swimming while we think about where to go next? Maybe Grammy Claire was talking about a different cave. And we can't go back home without an island suntan. It would be, like, illegal."

I can't believe we're actually having a normal conversation. Suddenly, my pulse is in my throat. I grab Riley's shoulder.

"Look! Down on those rock ledges under the water! Do you see that?"

"What, what?" Riley rolls back over and we lie shoulder to shoulder, our noses practically touching the water's surface.

My heartbeat crashes in my ears. "It's — it's a trunk! Or a chest of some kind. Sitting back under that ledge. You see it, right?"

Riley turns toward me and I can tell she's overwhelmed. "D-do you think — ?"

"Key Number Ten! I *knew* there was something else it unlocked, not just a dune buggy."

Pulling off my tank top, I fling it to the ground, then strip off my shorts so I'm in my yellow swimsuit.

Riley watches me, blinking. "What are you doing, Tara?"

"I'm going in. Gonna swim down there and see what that box or trunk is."

"But you've never swum in a lake or the ocean before. Wading is not swimming."

"I've had swimming lessons. I can do it. Besides, I body-surfed with Eloni yesterday."

"But what about all those fish down there? And the sea turtles? What if they attack you?"

"People snorkel and scuba dive all the time — just to see turtles and fish up close. They're not going to hurt me."

She gives me a peculiar look. "I've never seen you so brave. You're always such a straitlaced priss."

I find myself chewing on my hair, staring into the deep water, so clear, so filled with amazing creatures. Why *am* I doing this? What's happened to me in the past few weeks? Is it Grammy Claire, the ten keys, Eloni, Mamma? Or is it the *nipwisipwis* — the overwhelming need to learn their secret? To protect their secret. Grammy Claire had sent me on a mission and every moment felt like time was running out.

"I'm going in," I say, sucking in air. "Are you coming with me?"

Riley stares into the water, then at me, then back into the water. "I'll wait here and make sure you get down there okay. If not, I'll save you. Or get help." She glances around, looking suddenly frantic. I've never seen *her* like this before. "Wish we had some rope so I could tie one end to you and hold on to the other end."

"I'll bet it's not more than ten feet to that ledge. Like going to the bottom of a swimming pool. And it's warm. I'm not going to cramp up."

"What will I tell Mamma if you drown?" Riley gets more agitated. "This is crazy. We should get help."

"No! *Nobody* can know about this. Grammy Claire intended for me to come here. I have to get that chest out. If it was too dangerous, she wouldn't have given me the key."

"Weeelll, that's true," Riley says, finally letting go of my arm.

"I'll bet Grammy Claire put that trunk on that ledge herself."

"Or Eloni did," Riley says slowly.

My brain clicks and a few things fall into place. I can picture Eloni here, diving down, Grammy sitting on the ledge, giving out instructions.

Riley pulls me back from my diving position. "Maybe we should get him to do it."

"No!" I say again. "We don't know if we can trust him, either. Grammy Claire gave *me* the key, not him." I shiver, thinking of all the people out there I didn't trust any longer. "Whatever we find in that trunk is for us. Our family."

Riley presses her lips together. "Take a huge breath, Tara, and if you run out of air, come straight back up, okay? Promise?"

"I promise."

She reaches out and hugs me tight, then releases me. I can't remember the last time my sister hugged me. Impulsively, I throw my arms around her neck and hug her back. Her skin is soft and warm, even if her hair is like porcupine bristles against my cheek. "I love you, Riley," I whisper in her ear.

She gives a little choke. "Me, too," she says, so faintly it feels like an echo off the rocks.

I expand my lungs, breathing deeply over and over again. Then I take a final lungful of air as I lean over the ledge, staring straight into all the deep, gorgeous blue — and then fire off the edge. My fingers slice the water as I plunge, and I think I'm six or seven feet down within two seconds.

Stroking hard, I pull myself deeper into the underground pool.

The fish and sea turtles ignore me. They're about fifteen feet farther down, busy with their own lives. I swim past all that purple and orange and pink coral, and it feels like I'm *inside* an aquarium. Inside the cozy warmth of the belly of the island.

The next stroke of my arms and I'm at the shadowy ledge along the canyon's wall, my cheeks puffing out, trying to hold in air for as long as possible. My fingers brush against the metal straps of the rounded trunk. A treasure chest. I hear Riley calling to me from above, but her voice is garbled and muted, far, far away.

I'm running out of air. And I forgot Key Number Ten. I stuck it in the pocket of my shorts after Riley parked the dune buggy.

It's probably better to bring the chest up anyway. I don't have time to open it down here without an oxygen mask. I also don't want to lift the lid and have the contents float away. Or get snapped up by a sea turtle.

I wonder if it's filled with jewels and gold and silver — which is completely silly. Grasping the handle, I pull out and then up away from the ledge. Amazingly, the chest seems light. What if it's empty? Is this some local kid's idea of a joke? Eloni's? Or maybe Tafko is trying to drown me by luring me to the treasure chest!

Kicking hard with my legs, I reach for the surface again. My lungs are bursting, all the air whooshes out, and my eyes bulge. Riley grasps my arms and pulls me out of the heavy, warm water, placing my palms on the rock edge so I don't float off. "Breathe, Tara, breathe!" she cries out as I inhale all that lovely oxygen.

Water rushes off me, and I feel like a drowned rat, but I'm elated. "I did it! I did it!"

"Hey, this treasure chest is pretty light," Riley says, sliding it across the ledge so we can open it. "Maybe it's empty."

Scrambling to my knees, I reach for my shorts. "That's what I'm afraid of." After all the keys and letters and clues, were we just going to be completely disappointed? Grabbing the key, I glance up and my eyes meet my sister's. There's fear and hope and love all mixed up together.

Riley gives me an encouraging smile. "Here goes nothing."

"Please, please, please," I whisper to the cavern, not sure what I'm pleading for. No matter what's in that box, Grammy Claire will still be dead. Nothing will change any of that.

My hands are shaking as I stick the key into the lock. "It fits!" I whisper hoarsely.

"I feel like we're in a movie," Riley adds excitedly.

My head lifts. The shadowy grotto darkens a couple of shades as the afternoon disappears. "Do you hear something?"

"Nope. Open it, Tara, I can't stand it."

I turn the key and the lock snaps as I lift the lid and pull it back. There are no jewels or gold medallions clinking together to form a lovely pile of wealth, but there is a thick manila envelope in a waterproof plastic bag that has *Tara Doucet* written in Grammy Claire's handwriting. *For Your Eyes Only — Urgent and Vitally Important.*

"More clues?" Riley bursts out, obviously disappointed as she helps me unwrap the plastic.

Tearing open the envelope, I pull out a thick sheaf of papers. Scientific formulas spread across the pages. Chemistry formulas. Lots of math. Lots of pages. Typed-up notes. Analyses written in professor-type jargon. Piles of it. It would take a month to read through all this. And I wouldn't understand a word of it.

"Mumbo jumbo," Riley mutters. "Why did Grammy Claire put all this in here? And why put it in this cave?"

I stare inside the thick envelope, trying to focus. Words jump out at me. *Nipwisipwis* is written over and over again on every sheet. *Giant Pink. Experiments. Turn back time.* "This is Grammy Claire's research about the butterflies. Research she wants to keep secret."

"But why?" Riley asks. "I mean, butterflies are great, they're beautiful, but top secret? Was Grammy Claire losing her mind? Was she paranoid?"

My mind is going a mile a minute. "Think about those photographs of Grammy Claire in her bedroom. Think about

Eloni's grandfather, who looks so young. The Giant Pinks must have some sort of unusual chemical property. A gene or chemical that can turn back time. The butterflies make people younger. Maybe they make people live longer, too, I don't know. Grammy Claire hid her research because she was afraid someone was going to destroy the *nipwisipwis* to harvest them. Someone out there wants to kill them all and take their power."

The reality of it sinks in. The reason my grandmother never talked about her work here. The secrecy. "Maybe —" I start, tears pricking at my eyelids. "Maybe it's the reason she died."

"That's crazy, Tara. Nobody killed her. It was an accident."

I bite at my hair. "Maybe. Maybe not. If this is true, turning back time, making people young again — this would be worth millions. Billions! If it's true, there are a lot of people who would steal her research. And, oh my gosh, the letters!"

"What?" Riley practically shouts.

"Grammy Claire kept saying in her letters that the Giant Pinks were in danger. And that there were people who wanted to steal them. Destroy them. Experiment with them. Kill them. Maybe destroy this whole grotto. Our grandmother was trying to save them from extinction!"

Riley goes still as a statue. "We have to turn this research — all these papers — over to a laboratory or institute or something."

"No! Grammy Claire wants *me* to save the *nipwisipwis*! She wrote all those letters in case she died. But she couldn't come right out and say it. She had to let me figure it out. So that whoever wants to kill the Giant Pinks wouldn't be able to find her research."

"Look!" Riley says. "There's something else on the bottom of the chest."

Another envelope is taped to the bottom. When I rip it open, a new key falls into my palm. "It's for a safety deposit box," I say, shocked. "Look, here's a number and the name of the Island of Chuuk Bank. She must have reserved a new one — in case the first box got raided."

Somehow, when I unfold the sheet of paper included with the key, I know it's the last letter Grammy Claire wrote and hid away. I hold off for a moment, blinking back tears, wanting to savor each word.

Dearest Tara,

You're a smart girl and I'm sure you are piecing everything together if you've found the chest in the underground grotto and you're reading this last letter.

I compiled the most important parts of my research and moved it here. The rest of it I've burned. With the new bank deposit key, you will find my last will. The one I created and signed

*right after I booked my ticket for my trip to visit
you. Whatever Last Will and Testament you may
have seen or heard this past week is <u>not</u> mine. It's
a fake. I don't know who concocted it or witnessed
it. I do not know what's in it, but I suspect that
none of my life's savings were given to you — and I
also suspect that what is left of my laboratory is
being given to some other scientific research lab
that wants to harvest the Giant Pinks.*

"I knew Grammy Claire's will seemed wrong!"
"A fake," Riley repeats, shaking her head. "Keep reading!"

*The "Pinks" are migrating to a different
island, Tara. As though instinctively knowing
their numbers are dwindling. The <u>nipwisipwis</u> are
a true phenomenon. An absolute miracle. Each
species has a particular chemical makeup or
gene. I've been trying to isolate it and learn more
about how it works. You'll probably discover each
butterfly's individual *magic* after you've spent
more time with them.*

I think about the soft angelic music I hear each time the purple *nipwisipwis* comes near or lights on my finger. I wasn't
imagining it. I'm not going crazy.

298

Once you get to the bank and open the box that this key fits, you will see that I've left you and Riley and your mamma everything. My life's work. My money. Your grandfather's inheritance. Everything.

I hope you'll search deep within your heart and that over the next few years you will find the right scientists and chemists and biologists to help you save the _nipwisipwis_. Scientists who will love them as I do — as you do. Learn why they live here on Chuuk, and how they can help the people of the world. Without being destroyed. Or used to line the pockets of greedy, evil persons.

Someone has been watching me. I feel their presence everywhere I go now. There is danger. PLEASE be careful. For your sake and for my beloved creatures.

Until you can get to the island where the Giant Pinks are fleeing to, I want you to move out of the tree house and go live with Eloni's tribe. They will keep you safe. The _nipwisipwis_ have been protecting them for centuries — and blessing them in remarkable ways. I suspect that you may already have figured that out, Tara. I've always been aware of your intellectual capabilities. And I know that deep down, you have a good heart. Life has dealt *you blows. Don't let it harden you. Don't allow it to make you unkind or ungenerous.*

Tears start rolling down my face. I think about this last school year and the broken pier. The kids at school. Shelby Jayne Allemond and Larissa from the antique store. All the terrible things I did to them and to other kids. Because I'm a seventh-generation Doucet and thought I was the most important girl in town.

Then I remember the letter I wrote to Miz Mirage and Shelby Jayne, pleading for their help with Mamma. My heart twists inside my chest, pricking my conscience. I want to be a better person. A better sister, a better daughter, and a better friend.

"Mamma," I whisper. "We *have* to bring Mamma here."

Riley's suddenly wiping her eyes, too. "It's getting dark. Wonder if the bank is still open."

"We'll have to go tomorrow. Tonight we need to sleep together in Grammy Claire's room. Lock the door until we can get to the bank and get the right will."

Riley shakes her head. "I don't think we should stay at the tree house, even if we do lock the doors. Whoever is out to get the butterflies and Grammy's research knows we're here. They've probably been watching us since we arrived."

I start shivering. "Do you think they'll try to hurt us, too?"

Riley gazes at me and bites her lips. "They already did. When I fell down the stairs. When they shot at us, at you."

I'm suddenly very, very cold and very, very afraid. "They'll try again, won't they? They might be on their way this very minute."

A terrible urgency fills the air. "We gotta get out of here," Riley says, and we both stand at the same moment.

Quickly, I lock the papers up inside the chest again and pull my clothes on over my wet swimsuit. Clutching the treasure chest, I crawl my way out of the beautiful cavern behind Riley.

The sun is low on the horizon, but it's barely dusk. The air is hazy. Waves are whispering along the shore. Riley and I barely take two steps toward the dune buggy when I hear someone breathing behind me.

I whirl around as footsteps race toward me. Suddenly, I'm tackled from behind and flung to the ground.

Chapter Twenty-six

Just like the butterfly, I too will awaken in my own time. . . .
~DEBORAH CHASKIN~

The treasure chest launches out of my arms and I get a mouthful of sand. Then someone huge and strong reaches around and claps their hand across my mouth. A whiff of cologne and sweat mingle together, but it's faint and I can't place it.

"Let me go!" I yelp, squirming as sand crawls up my swimsuit. And I am *not* a girl who enjoys itchy, pebbly sand up her bathing suit. Even if I am currently on the beach.

Somewhere to my left, Riley screams like a maniac, but I can't see her. Whoever has me in the armlock sticks a knee into my back, and I can't even twist my head. Across the water, the sinking sun burns a hole right into my eyes.

I hear kicking, grunts, then more yelling. Is Riley still wearing her combat boots? I can't remember, but I hope so. And I hope she kicks and slams everyone in sight. Tears start leaking out my eyes. Mostly, I hope she's okay. The hands holding me are strong, muscular. It hurts, and I suddenly worry that Tafko has me in his grip. Don't people who play things like guitars and banjos have strong fingers?

I lie still for a moment, catching my breath while male voices mumble overhead. I try to flip my body over, but I feel as helpless as a bug, my arms and legs flailing stupidly. "Get off me!"

Nobody answers. I don't think they care that they're hurting me. I try to calm down and listen to see if I recognize their voices, but my heart is pounding too hard. Then I realize that they must have masks over their mouths because their voices are so muffled, the words brief, clipped.

"Rope."

"No. Grotto."

"You mean drown?"

"Hmm . . . might be easiest."

". . . found Claire's hidden chest. Look like they drowned getting it."

They're going to drown us? If there is any method of dying that terrifies me, it's drowning.

Think. Think!

Even though Grammy Claire had said in her last letter that I was smart, my brain is muddled. I'm panicked, petrified. And where is the treasure chest? I'm supposed to guard it with my life! Grammy Claire died for the *nipwisipwis*. Surely I can fight for them!

Instead of lying motionless under somebody's foot, I start screaming and clawing, trying to get out from under him. Riley must have the same idea because I suddenly hear her fighting somewhere across the sand.

It doesn't take long before I'm exhausted, but all at once I realize that the air is filled with shouting voices. Not just mine and my sister's but other people's.

I swear I hear drums. The pounding of feet — or is it the surf? Enemies or friends? I pray Butler Reginald has come to our rescue! He's tall and big and I'll bet that even though he's our butler/nanny, he's secretly got a black belt in karate. If I could just get two seconds to run for the tree house, Butler Reginald can call the island police. We can lock the doors and fend off these evil people. I picture him brandishing a sword. No, a gun.

I think I'm hallucinating.

My head hurts. Strangely, my teeth do, too. I think I slammed my mouth together when I was knocked down. My arms and legs and wrists are aching, and I'm trying not to cry.

The next second, someone flips me onto my back. The world tilts. I spit out sand and drool dribbles down my mouth. I try to look for Riley but can't move. Someone has my arms and legs pinned.

In the deepening twilight, a big man looms over me, kneels down, and grabs my jaw in his fist. "Give me the key!"

I stare at him and begin to choke. Literally. I can't breathe. I'm going to die. Not because they're going to kill me but because I'm in shock.

Still clenching my face in his hands, he orders, "Shoot off the lock. Don't have time to waste. There should be formulas in there, everything we need. And a map to the island where the Giant Pinks are going. There should also be another key. To Claire's new security box. The one she hid from me."

I hear a shot and the ringing deafens me. Feels like my hearing got blasted. A moment later, it clears and I hear another voice. A voice I know well. "Got it open. Documents are all here."

A whimper rises in my throat. They've got Grammy Claire's secrets!

Two large shadows hold Riley to the ground. And two more hold me down. My sister is cursing up a storm. Calling them every name in the book — some I've never heard before.

The man barks out four names I don't recognize. "Take them back into the grotto and hold them under the water.

After they sink to the bottom, nobody will find them for months. I can see the headline now: 'Sisters accidentally drown while on vacation — in a spot they should never have been swimming.' "

He gives a harsh laugh and his face looms over me. Tears spill down my cheeks, and I fight to hold them back.

The English accent is as warm and beautiful as ever.

He was the man who was supposed to save us.

The man Grammy Claire told me I could trust.

I try to lift my chin and spit at him, but only manage to drip more drool.

Butler Reginald just laughs. "Take them to the grotto — and make it fast!"

"Wait, wait!" I hear Riley desperately yell. "You have the treasure chest. What more do you want?"

"You don't get it, do you? Claire Chaisson's granddaughters need to be out of the picture. With you both dead, and your mother safely put away in an institution, the research, the butterfly potion, and the money all belong to me."

"What don't I get?" Riley flings back, and she sounds so unafraid I can't help being impressed. "That you're a kidnapper, a thief, a liar — a *murderer*?"

Butler Reginald's voice is full of disdain. "Such is life when those Giant Pinks are worth billions."

My throat burns as I try to swallow. "You're going to kill

them all?" The most beautiful butterfly I've ever seen is going to be . . . gone . . . forever?

"Killing them is the fastest way to harvest the chemical compound they possess," he says. "Claire figured it out just a few months ago — as I served her iced tea and watched from the polite silence of lawyerly butler-hood. We'll keep a few for reproduction, but it will be in a carefully controlled and monitored environment. Back in the States. Not out here on this godforsaken island where supplies are nonexistent. Your grandmother was an idiot when it came to true laboratory methods. We could have multiplied the Giant Pinks ten times by now, but she wanted to go slow. Retest over and over again. Stupid, sympathetic women scientists!"

My blood starts to boil. "Yeah," I say sarcastically. "Men who murder and steal make better scientists!"

Riley yells encouragement. "You tell him, Tara!"

Instead, I get a slap across the mouth for my insolence. It stings so bad, I'm really crying now.

The men lift me up by my arms and legs and start dragging me back to the grotto. Their faces are dark, unfamiliar shapes in the hour after sunset. As we lurch over the rocks, it feels like they're pulling me apart. My entire body aches and my eyes are swimming with terror. They're really going to drown us!

"Let me go!" I scream. "Help! Help!" I yell over and over again, but all I can hear are the waves rushing in and out. Even though we're miles from Eloni's village, I keep screaming. Riley screams along with me in the slim chance somebody might be out there to hear us. Unfortunately, all the dive boats came in for the night long ago.

I don't recognize Tafko, but I think one of the men holding me might be Mr. Masako from the bank. I want to spit at him, too. Anger bubbles up over his pretended sympathy the day I went there. He's also one of the fake witnesses to Grammy Claire's "new" will.

Just as my head is shoved under the rock overhang, I hear the sound of drums again. Is the sound coming from one of the *nipwisipwis* species? Like the purple butterfly who creates music?

The grotto is dark now, but the men have flashlights, the beams bouncing off the rock formations. I hear the gurgle of water, smell the salt. I can picture the crystal-clear pool just two feet away from me. And I start shivering uncontrollably. How long can I hold my breath?

"Hold their heads under," Butler Reginald orders. "But hang on to them so they don't get away."

They hold me over the ledge and plunge me into the water, still gripping my arms and legs, even though I'm thrashing like a maniac.

Riley screams, "Taraaaaaaaaaaa!"

Her voice is instantly muffled as a hand roughly shoves my head under the water. I never get a chance to take a decent breath. Almost immediately, bubbles escape my nose. After twenty more seconds, my eyes bulge, trying to see in the dark water, staring up at the cavern roof. Beams of light flash here and there, squiggly and hazy.

I'm losing air; it's growing darker. The heavy male hands keep pushing at me as I try to reach for Riley, but they're holding me so tightly, it's impossible to touch her. I can feel her legs flailing, the water moving next to me. Desperately, I try to reach for her fingers, a foot, anything. If I'm going to drown I want to at least drown in my sister's arms.

Now I'm bursting. I truly am drowning. My lungs are on fire. I'm going to die! Die!

"Grammy Claire!" I scream as my mouth finally opens and salt water rushes in.

Then, suddenly, the men's arms release me, and I'm floating away.

My legs and arms feel dead, heavy. I can't move, can't swim. I start to sink.

A second later, Riley's hand catches mine. She's pulling me up, toward the lights, which are bright as day now. Where did they come from? Am I in heaven? But why am I still underwater if I'm floating toward heaven?

My head breaks the surface of the lagoon, the fog clears, water streams out of my nose and mouth. My throat is burning, my lungs have collapsed, but I start to cough.

And then I hear the strangest sound of all. My mamma is screaming my name. "Tara! Riley! I'm here! I'm here! *Get my babies out of that water!*"

I choke on the sting of salt water. I must be dreaming. My mamma is thousands of miles away. Maybe I really am hallucinating. Maybe this is what it's like to drown. I'm seeing my life flash before my eyes.

As I keep coughing, I never realized how truly horrible and nasty it is to swallow seawater. It's coming out of my nose and my eyes, and I'm gagging it up. And yet I'm above water, even though the grotto rock ledge seems a mile away. I can't swim the distance. It's impossible. My arms and legs feel like dead weights; I can't get them to move.

As my ears and eyes clear, I finally realize, in the noise and flashing lights, that the grotto is filled with Chuuk Island Police. Every one of them is holding a gun in their hand. Both hands. In a stance, and ready to fire. I shiver when I see that all those guns are trained on Butler Reginald and Mr. Masako and the other men I don't even recognize. Are they members of Eloni's family? I have no idea.

Riley yells in my ear, pulling at me. "I got you, Tara, I got you! Swim already, swim!"

For the first time in my life, I obey her and manage to pull myself through the water. Arms reach out and lift me up, scraping my legs along the rock ledge. Finally, I'm hanging on to the ledge on my own, still coughing and spluttering.

I see Eloni. And Tafko, his brother. And his cousins and uncles. And I can smell the scent of barbecued pig filling the grotto. Eloni had rounded up his family and they'd come looking for us. He knew I'd planned to come here to the Butterfly Lagoon.

Before I can comprehend anything else, I let out a gasp. My heart pounds so fast, I think I'm gonna faint dead away.

On the outskirts of the police and Eloni's crowd of family, I see a small woman with dark hair and sturdy black shoes. Madame See.

Straining my burning eyes through the haze of flashing lights, I want to have the satisfaction of seeing the woman handcuffed and hauled away. Instead, my mamma drops to her knees in front of me like an angel. She's scooping me up in her arms, kissing my forehead, smoothing back my tangled, salty hair. "Are you real?" I whimper, grabbing at her.

"Yes, Tara, I'm here, I'm really here." She kisses me again and holds me tight against her.

"Where's Riley?" I croak, my throat swollen from the salt and screaming.

"Shh, Tara, she's right here," Mamma whispers. "Don't talk no more. You're gonna be okay. We're all gonna be okay now."

Turns out, Riley's been sitting next to me the whole time. She crawls over and throws her arms around me. We're both drenched, salty, a mess, and have sick all over us, but I hang on tight. And then I start to cry real hard. As hard as I did the day

Grammy Claire was killed in the car accident. I think I'm more terrified now that it's over. Riley and me were drowning. We were really going to die. I realize that I almost never saw my mamma again.

"We got Grammy Claire's treasure chest?" I ask.

Riley shakes her head. "Don't know where it ended up, but we'll find it, Tara. Now hush up before they take you to the hospital and stick some tubes down your throat."

I close my mouth, but it's okay because all three of us keep holding on to each other. In the distance, I hear sirens, police shouting orders, noise and confusion as they haul several dark shadows out of the grotto.

I stay quiet for about two seconds because I can't quit asking questions. "Mamma, how'd you know to come out here to Grammy Claire's *Nipwisipwis* Lagoon?"

Under the flickering torches, I see her smile. "I got a letter from your Grammy Claire."

Dawn is brushing pink strokes across the sky when I wake up to the sounds of rustling the next morning. I yawn and roll over, trying to figure out where the noises are coming from.

Mamma and Riley and I stayed up half the night talking and talking and talking. Long after midnight, Riley finally crawled off to her own bedroom and Mamma crawled in with me, sharing Grammy Claire's big bed. I slept hard and deep, better than I had in three weeks.

Now, next to me, Mamma is softly breathing, her dark hair spilling over her pillow.

I watch the room lighten and hear the rustling noises draw closer. Footsteps creep along the walkway between the outside staircase and the walkway to the master bedroom tree.

Who is that? All my senses go on high alert.

Slipping out of bed, I kneel on the rug next to the door. Someone is crouching on the opposite side of the wall next to the bedroom door. I can see cracks of daylight filtering through the bamboo — and the shadow of a person.

Hardly daring to breathe, I wait and watch. Who can it be? Riley playing a joke? Hardly. She'll probably sleep until noon.

A scratching noise comes next and suddenly I see an object being pushed through the slits of the bamboo. Something wooden with a golden burnish.

The stick comes into view, inch by inch, and now I see a leaping fish, sea drops glistening on its carved wooden scales, sprays of stars and a sliver of moon etched into the other side.

My heart flutters just like a butterfly.

The stick slides through until the whole piece is in view, the end of it held on the other side by someone I can hear breathing. I wonder if his heart is pounding as hard as mine.

I wait. He waits.

A laugh tickles my throat as I finally reach out and grasp the stick, pulling it toward me. I think my heart is gonna burst right out of my chest any minute.

Once the stick is through, I hold it in my hands, studying the beautifully carved pictures. It's still warm from someone's pocket. I run my fingers along each nick and groove and deeply cut line. And I know that I will treasure this.

The shadow still waits, so I get down on the floor and lie on my stomach, peeking through the bamboo. The shadow has big brown eyes. He finally whispers, "Tie the stick into your hair, Miss Tara. Then I'll know for sure."

"Okay, I will," I whisper back.

When Mamma gets up, she helps me wash my hair. I dry it on the balcony in the sea breeze. Then she helps me wrap my Pantene Princess hair around the love stick, knotting it in swirls so it stays tight on the back of my head.

Mamma finds a bouquet of red hibiscus on the dining room table and inserts a big red flower above my ear. "It's perfect," she says as we admire the effect in the hall mirror. "I think you're an island girl now."

"I'm so glad you're here, Mamma," I tell her as we stare at each other in the glass.

"Me, too, Tara. I think I needed to get out of that house for a while. Been suffocating me ever since your daddy left. This island is like a breath of fresh air."

"It's sea air. Literally!" I add, and we laugh together. For the first time in a long, long time.

Everything feels almost perfect. Almost. I only wish

Grammy Claire were here to see me dressed up with Eloni's beautiful stick in my hair.

Later that morning, Eloni and I sit side by side on the beach of *Nipwisipwis* Lagoon inside the Beautiful Empty. Which isn't empty at all when there are thousands of butterflies swirling overhead. "The Giant Pinks never showed up yesterday," I tell him. "When Riley and I got to the grotto in the dune buggy, we never saw them. Do you think they're dead? Did Butler Reginald capture them before we got there?"

Waves lap the shore in a soothing motion. The sea caresses the island like a mother stroking her child. I can't stop thinking about Key Number Eleven — the key to the box where the new will is hidden. Plus the envelope thick with Grammy Claire's secret research. I gotta get to the bank. I wonder if Alvios will take me in his taxi. Tafko might drive me to town himself. Eloni has been telling me how worried his quiet older brother has been about me and Riley. After the gunfire, he'd darted off into the trees, chasing after Mr. Masako.

Eloni touches my hair where I've tied his carefully crafted stick, and his eyes smile. "I like your flower," he says.

"Thank you," I say, feeling prim and shy.

He scoops up a handful of sand and lets it sift through his fingers. "Maybe it was the day the Giant Pinks left to go to their new island."

"Do you think they knew they had to leave? Did they know someone was going to kill them? Harvest them?"

He looks thoughtful. "We don't know what they think. No *nipwisipwis* can talk — yet." He grins and I can't help smiling back. What if there really was a butterfly that could communicate — or talk!

"Did the police find Grammy Claire's treasure chest?"

"Tafko found it broken on the beach. Don't worry. Everything is still there. The envelopes and key. He rescued it and we got it hidden. But you have to come to my family's party tonight to get it."

I glance at him. "Another party?"

"To celebrate your life. And that the butterflies are safe now."

We smile at each other, and I look away and start sifting sand myself. Bury my toes in the warmth of it, feeling pebbly, itchy sand go right up my swimsuit under my new sundress. But I don't care anymore. The island almost swallowed me last night. It's part of me forever now.

Eloni bumps my shoulder with his. "Come for a boat ride with me and Tafko and my grandfather?"

I stare at those dark brown eyes, and my stomach leaps into my throat. "You know where the secret island is, don't you?"

He gazes back at me, and then he leans in to whisper, "Yes, Miss Tara, I do!"

I clap my hands over my mouth. "You've been there with Grammy Claire, haven't you?"

Eloni doesn't answer. He just heaps a big glob of sand over my toes. Which need a fresh coat of nail polish and more glittery stars. They look pathetic, but I don't care about that, either, at the moment.

"Oh, my gosh," I hiss, staring out at the blue, blue ocean shimmering under the sun. "I *have* to go! Now! Today! I have to see them again. We have to keep them safe!"

"They will be safe, Miss Tara. My people will help to keep them safe."

A breeze lifts the hair off my neck and I raise my face to the salty, beautiful sky. I'm going to Grammy Claire's secret butterfly island! "How far away is it?"

"Not gonna tell," he says, copying my bayou accent. "Pack food. And another one of those swimsuits."

I turn my head, frowning. Then my gut drops and I clutch Eloni's arm. "Look! Over there! That's — that's Madame See!"

"Who?"

"Madame See! She's been following us. She stole Grammy Claire's money! Why didn't the police arrest her? She was in the grotto last night; I saw her myself! I thought she was going to jail! She was spying and planning to kill me with Butler Reginald!"

"Why do you think that? That woman called the police while my grandfather got the men in my village to rescue you. She had a cell phone. How do you know her?"

"I thought *you* knew her!"

"Nope. Never saw her before last night."

"She was with Butler Reginald at Grammy Claire's house in Louisiana! Then she secretly came back here."

Eloni lies back on his beach towel. "Maybe she's a scientist, too."

I watch the strange woman stand near the water. She's only about a hundred yards away now, and my stomach tightens. I wouldn't trust her as far as I could throw her. Even if she did call the police, she's still a thief. And a liar.

Narrowing my eyes, I continue studying her. Why does Madame See wear those ugly black shoes to the beach? Doesn't she own a pair of flip-flops? She must be hot in all those clothes.

I watch the woman scratch her neck. She looks sweaty and uncomfortable. Is she waiting to steal more money —.or steal the butterflies? Maybe she's actually been a spy for Butler Reginald all along.

Beyond her, out on the water, a diving boat sails, cutting across the waves, the ship filled with tourists. I listen to the ocean and sometimes it feels like it's talking to me. I want to lie back on my towel, enjoy the sun. Open up the picnic basket Mamma packed for us. Eloni said he'd build a bonfire and we'd roast hot dogs and marshmallows for lunch as soon as Riley and Mamma get here.

My eyes cut back to Madame See.

She stands stock-still at the shoreline. She's looking out to sea. I wonder if she came from China or Hong Kong. I wonder if she's homesick and just trying to get back to her family. Doesn't matter. I'm not gonna feel sorry for her!

As I'm watching, she raises her right leg and rubs the side of her foot along her left leg. Like she's scratching an itch. Then she rests her foot there, standing just like a stork.

Wind ripples the water.

Goose bumps rise along my arms.

Madame See rubs her foot along her leg once more. "Oh, my gosh, oh, my gosh, oh, my gosh!" I let out in a gigantic, almighty breath.

"Hey, ready to go swimming?" Eloni asks.

I don't answer. I leap to my feet, tearing straight for Madame See as fast as I can. My flip-flops go flying out from under my feet. My hair whips straight out like a flag as I pound the sand with my bare toes.

I reach the woman in about five seconds flat. And grab her arm and whirl her around to face me. Then I grab her hat and rip it off her head.

I pull at her sweater, yanking it halfway down her arm.

Then I touch her short black hair.

And pull. Hard.

The wig slides off her head and falls to the beach.

Long, silvery gray hair tumbles down her shoulders. Pantene Princess hair turned gray.

I've never stood this close to Madame Erial See before. She was always just a shadow in the kitchen. Quiet as a mouse. Hovering, watching. She really *was* a spy.

But her eyes aren't black at all.

Her eyes are blue, the very same color as mine.

I reach out and touch her hair, and it feels just like mine, too. Soft and silky, but without any sucked-on ends.

Madame See smiles softly, her eyes crinkling at me. "My dearest Tara," she whispers. "Oh, how I've missed you!"

"Grammy Claire, it's *you*! It was *you* all this time!" I throw myself into her arms and great big sobs wrench out of my chest. My throat is raw and painful as she clutches me back, tight as can be. My arms clasp her neck, but I still can't seem to get close enough as she whirls me around on the sand. "You're not dead! You're alive! We gave you a — a funeral!" Then I run my hands along her arms and touch her hair. "How can you be alive?"

She gives me a wry smile. "Because I'm smarter than Reginald Godwin, that's why!"

"What kind of a name is Erial See?" I burst out as another avalanche of tears floods my face. My nose starts running, but all I can do is keep on hugging her. We fall to the sand, hugging and laughing.

Grammy Claire gives a snort. "It's *my* name, silly girl. And I know you're smart enough to figure it out."

My mind instantly turns her words around. *Erial See*. That's how I'd heard it from Butler Reginald, but he'd never spelled it out. Heck, he didn't even know it himself! *Erial See*. Or *Erial C.* — backward — was *Claire*. For *Grammy Claire*.

"But why?" I ask. "Why?"

We sit at the water's edge, soft waves rushing over our toes. Tears keep spilling out of my eyes as she strokes my hair. I think my heart is going to leap out of my chest every time I look at her. "I had to do all this crazy scheming and lying and sneaking around for the *nipwisipwis*. I had to find out who was stealing my research, and who was killing them. There were so many suspects. After a couple of strange 'accidents' in my laboratory and tampering with my dune buggy, I knew it was only a matter of time before somebody actually succeeded in killing me. Somebody who didn't want to save the *nipwisipwis*. Somebody who only wanted the wealth they could get from them.

"So I hurriedly wrote those last letters. And staged a car accident with the help of my insurance company and Bayou Bridge's sheriff, your best friend's father."

My eyes widen. "You mean Alyson's daddy? Sheriff Granger?"

"The one and only. He was an enormous help to keep everything hushed up and out of the news. Just about did me in when I thought of you and Riley and your mamma grieving so horribly, but I finally had to go through with it — if I didn't want you truly mourning my murder down the road."

I rest my head in the crook of her neck and weep some more. She was here all along. In the shadows. Watching over us.

"You got Mamma to come, too, didn't you?"

Grammy Claire shakes her head. "No, Tara, that was you. *You* wrote the letter to my old friend's daughter Mirage Allemond. Mirage helped your mamma get some medicine and a dose of prayer. Then Mirage, along with her daughter, Shelby Jayne, helped your mamma pack her luggage and took her to the airport. That was your doing, my strong, wise granddaughter."

"But Mamma said she got a letter from you."

"After she arrived here. It was waiting for her at the tree house. The message told her to immediately go to the butterfly grotto, along with a map."

Tears fill up my eyes again so I can't hardly see no more.

"Saddest part is learning that my trusted attorney and friend was working behind my back all this time. Greed and envy are dangerous traits. But the butterflies fought back."

"What do you mean?"

"The *nipwisipwis* are amazing creatures, Tara. Each species has its own uniquely special ability. They follow those with a pure heart. Those who love unconditionally."

"Is that why the Giant Pinks left this island? Because they knew Butler Reginald wanted to kill them?"

"That's my theory. Reginald decided he wanted to control the *nipwisipwis*. He produced a false will, had it signed, deceived everyone, even me — until yesterday. I knew there was some-one, but I wasn't sure exactly who it was. My keys and letters to you were also a trap. To lure in the person who was trying to hurt me and the *nipwisipwis*."

"You found some dead Pinks in your laboratory, didn't you?" I ask her, realizing that it was Butler Reginald who killed the Giant Pink back home to run tests on it or take its DNA for himself. "I saw you that night. In the hall. I was hiding behind the clock."

Grammy Claire laughs. "I was busy following Butler Reginald, but he faked me out and I never actually caught him doing anything wrong. That's when I spent far too long sus-pecting Tafko or Alvios or Mr. Masako."

"And I was too busy watching you," I tell her. "I guess some of those noises were actually Butler Reginald all along." Butler Reginald stole my two thousand dollars! "He took the money so Riley and I couldn't escape once we were on the island."

"He needed you and those keys desperately, Tara. Eternal youth — eternal life — is a coveted commodity. Those who seek it must do so carefully. And the *nipwisipwis* instinctively know to save themselves. They were here to help the island people, who revere them and hold them sacred."

I try to take in everything she's telling me, but it's so over-whelming. I think about Butler Reginald now spending his days in the local jail. Then a trial and prison.

"He tried to drown me and Riley — and he was the one that sabotaged those stairs that almost killed Riley, too." I swipe my hands across my eyes. "I want to help you, Grammy Claire. I want to save the Giant Pinks. Teach me what to do. I knew they were smart and wonderful and magical the moment the first purple butterfly flew into my room."

My grandmother looks startled. "They came to you? The *nipwisipwis* found you?"

"The first butterfly came the day after your funeral. Flew right into my bedroom window. The purple-and-yellow one — the one that makes angel music."

"Oh!" Grammy Claire chokes out, and then she begins to weep herself, tears rolling down her beautiful, wrinkled cheeks.

"What is it?" I grip her arm, frightened. "What's wrong? Why are you crying?"

Grammy Claire pulls me close, and I can feel her trembling. "I asked the *nipwisipwis* to watch over you. The day I left the island. And the day I left my old home, not knowing if I'd ever return. And they *did*." She sounds completely overwhelmed. "They came to you — they really *came*!"

"Grammy Claire, what does it mean?" I think about the purple butterfly, the transparent butterfly, and the Giant Pink that flew into my grandmother's bedroom window.

"It means they heard me. They understood. And they found you. They have even more capabilities than I realized."

324

I want to cry and laugh with happiness. Excitement bubbles up my throat. Mamma and Riley are at the tree house, and I want them to be here with us, to share everything with them. I have a feeling we're not flying back home in two days any more. The tree house still belongs to Head Lepidoptera Scientist Professor Claire, and the whole summer is ahead of me. To spend with Grammy Claire. With my family. And with Eloni.

Something fizzy and stupendous shoots straight up my spine. "What do we do now?"

"Get your shoes and your shorts, my dear, because we're going to take a voyage across the ocean. To a place you will not believe. A place of dreams. An island inhabited by the *nipwisip-wis*." My grandmother pulls me to my feet and turns me around. An outrigger canoe has pulled up along the shoreline, just beyond the waves.

"Eloni!" she calls across the beach. "Hurry!"

Eloni races over, kicking up sand as if he's just been waiting for permission to join us. "Professor Claire! It's you, it's you! Today is the happiest day of my life!"

"Yes, it's really me, my dear boy." He starts to bow to her, but my grandmother tsks her tongue and grabs him in a big hug. When she releases him, I see tears in both their eyes.

"Do you remember the way?" Grammy Claire asks.

Eloni's face shines. "Yes, Professor Claire, I know the way. It's the island of all things beautiful, the home of eternity."

"Then let's make sure the Giant Pinks have arrived safely. We need to get back tonight, you know."

"Why?" I ask as I glance between them.

Eloni takes my fingers in his for a moment. "We're having a party, remember? I found a purple orchid for your hair, too."

I feel my face lighting up into the biggest smile of my life.

Grammy Claire grips my hand as we walk down the shoreline. Steadying the outrigger canoe, she helps me climb inside. I sit down in the middle, recognizing Tafko and Alvios, and a few of Eloni's uncles and cousins, ready to row us to the island.

Eloni hands me an oar of my own. "We get to row, too. I promise you'll like it."

The sun blazes overhead as the barefoot men push the outrigger into the surf and steady it. I dip my oar into the clear water, just like my daddy taught me when I was a little girl and he took me down the Bayou Teche. I think about seeing him again one day. Maybe I'll call him. Or Skype on Sundays.

Grammy Claire squeezes my shoulder and kisses my cheek. "Look, Tara," she whispers. "The butterflies are coming!"

Whipping back my head, I see the sky filling with purple butterflies edged in lemon-pound-cake yellow. They're following us to the secret island of the *nipwisipwis*!

As I pull hard on my oar, thousands of wings flutter while angel music saturates the sky and fills up every single corner of my heart.

Over the edge of the boat, I spot rainbow coral, and sea turtles, and polka-dot fish swimming below us in the ocean's depths. Soon I will swim with them, while *nipwisipwis* drench the skies.

Fluttering.

Joyful.

Magical.

My heart pounds in my throat as I gaze overhead, surrounded by all those hundreds of exquisite purple butterflies. We're being guarded by a cloud of *nipwisipwis* as we cross the water.

They're singing us over the sea.

Acknowledgments

They say stories are created by writers who spin and weave the many threads of plot twists, characters, and setting, as the Muse and a Deadline sit on their shoulders. While this may be true, it takes a whole bunch of warm and wonderful island village friends to help turn all those pieces into an actual book you can hold in your hands.

I couldn't do any of it without the love and support of my dear husband, Rusty; my son Jared, who critiqued and brainstormed *When the Butterflies Came* with me; my son Adam, who designs fabulous bookmarks and postcards; and Milly, my daughter-in-law, who takes me seriously when I go crazy with promotion ideas — and then helps me create gorgeous charm bracelets and butterfly necklaces and decorated cakes for bookstore events, along with PowerPoint presentations — while three toddlers cling to her legs (llama!).

Much love to my generous and nurturing editor and agent, Lisa Ann Sandell and Tracey Adams. You both are a gift in my life as you help me bring out the best in my work, and make the entire publishing process an exciting, dream-come-true journey.

I'm extraordinarily blessed to have good friends Cindy-Rae Jones and Bet Fonua at Nua Music, who create the most spectacular and magical book trailers for my novels, complete with original music and a whole lotta love.

I want to give a special thank you to longtime friends, Melanie Park, who generously let me camp out at her empty house to draft two different books when I was under tight deadlines, and Carolee Dean, who has buoyed me up over the long haul of this crazy writing career, and is a brainstormer and critiquer of great repute. Many thanks as well to Garrett Frei and Kevin South who spent time telling me about their life on the islands of Chuuk and their love of the people on those beautiful islands.

Endless thank yous and hugs to my brother Kurt, my sister-in-law Brenda, and their fabulous (and very hardworking!) children, Brandi (with BFF Megan), Cole, and Lexi, who built a gorgeous writing cottage for me during December with snow on the ground — in only a week! Thank you, as well, to my son Aaron, as well as to Milly and dear hubby who spent the week on the roof, becoming intimately acquainted with the shingles, and were all-around-terrific nail pounders and drywall hangers and painting pros.

The team at Scholastic Press is simply amazing, and every step of this journey has been filled with the most wonderful and generous people: My publicist, Emma Brockway, is cheerful, tireless, and adorable. Antonio Gonzalez, School Visit Coordinator, came to my rescue in the nick of time, and I'm grateful to the very talented book designer, Elizabeth B. Parisi; my copy editor, Monique Vescia; production editor, Starr Baer; associate editor, Jody Corbett; and editorial assistant, Jennifer Ung.

Special thanks to Deborah Kaiser, Theresa Frei, and Michelle McGilley, who set up school visits with the Book Fairs and carted me around the Bay Area, making sure I was fed and happy.

I'm also thrilled to have another gorgeous and mesmerizing book jacket by artist Erin McGuire — thank you!

I look forward to writing many more books and working with you all — all over again.